Bellaria di Rivergaro circa 1910

Bellaria
Di
Rivergaro

By
Louis E. Tagliaferri

Published by Talico
Ponte Vedra Beach, Florida

This is a work of historical fiction. Most of the characters and places portrayed in this book are real and most of the incidents occurred; albeit, in many cases the incidents have been fictionalized. Other characters, places and incidents, while based on historical research, are entirely the product of the author's imagination.

Cover illustration by and through the courtesy of Pietro Zangrandi, Piacenza, Italy.

Printed in the United States of America.

Library of Congress
ISBN - 13: 978-0615956121 (Louis E. Tagliaferri)
ISBN - 10: 0615956122

This book is dedicated to my wife, Judy, whose help and support made it possible, and to my grandfather Luigi, his parents and siblings whose lives gave rise to the incredible story of Bellaria.

Preface

BELLARIA DI RIVERGARO is a novel of historical fiction that is based on a real place and real people. Emilio and Evangelina were my great grandparents. Their son Luigi was my grandfather and his sisters and brothers were my great-aunts and great-uncles.

The story of Bellaria is derived from many sources including family oral tradition, documents, mementos and photo albums, public records, extensive Internet research, and personal visits to Italy. Most of the family-related incidents cited in the book actually happened. However, due to the lack of details about those incidents, it was necessary to fictionalize the circumstances surrounding many of them. Other events, places, and characters are entirely the product of my imagination, although they are feasible considering the history of the period.

In the end, the story of Bellaria is the story of an important part of my family heritage. I have done my best to tell it in a way that is historically accurate and that respects the memories of my family members, both living and deceased.

Louis E. Tagliaferri

Author

Prologue

ACCORDING TO ERNEST HEMMINGWAY, the Val Trebbia is one of the most beautiful valleys in the world. He was undoubtedly correct. The Val Trebbia is a picturesque valley that runs through a series of mountains, hills, and steep gorges in the Ligurian Apennines in northwest Italy. Coursing through the valley is the Trebbia River, one of four tributaries in the province of Piacenza that extend south from the Po River, the longest river in Italy. The source of the Trebbia is a spring 2,600 feet up the south slopes of 4,616 foot high Monte Prelà. From this source, the clear, clean water of the Trebbia flows seventy-three miles northeast, past the towns of Bobbio, Travo and Rivergaro, until it reaches the Po just west of Piacenza in the region of Emilia-Romagna. The Po begins at the base of the Alps west of Turin and winds its way eastward to Venice through the Pianura Padana, the broad, flat plain that is the breadbasket of the country.

The Val Trebbia is filled with ancient history. A few miles before flowing into the Po, the Trebbia passes the site where Hannibal and his 70,000 Carthaginian troops, with their terrifying battle elephants, defeated the Roman forces led by General Publius Cornelius Scipio in 218 BC. After later retaking the area, the Romans built a fortified city named Placentia on the banks of the Po that eventually became the modern city of Piacenza, the seat of the government of the Italian province with the same name.

There is a special place at the base of the rolling hills and low mountains of the Val Trebbia that has its own

1

fascinating history. The ancient Romans built a road connecting important commercial and military centers of their empire that ran past where this place is now located. It lays nestled within a region filled with Roman style farm houses and centuries old medieval castles. Renaissance churches and old monasteries dot the surrounding valley and mingle among the picturesque countryside that frames it like a portrait.

In medieval times, countless numbers of *contadini*, peasant laborers, worked near there in the fields of the feudal viscounts. They guided their horse and ox drawn carts, with oversized wooden wheels, past its site as they took the products of their labor from Rivergaro to sell them in Bobbio, or even farther away in Ottone.

Through the centuries, armies marched through this area, crossing an important intersection that divides the road to Rivalta from the road between Rivergaro and Bobbio. Nearby also are reminders of more recent conflicts, such as the site of a former World War II prisoner of war camp and a major battle between Italian Partisan forces and Fascist and German troops.

This special place has a name. It is called Bellaria - Bellaria di Rivergaro.

Chapter 1

SHE WAS INCREDIBLY BEAUTIFUL. She wore a red silk dress and a short red bonnet that framed her face like the women in paintings Emilio had seen in the homes of wealthy landowners for whom he had worked. He did not expect this. Emilio had protested when his mother Luigia asked him to accompany her to Rallio di Montechiaro to attend the second anniversary of the dedication of the church of Sant'Ilario Vescovo to the eighteenth century bishop, Giovanni Scalabrini. Rallio di Montechiaro was well over an hour carriage drive from Statto, where Emilio lived with his mother. Moreover, located in the hills across the Trebbia River, it was difficult to reach. The only reason Emilio and his mother attended the celebration was that they were invited by a cousin of Emilio's late father, Giovanni. Now, after seeing the beautiful, young woman who was walking toward him he was glad he was there.

Like Statto, Rallio di Montechiaro was a very small hamlet. With its population of forty-six souls, it did not even warrant a priest of its own. In this sparsely populated part of the district of Travo, priests usually came from larger communities like Bobbio or Rivergaro to say Holy Mass, and then only on Sundays. After Mass, they quickly returned to their more comfortable rectories in the larger towns or cities.

Emilio tried to catch her glance. She was young, maybe sixteen or seventeen, but not too young. He was much older, having recently passed his thirtieth birthday. For the most part he had been too busy as a *falegname*, a carpenter, in the family business to be too concerned about women. He was not inexperienced. However, the women he had been with were usually the daughters of farm hands, who worked for the owners of the *cascini*, much like the peasants who worked for the feudal landowners of the past. Thankfully, to the best of his knowledge, nothing ever resulted from those brief unions – but how would you know?

Anyway, making slats and paddles and other wooden parts for the water wheels that powered the many *mulini*, where corn and wheat were ground for local farmers, was profitable and had provided his family with stable work, but at a cost. Much of the work was for landowners across the Trebbia as far away as Rivergaro and Niviano to the north or Ponte Dell'Olio to the east of Rivergaro. Because of the distance and the twelve to fourteen hour workdays, it was often necessary to remain at the site of the *mulino* until the job was completed and that was usually a week or more. That did not leave much time for socializing with women.

Emilio could not take his eyes off of her as she walked out of a small stone house across from the church with a woman he assumed was her mother. A rather stern looking man, perhaps her father, escorted the two women. Together with fifteen or twenty other people, including Emilio and his mother, the three walked across the stone paved piazza toward the church where the campanelli were loudly chiming that it was time for Holy Mass.

As the madonna dressed in red passed by Emilio, she turned, nodded her head acknowledging his presence and gave him the briefest but most tantalizing smile. Emilio immediately fell in love with her and at that moment decided that she would be his wife and that together they would have many children. He was a decisive and determined man.

Her name was Evangelina Piergiorgi. As he had observed, she lived in the little two-story stone house directly across the piazza from the church with her mother, an older sister and two brothers, who seemed to be very protective of her. Her father died almost seven years ago. The elder man accompanying them was her uncle. Emilio learned all of this after Holy Mass when everyone gathered in the piazza to chat about everything from how beautiful and moving the ceremony was to the weather, the quality of wool and milk from this year's flock of *pecore* and, of course, families and the newest *bambini*. Excusing himself from his mother and the cousin who accompanied them to the celebration, Emilio decided on a direct approach, which was his style in most things. He walked over to the family, who stopped talking as he approached, and introduced himself.

"Sono Emilio Tagliaferri, figlio di Giovanni e Luigia Tagliaferri da Statto," he said. "I am Emilio Tagliaferri, the son of Giovanni and Luigia Tagliaferri of Statto."

"Ah, Giovanni il falegname," the older male of the group replied. *"Piacere, Signore Tagliaferri."* "It is a pleasure to meet you."

"You knew my father then?" asked Emilio.

"No, not personally, however I recognize his name. I understand that he was a carpenter and that he made cabinets and other furniture and also waterwheels for the *mulini*, the grain mills," answered the elder family member.

"Yes," Emilio replied. "He was originally from Travo and I know that he did some work in this area."

The elder man introduced himself as Alessio Piergiorgi and then proceeded to introduce each one of the other family members, saving the only one that Emilio really wanted to meet for last.

"And this is my niece, Evangelina," he said.

Emilio was surprised when she looked directly at him and said in a soft, but confident voice, "It is a pleasure Signore Tagliaferri. I noticed you earlier. It is easy to pick out someone who is not from Montechiaro."

"Well, Statto is not really that far, but as you know it is on the other side of the river and it is not all that convenient to come over to this comune.

"Besides," he said, "most of my work is north of Rivergaro – as far as Quarto and Gossolengo – wherever there are grain mills that need paddles and slats for their waterwheels or any carpentry work."

"So, you are a *falegname*, yourself?" asked Evangelina's brother Enrico?

"I am," Emilio answered. "And a good one at that,"

"In fact, my brothers have the same trade. As a family, we do a very nice business," he added, trying to convey to Evangelina and her family that he had a skilled trade and a stable business – an issue, no doubt, that he would have to deal with at a later time when, not if, he approached the patriarch of Evangelina's family to request permission to marry her.

6

"The name Tagliaferri means 'iron cutter,' doesn't it?" asked the senior Piergiorgi. "But, you work with wood."

Emilio explained that according to family tradition, in the medieval period his early ancestors worked for the count of the Statto Castle across the Trebbia from Rivergaro making armor and iron implements.

"That was long ago," he said. "Now we have a new trade that lets a man comfortably support a wife and a family."

The conversation turned to the dedication ceremony and how moving it had been. Then Evangelina's uncle and her brothers were summoned to join some men who were speaking with the bishop from Piacenza. That left Evangelina in the company of her mother Giuliana and her sister Giaele, who both casually moved a discreet distance away from her and Emilio.

Emilio looked at Evangelina and said, "I apologize for interrupting your family discussion. However, I really wanted to meet you. You are very beautiful, you know."

Evangelina refused to be demure. She said, "Are you always this direct with people you do not know?"

"Only with the woman I intend to marry," he replied.

***

The view from the terrace of the Chiesa di Santa Maria Assunta was spectacular. That is why he brought Evangelina there; particularly on this day that he hoped would be so memorable for both of them. He knew that it would be a long ride from her home in Montechiaro to Travo, across the Ponte di Travo, then on toward Statto and finally the long climb up to Pigazzano, some 400 meters above the Trebbia. So, he left Statto very early that morning to ensure that he would have enough time to take her to Pigazzano and then return to Montechiaro before dark. He decided to take the *calesse*, a light two-wheeled carriage that he recently bought for his mother. A mare with a shiny chestnut coat that Emilio had just groomed pulled the carriage. He wanted to make sure that even the horse made a good impression on her.

Emilio had been concerned about winning the acceptance of Evangelina's family. Then luckily, a day came when her uncle and brothers needed a good carpenter to repair the *stalla* in which they kept the livestock and stored the hay that fed them. Evangelina's uncle "invited" him to replace the old, unsound timbers in the lower level and add planking to the wood deck on the second level. Typical of all of the *stalle* in that region, the animals were kept on the ground level and fodder was stored on the second level. Emilio knew that this was not actually an invitation but rather a command performance, so the men of the family could test his skills and decide the extent they would allow him to continue to court Evangelina.

At the end of a long and hard day's work, it was clear that Emilio had passed the test. In fact, Evangelina's uncle seemed to be particularly impressed with Emilio's knowledge of carpentry from rough to finished work and with his ability to quickly assess exactly what needed to be done and how to do it. Not that he received any compliments from them. But, he sensed their approval and then became certain of his acceptance when Evangelina's mother invited him to join them for supper. Later, she suggested that rather than make the long trip back to Statto that night, perhaps she could prepare a comfortable place for him to sleep in the loft of the *stalla*. That was several months ago and since then he had seen Evangelina every chance he had.

Emilio knew that Evangelina's uncle would never allow him to take her unescorted on an all-day drive in his *calesse*, the horse-drawn carriage that was used only for important purposes, such as taking his mother to church or to Rivergaro to buy the cloth she needed to make a new dress for herself or shirts for Emilio and his brothers. Because of this, he had invited Evangelina's older sister Giaele to join them. Evangelina and Giaele packed a picnic basket and all three set off as soon as Emilio arrived. After a two-hour ride, they picnicked in a field below Pigazzano owned by a friend of Emilio's late father, who had a large flock of *pecore* that supplied milk for the pecorino formaggio he made and sold in Rivergaro. They had a light picnic lunch of salume, formaggio, olives, pane, and vino rosso and then continued on to the church at the top of the hill. Emilio secured the mare and the *calesse* and then the three of them walked up to the upper level of the church's small piazza, where they now stood.

Evangelina noticed that Emilio seemed to be a little edgy and nervous, completely out of character because he usually projected a calm confidence. Giaele sensed that Emilio wanted to say something to Evangelina in private and discretely walked to the other side of the piazza, gazing over the railing at the magnificent panorama below them. Emilio slid his hand over Evangelina's and pointed to the vista of Rivergaro and the Trebbia far below.

Bellaria di Rivergaro

"Can you believe it is this clear today? He asked. "Look," he said, pointing out into the distance. "You can see how the land flattens out into the Pianura Padana beyond Rivergaro." "In fact," he added, "I can see Piacenza in the distance and the new railroad bridge that they built over the Po River."

Evangelina moved closer to him and moved her hand to his arm. She said, "It is so pretty, Emilio. I can even see the Alps from here and I know that they must be many kilometers away. And look, there is the Castello di Statto, your parish church, Sant'Antonio Abate, and I can even see the landing at Statto where people take the *barcone* to cross the *fiume* when the water is too high to ford. They all seem so little from here," she said, almost in disbelief of the view below her.

The panoramic view was indeed incredible. The courtyard of the church was 465 meters above sea level and it was possible to see the Alps at least sixty miles in the distance, including snow-capped Monte Bianca, the highest of the Italian Alps. Immediately below them, the gently sloping mountainside was spotted with neatly separated plots of land owned by the local farmers. In some of the plots, wheat waved gently in the wind and in others there were flocks of sheep tended by their herdsmen. Everywhere there were small vineyards. It was too early in the season for grapes, but the leaves on the vines were full and stretched toward the sun that warmed the soil nourishing their roots. The red tiled roofs of the small beige and sand colored stone houses, like the one in which Evangelina and her mother lived in Montechiaro, added a paintbrush touch to the deep green of the mountainside fields. At the base of the mountain, the

Trebbia could be seen twisting from Statto toward the north, past Rivergaro and beyond the Castello di Rivalta, where the hills gave way to the Pianura Padana.

A light, cool wind brushed the faces of the three of them and they could not break their gaze from the vista below. Evangelina looked up at Emilio. He was not a tall man, but he was a full head taller than she was. "Emilio, why did you bring me here today? It is all so perfect," she said. "The ride, the picnic, the beautiful little town, and now this incredible view," she added. "Why, Emilio?"

Emilio felt weak in the knees. His hands were sweating, although the air was dry and cool. It was as though his brain would not send the right signals to his mouth, preventing him from saying the words he wanted to say. Then finally, in a voice that was not at all as strong and confident as he planned, he blurted out loudly:

"Because I love you so very much, and because I want to marry you, and because I want you to be my wife forever and I want us to become a family and have many children," he rambled. Then he continued, "And even though I am a lot older than you are I..."

Giaele heard Emilio speaking in a loud voice and turned toward the two of them, obviously startled. Evangelina put her hand to Emilio's mouth, interrupting him, and softly said,

"Emilio, don't you know that I love you, too?" "Of course I will be your wife!" "No, you are not too old for me, and yes, we will have as many children as God gives us."

11

Giaele gasped. Emilio sighed with relief. Evangelina cried, then she hugged Emilio tightly and then the two of them kissed softly at first, then deeply, while Giaele wiped tears from her eyes. What an incredible day!

Chapter 2

AFTER THEIR WEDDING, Emilio and Evangelina lived in
the house of Emilio's mother Luigia. Emilio's father Giovanni
died a few years earlier and his mother insisted that they live
with her to help fill "an empty nest," as she called it. The
house was located below the Castello di Statto, the Statto
Castle, not far from the banks of the Trebbia. When Emilio's
father Giovanni was alive, the family operated a small
foodstuff store in part of the house. They also had a few
tables outside where they would serve food to the people
traveling between Statto landing and Rivergaro across the
Trebbia.

The house had only two bedrooms, although at first it
seemed to be large enough for everyone. However, only one
year after they were married, Elisa was born, to be followed
barely a year later by Luigi. Almost overnight, the house had
become too small. Any noise, like someone coughing or one
of the babies crying, would awaken everyone, making it
difficult to get a good night's sleep. This was not a good
situation. So, Emilio looked for another place for his growing
family to live and found a small, modest house called "La
Casella," the box, only fifty meters from the Statto Bridge.
Luigia continued to live in her own house. However, Silvio,
Emilio's younger brother, moved back with her so that she
would not have to live alone.

Emilio found that everything he needed for the family's
carpentry business was located conveniently nearby the Statto
house. He was close to the little *mulino* where they obtained

the wood they needed to make the slats and paddles for their customers' waterwheels. He kept the *barra*, with its two oversized wheels he used to carry heavy loads and ford the river, in the field next to the house, together with the horses and ox and everything else that he needed in his work. However, Emilio was concerned that most of his customers were now located on the other side of the Trebbia in Rivergaro and in the area north toward Piacenza. It was getting to be more and more difficult to operate his trade from the Statto side of the Trebbia.

***

Emilio awoke with the memory of that wonderful day in Pigazzano, now several years in the past, still fresh in his memory. He tried not to disturb Evangelina as he prepared to leave the Statto house before dawn so that he could begin work early across the Trebbia at the Sconti *cascina*. If he left before sunup, he would arrive at the farm by 6:30 AM and get a head start on the job so that he could be home by dark. Il Signor Giacomo Sconti was an important customer and one who had used the services of Emilio and his family often throughout the years. Today, Emilio and his brothers Giuseppe and Silvio would be working on the addition of an annex to the main *cascina* buildings of Ca'Sconti that would house two to four additional seasonal farm workers. It was hard work, but it paid well and Il Signor Sconti always paid promptly and in cash – not some form of credit like some of the other local farmers did.

As Emilio began to dress, Evangelina wakened and rose from their bed. Emilio was not surprised.

"Emilio, why do you try to sneak out of the house without even a light *colazione*? You know that is not good for you," she chided.

"What kind of a wife do you think I am that I would let my husband go off to work without something to eat? Let me make you at least a caffè and you can have one of the fruit-filled croissants that I made yesterday, your favorite kind – the ones filled with apricots."

Emilio quickly drank the coffee that Evangelina had made for him and ate one of the apricot-filled croissants. Then he threw the satchel with the salume, pane and a corked bottle of vino Evangelina gave him into the *barra*, a two-wheeled cart commonly used in the region to haul heavy loads of goods and material. Today, because of the heavy load of wood and tools, he hitched an ox to the cart and set off on the road to the Statto Bridge, which was the closest place that he could cross the river to reach the Sconti *cascina*. Emilio could have ridden in the *barra* because some time ago he built a seat atop it just for that reason. However, the road leading to the bridge was very rutted. He felt more comfortable guiding the ox with his hand close to the bit rather than taking a chance that it might pull the cart into a rut off the road where it could damage a wheel or, even worse, break its wooden axle.

During early spring in the lower valley, the heavy rain and snowmelt in the Alta Val Trebbia raised the river level by as much as five meters. However, for the rest of the year there was relatively little water in the river, most of it flowing in narrow channels, leaving a vast area of dry, rocky riverbed. For several months each year, the Trebbia in the lower valley was often no more than half a meter deep and the large two-wheeled *barra* could ford it easily, as long as it was pulled by a strong animal and driven by a person who knew how to navigate the uneven, rocky bottom.

When Emilio chose the Statto house for his young family, part of his decision was that the house was only fifty meters from the Statto Bridge. The house was fairly isolated, its nearest neighbor being a much larger farm complex called Casa di Marchesi several hundred meters away. Nonetheless, the Statto house provided Emilio with closer access to his customers across the river while still being within carriage or walking distance to his mother's house, to the church of Sant'Antonio Abate where he had the task of climbing the bell tower, the *campanile*, every Sunday to pull the ropes that rang the church bell, and to a family foodstuff store and *osteria* operated by a cousin.

Another way to cross the river was to simply ford it, either on foot, on horseback or in a horse-drawn cart. For those people on the Statto side of the river who were going to Rivergaro or Piacenza, the closest fording place was at the Statto landing, immediately below the Castello di Statto. That was also the site of the third way to cross the river, which was by a *barcone*, a small, shallow draft boat propelled by sculling and poling that could carry as many as ten to fifteen passengers. The *barcone* transited the distance between Statto and Rivergaro on a more or less regular basis. However, for Emilio's purpose, it had limited value because crossing the river at the Statto Bridge was the only way he could take his ox and cart with its heavy load of tools and lumber across at times when the river was high, as it was now.

16

A golden dawn broke over the hills in the east. Emilio guided the cart and ox across the Statto Bridge that had been built less than ten years earlier. He turned and caught a glance of the Statto house in the distance and could see a faint light in the front window, where he imagined Evangelina was likely nursing bimba Elvira. His mind drifted to the day he took Evangelina up to Pigazzano and proposed to her, and to the day soon after, when he rode the mare to Montechiaro to ask her uncle for permission to marry her.

Alessio Piergiorgi was not really Evangelina's uncle. During their brief courtship, Evangelina told Emilio she was the adopted daughter of Luigi Piergiorgi and his wife Giuliana. Evangelina's birth mother died at childbirth and soon after she was born, her father decided to emigrate from Montechiaro to Bellavista, Argentina. He asked his cousin, Luigi Piergiorgi and his wife to take care of Evangelina until he got a job and returned for her in a few years. However, they never heard from him again and as time passed, they assumed he was dead. By that time, Evangelina was six years old and the Piergiorgi's were the only parents that she ever knew. As time passed, Giuliana and Luigi decided to adopt her. Sadly, Luigi, himself met an early death from pneumonia and so Luigi's brother Alessio became not only Evangelina's adopted uncle, but also her father figure and protector – a job that he took very seriously.

Much to his surprise, there was no "inquisition" when Emilio asked for Evangelina's hand in marriage. It was obvious to Alessio and Giuliana that Emilio and Evangelina loved each other. More important, however, it was also clear that Emilio had the personal and family resources to support

Evangelina and any children that they might have.
Consequently, there was only a token discussion about Emilio
personally, his occupation and his ability to provide support
for Evangelina, and about Emilio's family, who clearly adored
Evangelina. When the formality was completed, wedding
planning began. Certain inter-family arrangements were
made and, even at this late time in the nineteenth century, a
small dowry was negotiated.

***

As he guided the cart across the, narrow 200 meter-long
bridge, Emilio's mind once again drifted to the wedding now
almost six years in the past.

Italian tradition called for the bride to wear a green dress
on the pre-wedding day and stay with her parents that night.
This was not a problem for Evangelina because she lived with
her mother. Luckily, Piacentini wedding customs differed in
some respects from the wedding customs in many other parts
of Italy. In Tuscany, for example, brides traditionally wore a
black wedding dress and carried a fan, even in winter.
However, in Venice brides wore their second best dress to the
wedding, saving their very best for the formal ball that would
follow the ceremony. Evangelina had other plans.

Emilio was a religious man. As a child, he regularly
served as an altar boy at the little church in Statto. There was
no daily Mass there because there were not enough
parishioners to justify the daily, arduous trip from Rivergaro
to Statto. However, a priest from Rivergaro made the trip to
say a Holy Mass at 10:30 AM every Sunday. Nonetheless,
Emilio found long, drawn out Masses tedious and something

to avoid. So, he was gratified to learn the traditional two and one-half hour wedding ceremony at Sant'Ilario Vescovo in Montechiaro was shortened to only an hour and a half; after the wedding, the priest had to travel to Travo to say another Mass.

The wedding Mass was set to begin at 10:00 AM on Sunday, the traditional day for Italian weddings. Emilio's brothers would comprise his wedding party together with Franco Grazolo, his best friend, who would be his best man. There would be four women in Evangelina's wedding party. Her maid of honor was her older sister Giaele. None of the young women in Evangelina's wedding party were married. Therefore, it was fortunate that over the past forty to fifty years there had been a change in the traditional make-up of a bride's wedding party. Previously, only married women could serve as bridesmaids or, for that matter, even attend a wedding. However, these were modern times and young Italian women relished their recently liberated status.

The wedding ceremony was simple but beautiful. Evangelina wore a red silk gown, hand-sewn by a friend of her mother who worked on the dress for several weeks. She chose red because that was the color of the dress that she wore when Emilio first saw her and fell in love with her. Emilio was dressed awkwardly in a black suit that ill-fitted him, as was obvious by his frequent squirming. Under the suit jacket he wore a white linen shirt and a red *cravatta*, a necktie that matched Evangelina's dress. The bridesmaids' dresses more or less matched Evangelina's in color and design; but there was a lack of uniformity in clothing among the groom's men – not surprising considering that such clothing for them was both uncomfortable and unfamiliar. In the end, it did not matter. The bride and groom, their relatives and all of the wedding guests later said this was the most beautiful event that they had ever attended.

***

As he neared the Rivergaro side of the bridge, Emilio allowed himself one last thought of his beautiful bride and of their lingering kiss on the altar after the priest had proclaimed them man and wife. He remembered exiting the church to the greeting of a happy crowd that showered them with rice, laughter and well wishes and the bountiful feast that followed, accompanied by an endless supply of vino, limoncello, and grappa, as well as music and dancing that went on until well after dusk. Emilio agreed with the wedding guests; it was the most wonderful event that he had ever attended. He would remember it for the rest of his life. However, the wedding was in the past. Now he had to focus on the present. He felt a growing need to provide a more comfortable and stable life for Evangelina and the children. The question was how could he do this?

Chapter 3

EMILIO GUIDED THE OX AND THE *BARRA* on to the
Rivergaro shore and began the long trek uphill toward the
Sconti property. The road turned left past the landing and
then ran straight toward the top of the hill. On the left, was a
large open field that sloped all the way down to the Trebbia.
The land seemed to be fertile; however, it was strewed with
rocks and clusters of trees. To the right of the road – not
much more than a cart path – the land sloped upward until it
reached the hill crest, not more than fifty to seventy-five
meters above the river level, where it connected with the
main road, the *Strada Statale*, that began in Piacenza and
continued past Rivergaro to Bobbio and then on to Genoa.

At the top of the rise, the land flattened for less than a
half-hectare. Emilio knew this place well because he stopped
there for a few minutes each time he was in the area. From
this level area, he could see across the gently sloping hillside
down to the rocky Trebbia and across to the Statto side where
he could easily see the Castello di Statto and his parish
church. He thought about how much Evangelina and the
children would like this place and decided to bring them here
after Holy Mass on the coming Sunday. It would be a great
place to have a picnic. Afterward, he could take the children
down to the Trebbia, so that they could throw stones in the
river and wade in the shallow water.

Interrupting his own thoughts, Emilio focused back on
what he and his brothers had to do at the Sconti farm. It took

him less than a half-hour to reach Ca'Sconti where Giacomo Sconti was waiting.

"*Buongiorno, Emilio. Come va?*" Good morning, Emilio. How goes it?

"*Bene, Signore Sconti. Si, tutto va bene stamattino. È Lei?*" Good, Signore Sconti. Yes, everything is going well this morning. And, you?

"*Beh, mezzo mezzo,*" he replied, suggesting that things could be better. He then told Emilio that his youngest son Carlo had informed him that he wanted to immigrate to America, where he heard jobs were plentiful and everybody gets rich.

"I told him that's a bunch of *merda*; that he better think twice about it because America is a very long way from here and if he goes there he is completely on his own. But, how can you reason with these young people?"

"How old is Carlo, Giacomo?" Emilio asked, reverting to a more personal level. Emilio's father Giovanni would never have considered speaking in such a personal way to a man like Giacomo Sconti, whose ancestors included a count in the Farnese family in Piacenza. Furthermore, the man was almost old enough to be Emilio's father. But times had changed and, although Giacomo Sconti was a large landowner and a successful farmer, he also respected Emilio, his brothers and Emilio's late father Giovanni as being successful tradespeople, who themselves had achieved a certain status in the neighboring communities.

"He will be twenty next month," Sconti replied. "The truth is that there is nothing keeping him here. He does not have a woman and the chances are he may soon wind up in the army," referring to a recent edict proscribing compulsory military service in the army of Victor Emmanuel III, Italy's monarch, for single men the age of the young Sconti. "It would break his mother's heart if he went to America. However, it could save his ass if The King ever decides to send his army to invade Ethiopia as he keeps threatening."

"Well, personally, I do not know anyone who has gone to America. However, Evangelina has a cousin who went to New York some time ago and who opened a grocery business in the part of the city where there are many Italian immigrants. If you like, I can get some information for you."

"*Grazie mille,*" Giacomo replied in appreciation. "Please see what you can find out. In the meanwhile, before your brothers arrive there is something that I want to talk to you about."

Giacomo Sconti led Emilio into the *cucina* of the farmhouse. Like most Italian country kitchens, the *cucina* of the Sconti house featured a large fireplace with various size kettles and skillets that were used to prepare meals in the past. However, as was fitting for a man of Giacomo Sconti's economic standing, the kitchen now also featured a modern wood burning stove that was Signora Sconti's delight.

"Maria, please make some caffè for Emilio and me," Giacomo said.

"*Buongiorno, Signora Sconti,*" said Emilio. Although under the circumstances it was acceptable for him to address

Giacomo by his first name, protocol absolutely prohibited Emilio from using any familiar form with the Signora Sconti.

"Buongiorno, Emilio," she replied. "Please sit over at the table and I will have some coffee for you and Giacomo in just a few minutes."

Earlier her husband had told her that he wanted to talk with Emilio, so anticipating the request for caffè, Maria ground the coffee beans and filled the top part of the stovetop *"Moka"* Pot with the ground coffee, making sure that the metal filter was in place. She then filled the bottom chamber with cold water from the well, screwed the top part on to the water-filled chamber, and placed it on the hot stove. As the water began to boil, the steam pot made a gurgling sound, signaling that the boiling water was extracting the essence from the coffee grounds. Signora Sconti waited until the *"Moka"* Pot began to steam and removed it from the stove. After letting the brew stand for about five minutes, she filled two small espresso-size cups with the brewed caffè and brought them to the men, keeping the inevitable refill in reserve.

Thanking her, the two men sipped their coffee. Emilio wondered what this was all about, hoping that there was no problem with the job on which he and his brothers had been working. Giacomo seemed to be pensive, his gaze fixed on his cup of coffee. Then he looked at Emilio and spoke in a serious tone.

"I have known your family for a long time. Your father Giovanni was a good carpenter and he did a good job training you and your brothers Giuseppe and Silvio in his trade so that you could carry on the family business.

"But, as I look at the three of you it seems to me that you are the one with the best sense of business. So, I have a proposition for you," the elderly Sconti said.

Emilio sat impassively, not knowing how to respond.

"You know that in addition to this *cascina*, I own a lot of property down by the Trebbia, "he said. "In fact, I own ten hectares between the *Strada Statale*, the state road linking Piacenza and Bobbio, where the turnoff runs to the Statto Bridge, Travo and Rivalta, and the river.

"I know it well, Giacomo," replied Emilio. "I have to pass though it every time that I work on this side of the river. In fact, today I stopped to rest for a few minutes at the top of the collina where you can look down to the crossing and even across the river to the Castello di Statto and my church.

"It's a beautiful view. Actually, I plan to take Evangelina and the children there on this coming Sunday for a picnic," he added, knowing that no landowner in the area would object to his undeveloped land used for that purpose by anyone else in the community. There was no concept of trespass among the local people.

"Well, how would you like to own that land?" asked Giacomo.

Emilio was stunned. Own that land, he wondered! How could such a thing be possible?

"I would give anything to own even a part of that land, of course," Emilio said. "But, even though I have some financial resources, they could not possibly be enough to buy all of that property."

"Perhaps not right now," the older man replied. "But, here is my proposition."

Giacomo Sconti then laid out his proposal to Emilio. Although he owned the property, he never developed it into farmland. Moreover, he did not need to do so; his other land holdings were more than sufficient to take care of the needs of him and his family. He thought about giving the property to his youngest son, Carlo, as a future wedding gift. However, Giacomo knew that Carlo was very serious about immigrating to America. Once there, he could use cash, instead, so that he could start up some kind of business. Further, none of Giacomo's other sons had expressed an interest in owning that particular property. Therefore, Giacomo decided to sell it.

"I know the majority of your family's business is now on this side of the river. In order to practice your carpentry trade, you need a good supply of timber. You cut and convert the timber to lumber the size you need to make blades and slats for the water wheels in the mills and for the timbers and planks you use to repair and build the *stalle*, like the one here that you are working on today," he stated.

"But now, you have to transport everything that you make and need across the Trebbia – a very tedious and expensive process."

"Yes, that is true," interrupted Emilio. "Of course, I would very much like to have my own mill to cut lumber on this side of the river. However, I still do not see how I could afford to buy your property."

"Initially, you would not own it outright," said Giacomo. "You would lease it from me, but you would have the right to buy it within ten years at a reasonable, predetermined price. I will even hire you to build a *mulino* at a place where you can channel water from the river to the water wheel that would supply all the power you will need to cut lumber and even grind wheat and corn," he explained. "In return, I want ten percent of all of the revenue that you generate from the *mulino* and from your use of the land. Thirty percent of that fee would apply to the purchase price of the property if you exercise your option to buy it within the next ten years. And, you can work the land anyway that you want."

At first, Emilio did not know what to say. On one hand, it seemed so unlikely that something like this could ever be realistic. However, Giacomo was quite sincere when he proposed the deal and, already, Emilio was thinking about the many possibilities that such an arrangement might offer him and his brothers.

"Giacomo, I truly don't know what to say. Your proposition overwhelms me in its generosity. I cannot imagine why you would make such an offer to me."

"Don't be misled, Emilio. Of course, I see a profit potential here. If I do nothing with the land, it will simply remain an undeveloped piece of property. If I am able to sell it at today's market price, which is not very favorable, I make a little money, but not much. However, I have a feeling that with the *mulino* and whatever else you do with the land, it will not be long before it starts generating decent revenue and I want part of that money."

"One question, Giacomo," countered Emilio. "I understand that I would pay you rent until I exercised my option to purchase the property, with part of that rent being applied to the purchase price. Must I wait for the full ten years or could I pay off whatever the balance on the option is before the ten years?"

"Of course," answered Giacomo. "You would have the right to pay the full option price at any time within 10 years. However, if you did not exercise your option by then, your right to that particular price would expire."

"There is one other condition, Emilio," he added. "I do not want to see that land remain idle. If you accept my proposal, I would expect that you will put it to good use."

The sounds coming from the *stalla* suggested that Giuseppe and Silvio had arrived. Emilio told Giacomo that he should join them and get to work on the repairs to the animal stalls and the expansion of sleeping quarters for the additional workers. Giacomo nodded in agreement.

"Let me speak with my brothers," Emilio said. "We will get back to you very soon. I do want to say again, Giacomo, that this is a very interesting proposition."

Emilio decided not to discuss Giacomo's proposal with Giuseppe and Silvio until they had returned to Statto. He knew that they would be as astounded by the proposal as he was and he did not want their reaction to interfere with the job at hand. In addition, Emilio wanted time to think about the proposal, its ramifications for him and Evangelina and for all of them. One of the traits that Emilio admired most about his late father was that Giovanni was a very good decision maker. He rarely made a decision about an important issue without thinking it through. Emilio realized that if there ever was a time to follow that practice it was right now.

***

The three brothers sat at the heavy wooden table in the kitchen of the house that Giuseppe built for himself and his wife Claudia about two kilometers past the Statto Bridge on the road to Rivalta. Giuseppe was the eldest of the three, brothers, having recently celebrated his forty-third birthday. Emilio was forty-one and at age thirty-five, Silvio was the youngest. Emilio explained Giacomo's proposition to them and the more they discussed it the less feasible it seemed.

"This is not for me, Emilio," Giuseppe said. "I am a carpenter, not a farmer. I have no idea what I would do with all that land and I do not want to take on any additional obligation, even though Il Signor Sconti's offer seems to be quite generous."

"There are certain conditions very favorable to him, you know," Giuseppe added.

"And you, Silvio?" Emilio asked.

Silvio was unmarried and lived with his mother in the family home and *osteria* below the Statto Castle. Like his two brothers, he also was a carpenter.

"It's much the same for me, Emilio. However, I do like the idea of the *mulino*. I think that it would be great if the three of us had a small sawmill on the Rivergaro side of the Trebbia. Most of the good timber is up on the Alta Val Trebbia and it would be a lot easier if we could simply bring it down to our own *mulino* on the Rivergaro side, cut it into lumber, slats and paddles right there without having to haul it across from Statto."

Giuseppe grunted in agreement.

"So, what do you suggest? That we ask Giacomo to sell us only enough land to build a *mulino*?"

Emilio's question to the other two met with silence. They debated the Sconti proposal for another hour without reaching any kind of consensus. At that point, Emilio decided to conclude the discussion.

"Look," he said. "We agree that it would be in our mutual interest to have better access to the timber in the Alta Val Trebbia and be able to cut it on the Rivergaro side of the *fiume* so that the cut wood we need is closer and more convenient to the work we get over there."

"Both of you seem to lack interest in working the land," he added. "So, if I personally bought the property and took responsibility for working it, would the two of you be willing to help me build the *mulino* and any outbuildings that we might need to operate it? We might even be able to make some money cutting lumber for other people, as well as having all we need for our own trade."

Silvio seemed to be enthusiastic about the idea now that it was clear that he would not have to do any serious farming.

Giuseppe was more skeptical, but nonetheless agreed that the idea could work.

"Besides," he said to Emilio, "We are a family, and what is a family if we cannot help each other?"

Three weeks later, Emilio contacted Giacomo and told him that he would like to discuss his proposition further. He also informed him that Evangelina had a cousin named Alberto Zanmatti who had immigrated to America several years ago and who now had a grocery supply business in the Italian district of New York. Zanmatti agreed to sponsor Giacomo's son for immigration purposes and offered him a job working in his grocery business. Sconti seemed to be very relieved to learn that his youngest son would be looked after when he arrived in New York and he readily agreed to meet with Emilio to discuss the matter of the property.

Emilio wanted to avoid the impression that he was overly anxious to obtain the Sconti property, so he waited until he had another occasion to be in Rivergaro to visit the Sconti farm and meet with Giacomo. He explained to the elderly Sconti that he alone would lease the property from him, although his brothers would be involved in building the *mulino* and operating it.

Emilio had another idea about how he would use the property, as well. However, he chose not to discuss it with Giacomo at this meeting. He did request that any other use of the land be at his sole discretion. Giacomo did not seem to have a problem with this, so he arranged a meeting with the *notaio* he used to handle the legal matters of his farm and other business interests to draw up the lease-option agreement.

During the next thirty days, the *notaio* had the property surveyed to ensure that there was no question about its boundaries. Then, Emilio returned to the Sconti farm with Giuseppe and Silvio, who together with Giacomo's sons served as witnesses to the transaction. The parties signed the documents and exchanged congratulations, fortified with a liberal amount of homemade Piacentino wine. As he left the Sconti farm, Emilio was already envisioning another use for his newly acquired land – one that would surely please Evangelina.

Chapter 4

EVANGELINA SPREAD THE RED and white checkered oilcloth over the wooden table Emilio built on their favorite spot at the top of hill. It was a perfect day for a picnic, just like the many others that she, Emilio, and their children enjoyed on this spot since Emilio acquired the property from Giacomo Sconti. Emilio was down by the river with his brothers who were cutting lumber in the *mulino* they had built. She turned toward her son Luigi and said,

"Luigi, go tell your father that lunch is ready. Let your uncles know that if they are hungry they are welcome to join us. There is more than enough food for all of us."

Luigi ran down the hill with the message for his father. Elisa helped her mother set the table and slice the salume, formaggio, and pane that together with the marinated vegetables would be their picnic fare. Meanwhile, Elvira and her sister Maria played nearby with willow hoops that Emilio made for them. Farther down the slope of the hill, toward the north, a few cows and sheep were grazing near the *stalla* that Emilio built to shelter them and to store the hay and willow that served as their winter feedstock. It was an idyllic, tranquil scene made more beautiful by the burnt orange-hue of the poppies that filled the green fields at this time of year.

Luigi shouted breathlessly at his father, "Papà, mamma wants you to come up for lunch."

"*Si, Gigi,*" Emilio responded, using the common nickname for Luigi. "*Subito!* Right away!" he said.

Luigi almost forgot the other part of the message his mother told him to deliver, but as he and Emilio turned to leave he said, "Uncle Giuseppe and Uncle Silvio, mamma said there is plenty of food for you, too."

"*Grazie*. Thank you, Gigi. Tell your mamma that if your Aunt Claudia had not already packed Silvio and me a fine lunch we would certainly join you."

Emilio and Luigi walked uphill toward the distant rise and the table where Evangelina and the girls waited for them. At one point, Emilio stopped and pointed to a rock half the size of a soccer ball.

"Gigi, pick up that rock and give it to me," he said.

Luigi bent over and began struggling with the rock.

"Is it a little too heavy for you, son," Emilio asked.

"No papà. I am strong. Look at my muscles!" The boy answered, finally getting a grasp on the rock and passing it to his father. "But, why do you want the rock?"

"I don't need the rock today, young one," Emilio replied. "But, I think that soon we will need many rocks like this one from the field, and also others from the river. I wanted to see if you will be able to help me take them to where they will be needed."

"Where is that, papà," Luigi asked?

"Later, Gigi. We will talk about it later. But, yes, you are a very strong young man and I think that in order to build even stronger muscles you need to eat a good lunch. So, come along. We do not want to keep your mamma and sisters waiting."

Evangelina always prepared delicious picnic lunches. However, this one was special. There were two types of salume plus some excellent aged prosciutto that was made by one of her cousins who lived in Lugagnano on the other side of the mountain, not far from the ancient walled town of Castell'Arquato. The formaggi she selected included Grana Padano, an economical, tasty hard cheese that was a close relative to the more costly Parmigiano Reggiano. She also packed a soft, blue cheese from the town of Gorgonzola, a good half-day distant from Statto and Rivergaro, but readily available in local markets. The olives were grown locally and cured from last year's crop. However, the roasted red peppers and pickled onions or *cippoli* were a product of the small *giardino* that Evangelina tended behind the Statto house. Boiled and then marinated in balsamic vinegar from Modena, together with a few spices that made up her private recipe, the *cippoli* made an irresistible accompaniment to any meal. The beverages were local, homemade wine and sparkling water – acqua minerale – from a natural spring farther up the valley.

As Evangelina walked back to the cart to retrieve the basket containing a chocolate dessert torta she had made especially for the lunch, a heavily loaded four-wheeled wagon drawn by two horses, approaching from the direction of Bobbio, passed by, the driver waving.

"Where are you coming from," she asked, not recognizing the man.

Bellaria di Rivergaro

"All the way from Genoa," he answered, reining the
horses to a stop. "It's been a long trip. I had to remain for the
night in Ottone, but today I must get to Piacenza by
nightfall."

"Rivergaro is only a half-hour from here. If you stay on
the *Strada Statale*, Piacenza is another couple of hours after
that. I think that you can get there before dark. What are you
carrying," she asked.

"A little bit of everything. A ship from England arrived in
Genoa a couple of days ago and I have some machine parts
that a man in Milan ordered. However, I also have many
sacks of rice from the Cavour Canal and even some bolts of
muslin and linen for the dressmakers in Piacenza."

"You are a merchant, then," she said.

"I am," he answered. "And a hungry one, at that," he
added, looking at the feast that Evangelina was laying out on
the table. "So, if I want to have supper in Piacenza I better get
moving along."

Evangelina cut a few slices of salume and a piece of
cheese.

"Well, here is a little something to tide you over until you
get to Piacenza," she said, handing the merchant the food that
she wrapped in a piece of the brown paper lining one of the
baskets.

"*Grazie mille*," he said, as he snapped the reins urging the
horses on. "You should put up a kiosk here. It's a good place
to sell things to travelers like me."

36

As Emilio and Luigi approached the picnic *pranzo* that Evangelina had prepared with the help of her oldest daughter Elisa, Luigi ran ahead to report to his mother that he had given her message to his uncles but that they already had a lunch packed by Aunt Claudia. He also proudly showed off his muscles to his sisters and told them that papà said that he was strong enough to help him carry rocks out of the field. That brought on the usual taunting that his three sisters loved to give him.

"Papà," said Elisa, "Why do you want Gigi to help you take rocks out of the field?"

The three girls ran over to Emilio who stretched out his arms to embrace all of them at the same time.

"Later, later," he replied. "First we will eat our lunch and then we will talk about it."

Emilio turned to Evangelina, who looked at him curiously. He had not paid much attention when she packed all of the picnic food in the baskets, even though he had loaded them into the cart. He had no idea that she had prepared such a lavish spread.

"Evangelina, what's this all about," he asked. "You have prepared a feast – not a picnic lunch. This is fantastic! *Mi è venuta l'acquolina in bocca*," he said, indicating that the sight and odor of all of the food on the picnic table would inspire anyone's appetite and provoke them to start eating! "The *pranzo* that you prepare after Holy Mass on Sundays with mamma, Giuseppe, Claudia and their children, Silvio and my sisters Livia, Giuseppa and Tilde is not much more elaborate than this," he exclaimed.

Evangelina directed the four children to sit at their places as she filled their plates with the cold meats, cheese, and the vegetables that she had prepared.

"Mamma," said Elvira. "I don't want to eat the *cippoli*! They're too sour and I don't like them," she whined.

"You will eat everything that I put on your plate," Evangelina said sternly, "or there will be no *torta cioccolata* for you for dessert!"

"Actually, this is a special occasion," Evangelina said to Emilio. "I have something to tell you and I thought that a little celebration would be appropriate."

Emilio looked at her curiously. He was not entirely sure what was coming, but nonetheless thought that it best if he sat down.

"Emilio, do you remember that day in Pigazzano when you proposed to me and said that you wanted to have many children?"

Emilio nodded in anticipation, waiting for her to continue.

"Well, I think that just might happen. We're going to have another baby!"

The children stopped eating in unison and looked at their mother with wide eyes. Emilio's mouth gaped open.

"Are you trying to catch flies, Emilio?" Evangelina asked. However, before he could muster an answer, she walked over to him, sat on his lap, and gave him a big hug. Emilio, embraced her tenderly, smiled broadly, and then smothered her with kisses. The children started shouting and clapping their hands.

Luigi got up from the table and put his hands on his hips defiantly.

"I want a brother," he firmly declared. "I've got too many sisters!"

Elisa said that she didn't care if she had a brother or a sister, while Maria said that she wanted a baby sister to play with her. Elvira decided that this would be a good time to grab a piece of the chocolate torta before her mother made her eat the *cippoli*. No one seemed to mind at all.

***

When lunch was finished, Emilio helped Evangelina pack the cart for the return trip to Statto. He told her that he would stay on with his brothers to help them at the mill. Evangelina gathered the children, except for Luigi, who asked to return with his father and uncles later in the day.

"Emilio, is there something about collecting rocks that I should know?" she asked.

"Yes, papà," Luigi chimed in. "You said that you would tell me later where we are going to put all of the rocks."

"We're going to put them right here, Luigi – many, many of them."

Emilio put his arm around Evangelina's shoulders. They walked along the top of the rise past the picnic table to where they could see the Trebbia a few hundred meters in the distance. A clean, cooling breeze flowed down from the Alta Val Trebbia, countering the heat of the day.

"The reason is very simple. We have outgrown the Statto house – even more so now that you are expecting another baby. I intend to build a house for us, right here on this spot," he said, turning and making a sweeping motion, as though he was showing her the picnic area for the first time.

"But, it will not be just a house," he declared. "This is where the road to Statto and Rivalta turns off from the road to Bobbio and Genoa. Anyone who wants to travel to any of those places must pass this very spot."

"I know," she said. "Earlier a merchant from Genoa passed by here and he said that it would be a great place to have a kiosk selling food stuff."

"I have something more than that in mind. You know, I promised Giacomo Sconti that I would develop this land and he gave me free reign to do what I want. Giuseppe, Silvio, and I built the *mulino* and it is working quite nicely. However, among other reasons, I am getting very tired of all of the travel, and being away from you and the children, that building and repairing *mulini* for people as far away as Podenzano on the Nure River requires. Giuseppe and Silvio do not seem to mind it so much, but I do – even more now that we are going to have another child."

"The children and I don't like it, either, Emilio. But, we understand that you are doing it for us."

"I think there is something that we can do about it," he said. "First, I intend to exercise my option to buy the property from Giacomo, early."

"Emilio, do we have the money to do that?"

"It's been five years since I signed the lease," he pointed out. "Part of the money will come from the thirty percent of the lease payments that Giacomo said would be applied to the purchase price. In addition, there is some money that we have saved over the past few years and, of course, I had certain savings before we were married. The rest of the money will come from the sale of our house in Statto."

"I do not understand, Emilio. If you give up your carpenter business, how will you earn any money?"

"This will not happen overnight, Evangelina. If everything goes right, we will be able to phase into the new business smoothly."

"What new business," she asked, at this point thoroughly confused. "And what do you mean by 'we'? Emilio, please, what are you planning?

"Our home, Evangelina – it's not just going to be a house. I am going to construct a building big enough so that it can also serve as a *trattoria* and a *locanda* as well as our home. The 'we' is you and me who will operate it with as many of our children as might want to join us in the family business."

"This is a perfect location!" he almost shouted in excitement. "Rivergaro is growing. They are already building a station here to extend the railroad line from Grazzano Visconti. That will bring even more people and more business to Rivergaro and many of those people, as well as those who travel between here and Bobbio and Genoa, will need a restaurant and a place to sleep. Even more people will pass by in the future, as they take advantage of the new Statto Bridge to reach towns on the other side of the river."

Evangelina looked up at Emilio with an expression of both shock and wonder. This was an incredibly exciting prospect, but a frightening one, as well. They already had four children and a fifth was on its way. Ever since they were married, Emilio had provided a good, secure living for them. However, he had used his skills as a carpenter and had the shared support of his two brothers in the business. But, this was different; Emilio had no personal experience running a restaurant or an inn, although his parents had operated a small café in their house below the castle in Statto. It seemed to Evangelina that he was taking a great risk. Yet, he was such a confident and determined man. No matter what, she realized. She would be at his side and it would be a risk that they would take together.

"Now tell me," she queried. "Who is going to build this place with you? You are a carpenter, not a stonemason." She was simply curious, not doubtful about his skill.

"He is," said Emilio, pointing at Luigi. "My son Gigi and I will build it; with a little help from my brothers, of course," he added smiling. "In fact, much of what we do on *stalle* and on farm houses is stone and brick work. *Mulini* are almost all stone or brick. So, you see, stone masonry is already part of our skills. But, if I need other help I will get it."

42

Luigi beamed at the prospect of helping his father build their new house.

"Papà, if our new house is going to be a restaurant and an inn, it has to have a name. What are we going to call it?"

The girls were curious about the conversation that their parents were having and had no intention of letting their brother be the only one in on the secret. They all ran down from the cart to where their parents and Luigi were standing. Elisa, the eldest, asked what everyone was talking about.

"Papà said that he is going to build us a new house and that it is going to be so big that it will have a restaurant and that people can sleep in it like a hotel," Luigi said.

"What are we going to call it, papà?" he insisted. "It will need a name."

Emilio looked up to the south. "The Alta Val Trebbia is in that direction," he said. "Do you feel that refreshing breeze coming down the valley?"

Everyone nodded that they did.

"Well then," he said. "I think that we should name it after the clean, fresh air that the breeze brings us. We'll call it 'Bellaria.' 'Bellaria di Rivergaro.'

Bellaria di Rivergaro

Chapter 5

ON THE WAY BACK TO STATTO, Emilio decided to stop for a few minutes to speak with Giuseppe and Silvio. Luigi accompanied his father while Evangelina and the girls remained in the *calesse*. Emilio could see that his brothers were chopping firewood and stacking the split pieces next to the *mulino*. Later, they would load the wood into a cart and take it into Rivergaro where they hoped to sell it. As Emilio and Luigi approached the two men, Silvio took a mighty swing at a log and then screamed out in pain. His axe hit the log a glancing blow, ricocheted and struck his leg. Silvio fell to the ground clutching his leg. Blood was spurting from the gash where the axe deeply cut into his calf.

Giuseppe dropped his axe and ran to aid his brother. Emilio took off in a run with Luigi trailing behind. By the time that Emilio arrived at the scene, Giuseppe had cut Silvio's trouser leg open so that they could see the extent of the injury. It was severe. Emilio took off his belt and tied it tightly around Silvio's leg above the gash. Then he told Luigi to run and get Evangelina and to tell her to bring something they could use as a bandage.

As soon as Luigi told her what happened, Evangelina leaped off the *calesse*, grabbed the only cloth available – a couple of extra white cotton napkins from the picnic – and ran over to the *mulino* to join the men. Evangelina could see that the axe cut deeply into the fleshy part of Silvio's left leg above the ankle. The tourniquet that Emilio had improvised with his belt was helping to reduce the bleeding; however, it was only a temporary measure. Evangelina did the best she could pressing the napkins into the wound. She secured the makeshift bandages by wrapping her scarf around Silvio's leg. It was clear that Silvio needed medical attention quickly. He was doing his best to hide the pain, cursing at his own clumsiness. Giuseppe offered a suggestion.

"Emilio, let's get Silvio to the *calesse* and take him to the Statto house. Then, I'll take the *calesse* to Travo to get the doctor."

Emilio and Giuseppe carried Silvio to the *calesse* and as gently as possible lifted him up to the front seat. There was not enough room for everyone in the *calesse* so Evangelina and the children followed on foot. When the men arrived at the Statto house, they carried Silvio inside and made him as comfortable as possible. Giuseppe sped off toward Travo to get the doctor. On the way back to the Statto house, Evangelina stopped at the house of her friend Melissa Spallazi, the village *ostetrica*, midwife. She knew that Melissa had some medical knowledge and that she would know what to do until the doctor arrived. As soon as Evangelina told Melissa what happened, she reached for the knitted bag that contained her medical supplies and hurried with Evangelina and the children to the Statto house.

It was over two hours until Giuseppe returned from Travo with the doctor, who followed Giuseppe on horseback. By that time, Melissa had cleaned the wound and wrapped it with fresh bandages. The wound was so severe, however, that it was still necessary to apply a tourniquet, releasing it briefly every fifteen minutes to prevent gangrene in the wound site. The bandages were soaked in blood. The doctor examined the wound, complimented Melissa for her first aid treatment, and sprayed the entire area of the injury with carbolic acid. He closed the gash with sixteen stitches and wrapped it thickly with sterile gauze to help prevent airborne microorganisms from infecting it. However, before he left, he told Silvio, not so gently, that he was as clumsy as an ox and that he would be lucky if he did not lose part of his leg to infection.

***

A few days after the incident at the mill, Emilio, Giuseppe and Luigi returned to the place where Emilio planned on building Bellaria. Silvio wanted to join them, but he was still not able to walk on his injured leg. The purpose of this trip to the top of the hill was to survey the area where Emilio planned to construct Bellaria and to get an idea of the size building that would fit in that space.

"This flat area at the top of the hill is just a little less than a half-hectare, Emilio," observed Giuseppe. "It will need some grading to make it level, but not a lot. I think that you have plenty of room for a good size house."

Emilio nodded in agreement. "Yes, the main issue here will be how we layout the building. It should probably face the road between Rivergaro and Bobbio. That way, the heaviest traffic will pass directly in front of it, which is exactly what we want for business."

Emilio had barely finished speaking when Luigi tugged at his arm.

"Papà, look!" he exclaimed, pointing down the road in the direction of Bobbio. "Look, papà, soldiers – lots of them!"

Coming in their direction were several dozen soldiers, not marching in unison, but rather half-shuffling in a rag-tag, disorderly way. The men seemed to be tired and their uniforms were dirty and untidy. Following them were two horse-drawn artillery pieces and a wagon carrying additional men who were obviously injured. The trio stared as the weary troops trod past them.

"What are you staring at," one of the soldiers asked, as he and his comrades passed them. "Take a good look. This is what happens when the stupid generals send 17,000 good Italian soldiers to fight 100,000 Ethiopians," he said. "Long live Crispi," he shouted in a mocking voice, meaning Italian Premier Francesco Crispi, whose government had ordered the ill-fated excursion into Ethiopia the previous year.

The exhausted soldier was referring to the humiliating defeat of the Italian forces under the command of Italian General Oreste Baratieri at the battle of Adwa in north-central Ethiopia just a few weeks earlier. The defeat ended Italy's hope of becoming a colonial empire in Africa comparable to that of the British or the French. Although greatly outnumbered, the Italian forces had a significant logistics and technological advantage over the poorly equipped and near starving Ethiopians, who had been living off the land for several months. However, a tactical blunder, plus an unforeseen event, resulted in the Italian forces being caught in a lethal crossfire, leaving 7,000 Italian soldiers dead, 1,500 wounded and 3,000 taken as prisoners within just a few hours. The remaining forces retreated to the port city of

Eritrea where they were given transport back to Italian ports including Naples and Genoa.

"Shut up, you damn fool," ordered a sergeant. "The lieutenant will hear you. Besides, you are lucky that you aren't one of those," he said, gesturing at the wagon carrying the most seriously wounded soldiers that was now passing by Emilio and the others.

Emilio was stunned. He now understood why Giacomo Sconti had preferred that his son Carlo immigrate to America rather than face conscription into the Italian army, where he would likely have been sent to Ethiopia. Emilio looked at his brother Giuseppe and then at Luigi, who was staring wide-eyed at the incredible sight passing by in front of him.

"Papà, I don't think that I want to be in the army when I grow up," he said.

"No, Gigi, I don't want that for you either," he replied, as the three left the future site of Bellaria and walked back down the road toward the river.

***

When he returned to the Statto house that evening, Emilio found Evangelina in the kitchen with his mother Luigia. The two women were busy rolling out egg pasta, making each sheet as thin as possible without tearing it. Earlier in the day, they had made the pasta by adding seven eggs, a little olive oil and a little water to ten cups of flour. They kneaded the mixture by hand until it was firm enough to form a smooth ball. Then they let it set for a couple of hours before they began to roll it. Evangelina looked up and noticed the dour look on Emilio's face.

"Is there anything wrong, Emilio?" she asked.

"You look tired," Luigia said. "Sit down and have a glass of the Gutturnio Frizzante that your cousin Angela brought when she and Gianni were visiting us last month," she suggested. She brought out a tumbler and a bottle of the prized, lightly sparkling red wine from Colli Piacentini, near Bobbio.

Emilio decided not to tell the women what he, Giuseppe and Luigi had just witnessed. He knew about the war in Ethiopia and often discussed it, along with other events of importance, when drinking wine, smoking cigars and playing cards with his friends at the little *Antica Trattoria* down the road from the Statto house. However, none of them had any knowledge of the defeat of the Italian forces – until now. Nonetheless, this was not the kind of subject that should be discussed in the presence of women.

"Yes, I am a little tired," he said. "However, we surveyed the top of the *collina* and there is more than enough room to build a large house now and, then later, any additions that we might need in the future."

Luigia began mixing the finely chopped spinach and ricotta cheese that would serve as a filling for the *agnoli* that they were preparing for supper. Evangelina was already cutting the rolled pasta into squares almost the size of a playing card. The women put a spoon full of the ricotta-spinach mixture on each square, folded the points of two sides over the mixture and then pinched and formed the pasta into the delicate elongated shape characteristic of this type of ravioli. When it was time for supper, the women placed the pasta in boiling water for only seven minutes. They, they lightly mixed it with melted local butter. Served on a plate and sprinkled with grated parmesan cheese, the delicacy brought contentment to even the fussiest diner. In the next few years, this local specialty would become a signature dish at Bellaria's *trattoria*.

"Evangelina, I've been thinking about Luigi. He has now completed his third year of school. He's a bright boy and can read, write and do arithmetic as good as some of the children much older than him. I think that it is time for him to learn how to be a carpenter. Besides, he can help me build our Bellaria"

Luigi, who had been keeping still so that no one would notice he was listening to the conversation, beamed at that thought.

"I am not sure, Emilio. Yes, he is bright. However, that means that he should stay at school and maybe someday he can be lawyer or a doctor or even one of those people who design bridges and tall buildings. I think that he should stay in school. What do you think mamma?" Evangelina asked as she turned to Luigia who was mixing a new batch of filling for the *agnoli*.

Emilio's mother replied diplomatically, "That's for you and Emilio to decide. You are his parents."

Knowingly, both Emilio and Evangelina waited for the inevitable advice that would follow.

"On the other hand, how many children actually go to school past the third year? It might be different if we lived in Rivergaro and Luigi could go to the school at Sant'Agata that is run by the nuns. Neither of you went past the third year in school; neither did your brothers or sisters, yet all of you have done just fine."

"Well, I don't know," said Evangelina pensively. "I suppose that he could continue to learn by reading books and perhaps when we all move to Rivergaro he could attend the school at Sant'Agata then."

It was close to suppertime so the adults agreed that they would talk about Luigi's schooling later. Right now, however, the women were ready to put several dozen *agnoli* in the big pot of boiling water that was on the stove and Elisa and her sisters were setting the table with plates, tumblers for water and wine and, of course, an ample supply of grated cheese. Emilio stood up and walked to the small porch immediately outside of the kitchen. He lit another cigar, knowing that he would only be able to take a few puffs before Evangelina called him to supper. He gazed out across the Trebbia, up toward the top of the hill where he would build Bellaria. No, no more school for Luigi, he thought – at least not for now. There was something more important do. It was time to begin building Bellaria.

Chapter 6

EMILIO AND HIS BROTHERS KNEW HOW to build a house. They had been building *stalle* for the local *cascina* owners for years to shelter farm animals and to store hay. They built additions to farmhouses and various farm outbuildings and they had built the house where Giuseppe now lived. The first task that Emilio tackled was to sketch an outline of the house, including its various rooms. He decided that Bellaria would consist of three floors, including the ground floor. The *trattoria* or restaurant would be on that floor, together with a small *salumeria*, delicatessen, where the family could sell local produce such as vegetables, wine, eggs, salume, and other products. The first floor (the floor above the ground floor) would house four guest rooms that would comprise the *locanda*. The family quarters occupied the entire second floor on the third level of the house.

Emilio estimated that it would take about one year to build Bellaria. First, he had to meet with Giacomo Sconti to finalize the purchase of the property; so, he set up a meeting with Sconti for the following week. Next, because the house was to be constructed mostly of local stone, a huge supply of rocks and stones from the fields on the property and from the river had to be gathered and stacked next to the building site. There was much to do and Emilio decided to begin as soon as possible.

The meeting with Giacomo was cordial and productive. As usual, when Emilio visited the Sconti farm, Giacomo ushered him into the *cucina* of the main house where Signora

Sconti made caffè for the men and served them a sampling of her excellent pastries. When the two men were seated, Giacomo began the conversation with "family talk."

"How is your brother Silvio's leg?"

"Much better, thank you," Emilio answered. "He will be fine, but for now he walks with a slight limp."

Giacomo nodded in understanding.

"I don't know if you are aware, but I have received several letters from Carlo. He seems to be doing quite well in New York," he said.

"I'm glad to hear that. How was the trip over to America?" Emilio asked.

"Not good if you are traveling steerage. These steam ships are not much better than the cattle cars on the railroads. Men, women, and even married people are assigned to separate compartments. Carlo said that the compartments are very crowded with perhaps 150 to 200 or more people crowded into a one of them, and there are many compartments. Everyone is assigned to a bunk bed but the unlucky ones don't have a mattress. They simply spread a blanket or a heavy coat over the wire springs and get what sleep they can. There is almost no ventilation and the food is poor. Carlo said that it gets very bad when there are heavy seas and people begin getting sick. To make matters worse, the toilets often clog. The wealthy people, of course, have much more comfortable facilities. All-in-all, Carlo said it was a trip that he would rather not take again."

"I can imagine," Emilio empathized. "It is not something that I would want to do, either. On the other hand, how else can you get across the Atlantic?"

"Yes. However, the trip seems to have been worthwhile; not that Carlo cares much for New York City. What is important is that Carlo immediately got a job working for your wife's cousin, Zanmatti. We are very grateful for that."

"What is he doing for Zanmatti?" Emilio asked.

"Delivering groceries to the markets in the Italian section of New York," Giacomo replied. "Carlo said that there is a very large section of Manhattan, which is part of New York City, where so many Italian immigrants live that it is called 'Little Italy.' In fact, he said that most people there still speak Italian, although some are learning to speak English, and most of the signs in the storefronts are in Italian. Can you imagine that?"

"Incredible. Why go to America in that case?" Emilio wondered aloud.

"Well, according to Carlo, a lot of Italian immigrants, especially those with some kind of skill, eventually move out of New York and go to other places where their skills are in demand and where the living conditions are better."

"Good carpenters, by the way, seem to have no trouble finding a job. It is the same for masons, stonecutters, tile setters and most people in the crafts and skilled trades. Carlo said that there are even good job opportunities for people who come from the farms, especially if they know anything about cultivating and growing grapes," Giacomo explained.

"It seems that those kinds of skills are in high demand in California."

"California! That's so far away from Italy, Giacomo. Who would want to go there?"

Giacomo decided to turn the conversation to the purpose of Emilio's visit. "So, you wanted to see me about the property down by the river," he said.

"I do, Giacomo," Emilio replied. "You know that I have already made certain improvements to the property. The *mulino*, for example, is doing fine and it is producing decent revenue that benefits all of us. In addition, my brothers and I have converted a hectare of the southern section of the property to a vineyard and that is just beginning to produce wine grade grapes. Of course, there are also a few head of cows, sheep, and goats that graze in the north section by the river where I built a *stalla*.

"However, I have decided to build a house there; in fact, not just a house but also a *trattoria* and a *locanda*," he added. "I think that it is time to exercise my option to buy the property as we agreed five years ago."

Emilio outlined his plan to pay for the property: a combination of cash, the amount of Emilio's lease payments that Giacomo agreed would be credited toward the purchase price, and money to be derived from the sale of the Statto house. Fortunately for Emilio, the elder Sconti was willing to accept his pledge of the sale of the Statto house as collateral for the final balance due on the purchase of the property. One week later, Emilio was the sole owner of 10 hectares of land three kilometers south of Rivergaro that extended from the road to Bobbio to the Trebbia – land on which he would build his and Evangelina's future home – a place he would call Bellaria.

***

The ancient Romans did not invent brick or mortar. However, they made significant improvements in both and, in addition, discovered that when volcanic ash is mixed with lime mortar the result is cement. From that point it was just a matter of time before they also discovered that when cement is mixed with sand, gravel and water, the mixture morphs into concrete that not only has great strength, but also can be applied underwater – a useful attribute that facilitated the construction of aqueducts and underground cisterns.

This important construction material enabled the Romans, and later other societies, to build incredible structures of brick and stone, continuing through the medieval period to the present time. Italy, in particular, is strewn with Roman ruins where the stone and brickwork still endure, as do countless medieval fortifications and castles in one state of preservation or another. In the Val Trebbia alone, there are more than eighty medieval castles, some of them still in very good condition. Originally, there were hundreds of castles, towers, and fortifications in the valley.

One reason for extensive development of stone and brick structures in the Val Trebbia is that as the valley formed, its torrential river and streams carried millions of tons of rock, stone, and gravel down to the alluvial plain at the bottom of the valley. Most of the buildings that have been constructed in the valley over the past two millenniums have been constructed of this plentiful material. The second reason concerns the availability in the valley of limestone that is a base material for mortar, cement, and concrete. All along the bottom of the Val Trebbia one will find natural outcroppings of calico in the form of calcium carbonate, limestone. When limestone is heated to great temperatures, as it is in the many *fornace* or kilns in the area, and then cooled, quicklime is produced. Mixed with sand and clay, also abundant in the valley, the lime forms an excellent mortar for stone or brickwork.

Master carpenters in the region where Emilio lived did not work from detailed plans when they built a structure. They thought out every detail in their minds before they began construction, made a rough draft or sketch of the planned building, and used building methods that were as old as the ancient Roman walls of Piacenza; and, that were continued through the medieval era, right up to modern times. Construction drawings and detailed building plans were tools used by the people who built the tall five to nine story buildings that could now be seen in cities like Piacenza, Milan, and Genoa. Of course, the famous Renaissance builders, who designed and built the magnificent cathedrals and churches, used building plans painstakingly drawn by an army of apprentices. However, the only apprentices that local artisans employed were usually their sons.

The construction skills of Emilio and his brothers were not limited to working only with wood. It was not possible to build a good *mulino* without also knowing how to build the stone walls that supported the waterwheels and the brick and stone structures that housed the mill's grinding stone.

Further, not all waterwheel hubs were made of wood. Many were made of cast iron. As builders of *mulini*, the three brothers also had a working knowledge of construction materials other than only wood and expertise in using them.

Soon after his meeting with Giacomo, Emilio graded an area at the Bellaria building site that was half again as large as what would be required for the structure. He anticipated that at some time in the future it might be necessary to expand Bellaria and he wanted the building site to be properly prepared for that eventuality. Meanwhile, the piles of rocks, gravel, sand and the bags of crushed lime grew until there was hardly room for anything else.

"Gigi, hold this end of the tape here and do not let go until I tell you." Emilio slowly unwound the metal tape measure from its case and pounded a stake into the ground every meter until he reached the end of one side of the trench that had been dug for the foundation of the house.

"Now come here to where I am, Gigi, and we'll do the same thing for the next side."

Luigi could not have been happier. It was a short leap in his mind from holding one end of a measuring tape in a foundation trench of Bellaria to building those tall structures called "*grattacieli*" – skyscrapers – that he had seen in pictures of the big cities in America.

"Papà, are you going to teach me how to build the whole house?" Luigi asked.

"That and a lot more," Emilio answered. "Before you know it you will be as good a carpenter as your Uncle Silvio," he said, patting his younger brother on the back as the two men continued to stake out the line where the walls of the building would be built.

Silvio smiled at his brother and said, "Watch out, Emilio. Pretty soon Gigi will be asking you for a raise!"

"Gigi, watch as I make the mortar that we need for the walls of the house," Emilio said. "Now, you take the hoe and mix the sand, lime, and water together."

"It's hard, papà," Luigi complained, as he struggled pulling the hoe through the thick, viscous mixture.

"You have muscles, don't you?" Emilio said. Then he grasped the hoe with the boy and the two pulled the mortar back and forth until it was well mixed.

"You did great, Gigi. Now let's add a little gravel and some of that black volcanic ash to the mortar to strengthen it and we will be ready to pour it into the trench."

The brothers poured the mortar and then added rocks to the mixture, larger ones toward the inside and smaller and less rounded rocks toward the outside. Emilio showed Luigi how to use a trowel and smooth the mortar over the rocks that they had just put in place. They were careful to make sure that there were no voids, where air pockets could weaken the wall and eventually erode it. When all four sides of the foundation wall were filled with mortar and rocks to a height of about a half-meter, they went back to their starting point and began to add a new level to the wall. This was incredibly tiring work. However, it would continue for months until all four walls of the house were built.

Chapter 7

EVANGELINA HAD ENDURED PART of her pregnancy during the hottest months of the year. She calculated that her due date would be in early December, so she still had a full two months of her term left. Emilio's mother Luigia had been an angel, helping Evangelina with the children as much as a woman in her seventies could. Luigi was with his father and uncles most of the time, so at least she did not have to contend with an active nine year old boy. The girls were another matter, except for Elisa, who was her mother's "little helper."

"Mamma, why do we have to put all of the curtains in that big bucket?" Elisa asked out of curiosity.

"We do this every year, Elisa. This is starch that I am adding to the water in the buckets. We'll soak the curtains just a little bit and then we'll carefully hang them on the clothesline to dry."

"What does the starch do mamma?"

"It will make the curtains look beautiful, little one," Evangelina explained. "When we hang them back up over the windows they will be nice and straight and pretty."

"Elvira!" Evangelina said, noticing that the two younger girls who had been playing quietly together were now quarreling over a painted toy horse that their Uncle Giuseppe had made for them. "Stop fighting with Maria. Here, take this paper and these crayons and show Maria how to draw the fig tree that is behind the house."

61

Emilio's mother, Luigia, had silently been watching the scene with the children unfold and decided to intervene.

"Who wants to help grandma make a cheesecake for dessert tonight," she asked.

Immediately, three sets of hands went up as all three of the girls shouted, "I do!" The two younger girls were jumping up and down.

Evangelina thought that was a good idea and sent Elvira and Maria off to the kitchen with their grandmother. "Elisa, you can go, too, but first help me hang up the curtains."

Hanging clothes and linen to dry always had to be done carefully. The clothesline was stretched between two trees in the backyard high off the ground. Evangelina had to stretch to hang each piece of clothing or linen with the homemade wood clothespins that Emilio cut and notched for her. The weight of the wet laundry slowly brought the clothesline closer to the ground each time a piece was hung. The concern was the possibility that a washed item would touch or fall to the ground and become soiled again. It was laborious enough taking soiled clothes down to the river and scrubbing them on a washboard until clean; a task made tolerable only by the fact that it gave the women of the little community a chance to meet and gossip once or twice a week.

"Don't let the bottom of the curtain touch the ground, Elisa. Hold it up while I put clothespins on the top part. That's it, Elisa. You're such a good helper!"

When the last curtain was hung up to dry in the light breeze that was coming down from the Alta Val Trebbia,

Evangelina told Elisa that she could join her sisters and help Luigia make the cheesecake. Ricotta cheesecake was one of Luigia's specialties and was a two-phase process. First, Luigia made the crust, which she preferred to be on the dry side so that she could crumble it and press it along the bottom and sides of a pie pan rather than roll it, as she would do for a fruit pie. Then she pre-baked the crust in a hot oven until it was a light brown.

Luigia prepared the cheesecake filling from freshly made ricotta cheese, mascarpone, eggs, sugar, sour cream, melted butter and fresh cream. She let the girls help her measure the ingredients and put them into a big ceramic bowl with a rooster design on it. Then each of the girls took a turn using a wooden spoon to blend the mixture into a smooth batter. Because Elisa was the oldest of the girls, Luigia allowed her to pour the batter into the waiting crust. She then baked the cheesecake until its top was a puffy, golden brown. That same night the entire family would enjoy a special treat after *la cena* – provided the children ate all of their supper, of course!

***

The last few weeks had been difficult on everyone. Emilio, Giuseppe, Silvio, and even Luigi had spent as many hours as possible working on the walls of Bellaria. However, they also had work to perform for their customers. Luigi was now an expert mixing the mortar in the metal watering trough that at one time provided water for the animals when they grazed uphill from the river. When they could work on the house, the three men did the heavy work of hauling the rocks and setting them in the mortar that filled the forms.

Emilio was careful not to overwork his young son. He would often assign Luigi to go down to the *stalla* to check on the goats or to take a bucket to the river to bring back clear, cool water for the men to drink – any kind of task that gave Luigi time to take a rest or play break.

The hard work was not limited to the men. Fall was one of two times during the year when the women of the house did major housecleaning, the other time was mid-spring. This year that task was especially difficult for Evangelina because she would was entering her eight month of pregnancy and she had had a very tiring day. That night Emilio, Evangelina and the children were having supper with Luigia and Emilio's brother Silvio. Emilio seemed to be pensive and then began speaking:

"I have been thinking," he said. "It's time that we rest for a few days."

That caught the attention of the adults, including Silvio. They looked at Emilio waiting for him to continue. The children had not yet understood what he was getting at so they continued with their meal.

"We need to do something …different."

Now the children stopped eating and looked up at their father, wondering what he was going to say next.

"First, we are very fortunate. Many of the *contadini* in our province are very poor and have little to eat," he stated, referring to the poorer farmers who made up the peasant class. "They work much harder than we do and yet they eat only cornmeal and a little soup at almost every meal. Most of the *contadini* children wear wood shoes and sleep on hard wood beds with only cornhusks stuffed into their mattresses. All of us, and especially you children, have much more than that."

Evangelina spoke up, "We know this, Emilio. You provide for us very well. We are fortunate that you and your brothers have a skilled trade and do not have to work in the fields like the *contadini*. Planting all of those thousands of tomato plants, one after another, must be backbreaking work."

She was referring to farmers in the Pianura Padana that began just north of Rivergaro where the bottom of the Val Trebbia opened into a broad, fertile alluvial plain. Many hundreds of hectares of land in that area were under cultivation with most of it used for the tomatoes for which the region was famous, and the remainder for corn and wheat. Thousands of tomato plants were hand-set into the soil each year. Then, when the crops were harvested, there was the backbreaking labor of hand-picking the tomatoes, thrashing the wheat and picking ripened corn. During these times, the fields were filled with the *contadini* and their children, most of whom had never seen a day of school, even though schooling was free to all according to the law. For most of them, there was no time for school – just time for hard work.

"Yes. Well, I have made arrangements for all of us, except you Silvio, sorry, to spend the weekend with the Piergiorgi's, in Montechiaro." Emilio turned toward the children and said, "Your grandmother Giuliana and aunt Giaele are very excited that you will be visiting them and they have a special treat for all of us."

"Is grandma Piergiorgi going to make a chocolate cake for us?" asked Elvira, who seemed to be the chocolate lover of the family.

"I imagine so," said Emilio. "However, this weekend all of the larger towns in the Valley will be celebrating the chestnut harvest with a Festival. After Holy Mass on Sunday we will all go to Travo which, I understand, is going to have a very nice festival with lots of roasted chestnuts, fried cakes, and games for the children and even gelato."

Evangelina and Luigia were smiling in approval, but when Emilio mentioned the word 'gelato' the children began shouting and jumping and Evangelina had to tell them to calm down or maybe they would not go to Montechiaro.

"I think I will stay home," Luigia said. "I'll keep Silvio company and perhaps have Giuseppe and his family over to my house for *pranzo* on Sunday."

"No, no mamma, you must come with us," Evangelina said. The children chimed in pleading with Luigia to go with them.

"You go with them, mamma," said Silvio. "Besides, I might not be too much company for you. I have some things to do this weekend."

"Ah, perhaps like taking a trip to Niviano to visit a certain young lady?" quipped Emilio.

"I guess I can't keep a secret from you, big brother," Silvio replied in good humor.

"It's not exactly a secret, Silvio," Luigia replied. "Maria Borella is a lovely young woman and I am glad that you are seeing her."

"Mamma!" Silvio exclaimed. "How could you know that I have been seeing Maria?"

"You forget that we women gossip a little when we are washing clothes in the river. Remember the old saying in our Piacentini dialect, '*I an dit il donn in Trebia*,' I heard it from a woman in the Trebbia."

***

The drive to Montechiaro took a little over an hour and a half. Emilio, Evangelina, and Luigia sat on the front seat of the four-wheeled carriage, while the children occupied the back seat. October weather had set in and the day was mostly cloudy, the breeze flowing down from the Alta Val Trebbia bringing a chill to the air. Emilio decided to take the road from Statto to Travo and then cross the river at that point. It meant a slight backtrack from Travo to Montechiaro, but the scenery was especially pretty when viewed from the Statto side. As the carriage pulled away from the Statto house, Luigi spotted the Bellaria construction site and called out to his mother:

"Mamma look! You can see Bellaria from here. See how big our house is getting," he said pointing across the river to their left. "We already have the beams across the first floor and papà says that the roof might be on by Natale," he added, beaming that the construction of Bellaria would be that far along by the feast of Christmas. It was clear that although

Luigi had just passed his tenth birthday, he was learning quite a lot about the work of carpenters and stonemasons.

"Once we get the roof on, we can work inside the building even in winter weather," Emilio explained. However, if we get a lot of rain and snow this season, and if it is very cold, then the mortar will not set properly and we will have to delay much of the work until spring."

Luigi called out to his father again, "And there, papà," he said, pointing to a spot on the Statto Bridge, "is where you taught me how to swim!"

The three adults and even Elisa laughed. The way that Emilio had taught Luigi to swim was to drop him off the low bridge into chest-deep water where his Uncle Giuseppe stood guard, as Luigi paddled around like the black hound that the family adopted a couple of years earlier. Nonetheless, it worked and now on hot summer days, Luigi could often be found jumping into the river at that very spot with other boys from the little hamlet to cool off - when he was not helping his father at Bellaria, that is.

The road slowly rose as they headed south in the direction of the Alta Val Trebbia. On their right, the heavily wooded hills sloped sharply upward, limiting their view of Monte Pillerone. However, across on the east side of the river, there was a panorama of open fields and pastures that ran though areas thick with trees, now losing their colorful leaves. Stone and brick farmhouses and *stalle* dotted the landscape, where small herds of cows, sheep, and goats were grazing. It was a beautiful, tranquil scene that made Evangelina recall the time that Emilio took her up the mountain to Pigazzano to propose to her. She reached for his hand and tenderly squeezed it. He turned to her and smiled, knowing that they were sharing the same thoughts.

They reached Travo by mid-morning and took the bridge over to the small hamlet of Canova Ponte on the Rivergaro side of the river. From there it was less than a half hour to Montechiaro where Evangelina's mother, sister, and uncle were waiting for them.

It had been several weeks since the families had seen each other. Therefore, it was no surprise that many hugs were shared among the women and children and even among the men, in a culture where a 'handshake' was less common than an embrace. Emilio, Evangelina, and Maria stayed with Evangelina's mother and her sister Giaele in the stone house that bordered the piazza of the little town, across from the church. Elisa, Elvira, and grandmother Luigia stayed with one of Evangelina's cousins, while Luigi got to stay at Uncle Alessio's house all by himself. As to be expected, as soon as everyone was settled and rested, it was time for *pranzo*, the traditional Italian lunch that on special occasions, like this one, could easily stretch for two or three hours.

The food was spectacular and more than abundant - what else could be expected? During the lengthy meal, the keen eyes of Luigia focused more than once on Evangelina, who seemed to be in some state of discomfort. It was late afternoon when the meal was finished; including the chocolate torta that Elvira had been promised. The men congregated to smoke their cigars, play cards, and drink grappa, the clear brandy-like beverage made by distilling pomace, the skin, pulp and other parts of grapes leftover from winemaking. The boys were playing 'tag' and the girls were playing 'hoops' in the church piazza while the women gathered to chat and share information about what was happening in the comune. Giaele now also noticed that Evangelina did not seem to feel well.

"Lina," Giaele called, using the name that she had called her sister since childhood, "Are you alright, honey?"

"Yes, yes I'm fine," Evangelina answered. "I'm just a little tired. I must have eaten too much, I have some stomach cramps."

Giuliana suggested that perhaps Evangelina should go to bed early since it had been a long day and the drive from Statto had been long and tiring. By now, the sun was setting. As it did, the air turned sharply cooler. Most of the women in the group agreed that it had been a long, though wonderful, day and that it was time to gather the children and take them to their homes. The families slowly dispersed, the men reluctantly following.

When they returned to Giuliana's house, Giaele noticed that Evangelina's legs were swollen and that she kept rubbing her back. Giuliana and Luigia looked at each other with concern. Giuliana arranged two chairs so that they were facing each other and called to Evangelina.

"Lina," she commanded, pointing to the more comfortable chair. "Sit here and rest your legs on top of the pillows," she said, as she guided her daughter into the chair and helped Giaele raise Evangelina's legs onto the pillows that she had placed in the other chair.

"Mamma, I am really fine," Evangelina protested. "Please don't fuss so much. It's nothing but a little cramping."

"You can't be that certain about these things," Luigia said. "You are in the late part of your term and you can never tell what might happen if you don't get enough rest."

The door opened and Emilio entered, asking what was happening.

"I am just a little tired, Emilio," Evangelina said. "Everything is fine. Now, let's put Maria to bed and I think that I will follow shortly."

Emilio walked to the fireplace and started a fire that soon began to take the chill out of the room. Luigia went over to the table opposite the fireplace and sat down. Giaele, Giuliana, and Emilio were focused on Evangelina, so no one noticed that Luigia pressed her hand to her chest as she sat down, took a deep breath, and winced.

***

There was not a cloud in the sky when everyone rose the next morning. It was a perfect day to attend a festival – after Holy Mass, of course. Holy Mass at Sant'Ilario was at 9:00 in the morning, which meant that except for children under age seven, all other children and the adults had to fast from food and abstain from water until after Holy Communion. This was met with some grumbling from the adults, especially the men, and the pleading of the children for "just a little something to eat" or for "only a little sip of water." However, the more devout women of the family reminded the complainers what the priests and nuns had drummed into

71

them for many years – that if they dared to consume any food or water before they received Holy Communion they would surely suffer the pains of Hell. This admonition was usually enough to hold back the grumbling.

After Mass, Elisa, Elvira, and Luigi were escorted by their adult cousins and uncle to Giuliana's house where the entire family enjoyed a light, but most welcome breakfast, *colazione*. Evangelina seemed to be rested and more comfortable, so by mid-morning Emilio, Evangelina, Luigia and the children set off for Travo and the Chestnut festival.

In the center of Travo there is a medieval castle that was the twelfth century fortress of the family Malaspina. Piazza Trento, the main square of the little town, spreads out from the old castle and on this festival Sunday was filled with families strolling under the shade of the trees lining the square. Emilio hitched the horse to a post along the piazza and helped the women and children step down from the carriage, except for Luigi who decided to jump from the back seat by himself.

The weather was delightful; the day was cool, but sunny. Because it was Sunday, all of the shops in the town were closed. However, in the piazza vendors were everywhere, selling chestnuts that they were roasting over hot coals in black metal half-barrels, sugared funnel cakes that had their origin in the Dolomites north of Trento, ricotta cream-filled cannoli and gelato of many flavors - that incredibly delicious ice cream so uniquely Italian. True to his word, Emilio made sure that both the children and the adults enjoyed a sampling of these delights.

Emilio was standing in line waiting to buy another bag of roasted chestnuts when he heard Luigia call out.

"Emilio, come quickly! Something is wrong with Evangelina."

He turned and saw Evangelina slumped on one of the benches in the piazza and ran over to her.

"What's wrong?" he asked frantically.

Luigia was seated next to Evangelina, trying to hold her upright. She gave Elisa her scarf and told her to run to the fountain in the middle of the piazza and dampen it. Then she told Luigi to go to the carriage and bring back the jug of drinking water that Emilio had brought for the trip home.

Emilio knelt next to Evangelina and put his arms around her. "It's the baby, isn't it?" he said, more of a statement than a question.

"I don't know, Emilio," she replied. "I'll be alright."

Elisa and Luigi arrived with the damp scarf and the water jug at the same time. Luigia wiped Evangelina's brow with the cool cloth and gave her a sip of water. Evangelina seemed to recover a little and sat upright, still supported by Emilio, who spoke quietly but with authority.

"I think that we should go home, now," he said. "Elisa and Luigi, you bring Elvira and Maria and grandmother Luigia and I will help mamma get to the *calesse*." He was careful to remain calm to avoid frightening the children, who nonetheless were quite aware there was a problem.

Evangelina sat between Emilio and Luigia and, as before, the children sat on the back seat. Everyone was silent as Emilio snapped the whip and the mare began pulling the carriage toward Statto. Maria broke the silence.

"Mamma, are you going to be OK?" she asked.

"Yes, dear, Mamma is going to be fine."

They had traveled almost half the distance to Statto and were passing through the small hamlet of Buelli when suddenly Evangelina gasped and clutched her abdomen. Emilio immediately hauled in the reins of the mare, stopping the carriage.

"What's the matter?" He shouted.

Evangelina put her hand to her forehead and said that it felt like labor pains.

"But, this is too early," she cried, as she leaned against Emilio for support.

Luigia grasped Evangelina's right arm firmly.

"Emilio, please hurry! We need to get home now!" Luigia said.

Almost frantically, Emilio snapped the whip again and the mare bolted forward. The carriage leaped ahead and the children clung tightly to the side railings as their father drove as fast as he could on the rutted, rock strewed road. Emilio had one thought, to get his beloved Evangelina safely home as quickly as possible. In his concentration, he did not see the grimace on his mother's face as she once again pressed her hand to her chest to ease the growing pain.

Chapter 8

THEY SLOWLY WALKED UP THE HILL from the old stone house that had been Luigia's home for many years and that was the birth home for all of her children. The small group passed the Statto Castle to their right and continued their procession up to the church of Sant'Antonio d'Abate where the funeral Mass would be held. The priest leading the mourners was dressed in a white surplice over a black cassock. He wore a black mozzetta or cape over his shoulders to ward off the cold on this dreary late October day. On his head was a black biretta, a squared hat with four ridges across its crown. Behind the priest were his servers, the carriage, pulled by two of Emilio's horses, that bore the plain wooden casket, and a group of family and friends, all dressed in black – men, women, and children. The mourners were quiet and somber. The silence was broken only by the sound of carriage wheels rolling over the uneven road and the occasional wailing of a close relative or a friend.

Evangelina gazed ahead at the casket through her black veil, almost in disbelief that Luigia was gone. She loved Luigia as if she had been her own mother. She felt the same pain and loss she knew Emilio was experiencing at that very moment. The procession stopped at the top of the gravel road leading to the steps of the church. The pallbearers lifted the casket from the carriage and turned it so that Luigia's head would face the altar, as prescribed by the funeral rites of the Catholic Church. They then solemnly carried the casket into the church, followed by the twenty or so people who were attending the funeral Mass. Emilio and Evangelina ushered the children into the front pews that were reserved for the immediate family.

Luigia had been careful to conceal the chest pains that she had been having for several months from her family. Even Silvio, who was still living in his mother's house, did not notice anything unusual. If Luigia's caution lapsed for a moment or two, she simply smiled and shrugged off any grimace or wince of pain as being "just a little agita." It had become increasingly difficult to hide her pain during the past month. In fact, in the week before going to Montechiaro she seriously considered asking Silvio to take her to visit the doctor. However, the closest doctor was in Travo and that was so far away.

When Emilio reached Statto that Sunday afternoon, he went directly to La Casella where he got Evangelina to bed immediately. He then took his mother to her home below the Statto Castle. A full day of bed rest relaxed Evangelina and eased her false labor. However, a neighbor of Luigia went to Emilio's house at Silvio's request to tell him that Luigia was having trouble breathing. When Emilio and Evangelina arrived at Luigia's house, it was clear that she was having a heart attack. Silvio immediately set off to fetch the doctor. However, before they could return from Travo, Luigia slipped away.

After the Mass, the mourners followed the funeral carriage up the hill to the parish's small, stone-fenced cemetery where Luigia was buried next to her husband Giovanni. The formal mourning period for her would be at least six months. However, her family would miss and lovingly remember her for a very long time after that.

***

Two months later, the sadness of Luigia's death lifted somewhat when Evangelina gave birth to her and Emilio's second son, who they named Pietro. Despite her earlier labor difficulties, Evangelina did not have a problem with the delivery and soon everyone was celebrating the addition of another member of the family. The birth of Pietro also helped brighten Christmas that year, which otherwise would have been greeted more somberly because the family was still mourning the loss of Emilio's mother. At the same time, the combination of these events, together with the onset of an early winter, dashed Emilio's hopes to complete the walls and roof of Bellaria by Christmas.

Now, more snow had fallen during the night. The unfinished walls of Bellaria reached toward the cloudy sky as though they were begging the sun to break through. Emilio and Giuseppe stomped through knee deep snow trying to determine whether it was possible to continue any further work on the building until the snow was gone. Luigi trailed behind, stopping often to make snowballs and throw them at imaginary targets.

"I tell you, my brother, it could be much worse," Giuseppe said. "At least we were able to put the beams and planking across the two upper floors before the snow came. Until the weather breaks, we can work on the interior of the ground floor and the first floor upstairs. Then, we'll worry

77

about adding the roof and completing the family floor in a few weeks when the weather changes."

"*D'accordo*," Emilio replied in agreement. "What do you think, Gigi?" However, Luigi had spotted a squirrel stealthily scurrying along one of the lower beams of the house and had taken off after the animal, armed with several snowballs. "*Un momento, papà*," he said as he loosened a volley of snowballs at the hapless creature. Returning with a look of triumph on his face, he told his father that they should finish his room first so that he could move in and guard the house against the squirrels and other "critters" that had no business being there.

Work on the interior of the first two floors of Bellaria continued into March, when the weather moderated and the last of the winter snow had melted. Weeks later, Emilio and his brothers set the final layer to the walls and added the building's tile-over-wood roof. Emilio designed Bellaria so that the *trattoria* was on the ground floor. It was also facing the road between Rivergaro and Bobbio, giving it easy access by travelers and passersby. Inside the building there were two dining areas with enough space for ten to twelve tables. In nice weather, three or four additional tables could be set up outside in front of the building so that guests could enjoy the cooling breeze flowing down from the Alta Trebbia.

A stairway leading to the upper levels was accessed both from the restaurant and through a second front door. The stairway took inn guests to their rooms on the second level and the family to their quarters on the third and upper level of the building. A small kitchen was located to the left rear on the ground floor, next to a rear door that led to the road to the Statto Bridge and to an outhouse across the road. Emilio had designed the kitchen especially for Evangelina. He hoped she would be pleasantly surprised.

Emilio pulled the four-wheeled carriage up to the front of Bellaria and helped Evangelina, who was carrying baby Pietro, step down on to the road in front of the building. Luigi jumped off the carriage as soon as it stopped, but Elisa exited with her younger sisters more sedately. This was the first time that Evangelina and the girls had seen Bellaria in its completed form. Emilio was more than anxious to show his family the product of his many months of hard labor.

"Emilio, Bellaria is so big," Evangelina said, her eyes trying to take in the entire building in a single glance. She was correct. The building was large, especially compared with *La Casella*, the "Box," as the Statto house was called. Bellaria was three stories tall and was likely three times the size of the Statto house. The girls looked at the house wide-eyed. Luigi went over to them, pointing first to himself and then at the building, saying:

"I helped papà build Bellaria and I know where all of the rooms are!"

Then, as self-appointed tour guide, he began to lead the group into Bellaria through the front door. However, Evangelina noticed the arched grillwork over the entrance and stopped.

"Look children. See what papà did so that everyone will know that this is our house," she said pointing to the initials "T E" centered in the grillwork. "Tagliaferri Emilio."

"Papà wouldn't put my initials there," Luigi pouted. Then he added, "There's another one just like that over the doorway on the side of the house, too." With that, Luigi marched into the house, instructing the others to follow.

Directly in front of them, Evangelina saw the stairway leading to the two upper floors that divided the ground floor level into two separate rooms, both designed to serve patrons of the *trattoria*. Wooden tables and chairs, all made by Emilio and his brothers at the *mulino* down by the river, filled both rooms. There were four tables in the smaller of the two rooms and six in the other. A doorway to the right of the larger room led to a small terrace, which could hold another table or two during nice weather.

Then Emilio took over and led Evangelina into the *cucina*, the kitchen that would be her workshop as she prepared meals for the family and for Bellaria's guests and patrons. A new wood-burning stove stood against the back wall, connected to a chimney flue. Evangelina could not believe how much larger it was than the stove that she used in the Statto house.

"It must be larger. We will have guests to feed –not just us," he explained.

However, what really caught Evangelina's attention was a large sink next to the stove. "What's that?" she exclaimed, as she shifted the baby in her arms so that she could point to the shiny brass object bolted to the wood counter at the edge of the sink.

"As you can see, that is a water pump," Emilio responded. He walked over to the sink and began pumping the handle of the device. Soon clear water was pouring from the spout of the pump into the sink and then out of the drain at its bottom.

"We put a cistern under the terrace to collect rainwater. We can also fill the cistern with water that we bring up from the river in the *carro-botte*, the large wooden cask on the ox-drawn cart. The pump connects to the cistern. Now you can pump all of the water that you need for cooking, washing, and even for our baths right here."

Evangelina smiled at Emilio and handed the baby to Elisa. Then she put her arms around him and gave him a big kiss. "Evangelina!" he said, embarrassed by her open display of affection. "The children are watching."

"I certainly hope so," she replied. "They need to know what a wonderful man their father is!"

Luigi then reasserted his role as the family guide. He marched ahead of the group as they went from room to room on both of the upper floors. Except for the tables and chairs that had been made for the *trattoria*, the rest of the building was still unfurnished. Nonetheless, the children ran from room to room laying out claims to a space where their beds would be placed, while Evangelina tried to visualize how she would decorate both the family quarters and the *locanda's* guest rooms. Each of the guest rooms would require a bed, chair, nightstand and an *armadio*, wardrobe. All of the guest rooms had large windows that were shuttered, so no curtains were needed on that floor. However, the double hung windows on the family floor were smaller and had no shutters. Curtains were needed in those windows to ensure privacy. It was clear that there was a lot of work to be done yet before the family could move from the Statto house to Bellaria.

***

A few weeks later, Bellaria was finally completed and the family moved from Statto to their new home on the other side of the Trebbia. Evangelina once again became pregnant and gave birth to her and Emilio's third son, Giuseppe, in the summer of the following year. Meanwhile, Elisa was becoming a young lady and reveled in supervising the other girls, who were now old enough to help their mother with most of the household chores. Luigi, who was barely a year from becoming a teenager, seemed to grow taller by the week. Little Pietro had been the center of attention in the family, but now yielded that honor to baby Giuseppe.

Bellaria's early results as a *trattoria* and *locanda* were disappointing. An occasional passer-by would stop for *pranzo* and once-in-a-while there would be an overnight guest. However, the traffic was light and Emilio was concerned about the lack of revenue. He needed a plan to make Bellaria financially viable and decided to consult with his brothers and his friend Giacomo Sconti, who he invited to Bellaria to share their ideas and suggestions with him.

It was mid-summer and the four men were seated together at a table in the smaller of Bellaria's two dining rooms. The shutters of the tall windows were wide open in the hope that a breeze from the Alta Val Trebbia would enter and relieve the heat that was mounting inside the *trattoria*. Giacomo had come alone, but Giuseppe had brought Claudia, and Silvio was accompanied by Maria Borella. The two had recently announced their intent to marry. In fact, they made plans for the wedding banquet to be held at Bellaria the following April. The women joined Evangelina in the kitchen where she was baking bread and preparing the pizza that everyone would enjoy at the *seconda colazione*, the light lunch that was more common among Italy's working class than the more elaborate *pranzo* they enjoyed at family gatherings, feast days and holidays.

The three brothers expressed concern about how long it was taking to build Bellaria's restaurant and lodging business. Drawing on his business experience, Giacomo was more upbeat. "You cannot expect overnight success," he counseled. "It takes time to build a patronage for a place like Bellaria. For one thing, you need some special reason for people to come into Bellaria in addition to simply offering good food and comfortable lodging."

"I agree," said Giuseppe. "If we can get more people to stop here perhaps we can interest them in the *salumeria*, where they will see all of the cheese, salume, eggs, wine and the products we make in the *laboratorio*, the workshop."

"It will be easier to do this in the summer," Silvio added, "when we can attract customers with fresh vegetables. That's also when the sows have their litters and we can sell the piglets, as well. But, what do we do until then?"

There was silence around the table and then Giacomo spoke. "Well, there is one possibility and if it can be arranged I believe that you will see a rapid increase in people coming into Bellaria."

"My friend," said Emilio. "If you have a solution for us, please go on."

Giacomo reminded the brothers that anyone in the area who wanted to mail a letter or package, or who was expecting to receive one, had to make the trip either to the post office in Rivergaro or to the one in Travo. That meant an especially long trip for all of the people on the Statto side of the Trebbia. "I have heard from my friends in the office of the mayor in Rivergaro, *L'Ufficio del Sindaco*, that they have been considering petitioning the authorities in Piacenza to set up a postal substation somewhere between Rivergaro and Bobbio. So, why not set it up at Bellaria?" he wondered.

Emilio stood and placed his hands firmly on the table. "Yes, of course that would work!" he exclaimed. "Many people would come to Bellaria regularly to drop off their mail or to see if any mail has arrived for them. We could even have a section of the *salumeria* just for handling the mail. But, how can we persuade the mayor to petition Piacenza on our behalf?"

"I have some influence," said Giacomo who sat back in his chair with his fingers touching each other in a steepling gesture, signaling power and confidence.

Emilio was about to respond when suddenly Claudia burst into the room. "Oh God have mercy on us," she cried. "They killed the king!"

Chapter 9

THE MID-EIGHTEENTH CENTURY was a turbulent period in Italy called the *Risorgimento* or period of unification. In 1861, after much political and military conflict, the individual city-states of Italy, such as Venice, Milan, Rome and Naples, were unified into one Italian state, the Kingdom of Italy. The Risorgimento was not accomplished easily or without bloodshed. When Victor Emmanuel II, who was then the King of Sardinia and the Piedmont, wrestled power over the Italian city states away from the domination of the French and Austrian Empires, violent revolts broke out in northern Italian cities including Parma, Modena, Bologna and Milan, all not far from Piacenza and Rivergaro. Complete unification was not complete until 1870 when the Papal Forces of Pope Pius IX surrendered to the Italian Army led by General Raffaele Cadorna and Rome became the capitol of Italy.

King Umberto I was the son of King Victor Emmanuel II. He was born in 1844 in Turin, Italy and assumed the throne of the Kingdom of Italy in 1878, on the death of his father. While Victor Emmanuel II focused on unifying Italy into one kingdom, his son had more imperialistic ambitions and envisioned Italy as a colonial power in north Africa, rivaling the French and British in that region. Umberto I was a controversial figure. On one hand, he was called the "Good King" because of his good humor and personal generosity. On the other hand, he was unpopular among the many socialists and leftists in the region. The anarchists, of course, opposed anything connected with a monarchy, constitutional or not.

In addition, there was disenchantment among the Italian people as a result of the defeat of Umberto I's forces in Ethiopia in 1898 and the king's decision to become part of the Eight-Nation Alliance that participated in the Boxer Rebellion in Imperial China in 1900. The consequence of these political events was further social unrest in Italy, including violent revolts in Sicily and Milan in which hundreds of citizens were brutally killed by government forces. The socialists and leftists blamed Umberto I personally for these massacres. In an equally violent reaction to the killings, an anarchist named Gaetano Bresci stalked Umberto I when he made a political trip to Milan and on July 29, 1900 shot and killed him. Italy was once again thrown into turmoil, both politically and economically.

***

Emilio was already standing when Claudia entered the room. The other three men jumped to their feet when she said that the king had been killed. Complete shock permeated the room. The other women filed in after Claudia and all of them began crying. Elisa and the other girls followed, all crying also but not really knowing why. Luigi hugged Elisa and tried to calm her. Emilio nodded at his son with approval. The men were enraged. How could this terrible thing happen, they wondered? Silvio moved to Maria's side to comfort her and asked where they got such terrible news.

Bellaria di Rivergaro

"A man on a bicycle rode up to the front of Bellaria and told us that yesterday a madman shot the King when he was in Milan making a speech," Claudia explained. Everyone stood in silence until Evangelina asked, "What is going to happen now?"

Giacomo spoke up, again exercising his status as a patrono, a respected person of influence.

"This is a terrible thing that has happened. I think that we should go to Rivergaro to learn the facts. However, remember, it is not actually the King who controls the government, but rather Prime Minister Giuseppe Saracco. If Saracco was not injured then the government still stands."

A large crowd milled around the Piazza Grande in Rivergaro, waiting for more information about the assassination of the king. The Mayor of Rivergaro, Armondo Martinelli, and the members of the city council walked in unison around the corner from the city hall on Via San Rocco on to Via Genoa and paraded into the Piazza Grande. Martinelli was wearing the *Fascia Tricolore*, the tri-colored sash that served as his badge of office. The other members of the council each carried a small green, white and red flag with the Crown of the Two Sicilies centered in the white band, the official flag of the Kingdom of Italy. The crowd became silent, waiting for the mayor to speak.

"Subjects of the Kingdom of Italy, Citizens of the Province of Piacenza, People of the Comune of Rivergaro," the mayor said. "On the evening of July 29, 1900, our beloved King Umberto I was in the city of Milan awarding medals to the athletes of a sporting competition. As the 'Good King' returned to his carriage and sat down, an anarchist named Gaetano Bresci burst from the crowd and fired four shots that struck and killed the king. Bresci was immediately apprehended by the king's guards.

"A period of mourning has been declared by Prime Minister Saracco. The body of King Umberto will be taken back to Rome where he will be buried in the Pantheon next to his father, King Victor Emmanuel II." The mayor paused, his head bowed in sadness. Before he could continue, a lone voice in the crowd could be heard singing 'Brothers of Italy,' the first stanza of Mameli's Hymn, the stirring 'Song of the Italians' written by Goffredo Mameli in 1847 that was rapidly becoming Italy's national patriotic hymn.

More voices joined in the chorus:

'Italy has awakened…'

And in a moment, as if on cue, the entire piazza erupted in song:

'Let us unite

'We are ready to die

'Italy called…'

It was an emotional moment and when the song ended, there was silence. The mayor and all of the council members turned without further comment and returned to the city hall, leaving the crowd to speculate about what all of this meant for Italy and for the comune of Rivergaro. Emilio also wondered what it meant for Bellaria.

***

Bellaria di Rivergaro

Following the assassination of Umberto I, Italy gained a new king as Victor Emmanuel III succeeded his father. As Giacomo Sconti had surmised, the king's death did not affect the stability of the Italian government under Giuseppe Saracco, which had already survived many lesser crises. Giacomo's influence with Mayor Martinelli helped Emilio win the franchise for a postal substation and Emilio immediately built a bank of cubbyhole-like spaces behind the counter in Bellaria's store to hold mail for his customers. Evangelina learned how to sort both incoming and outgoing mail and prepare the necessary paperwork that she gave to the postman when he made his regular deliveries and pickups. As more people from the local community, including Statto and even Rivalta, stopped at Bellaria to pick up or drop off mail, Bellaria's business began to improve, at least at the store.

Business improved even more after Silvio and Maria held their wedding banquet at Bellaria. The banquet was a gift from Emilio to his younger brother in gratitude for all his help during the construction of the building. However, the event also served to introduce still additional people to the restaurant and inn. In a gesture of courtesy, but also shrewd marketing, Emilio invited Maria's parents to remain as guests in the inn so that they did not have to make the long, two-hour carriage drive back to Niviano after the banquet. It was not long afterwards that word spread from Niviano to Settima and the other small communities north of Rivergaro about Bellaria's wonderful *trattoria* and *locanda*. The improvement in Bellaria's business enabled Emilio to take advantage of a technological marvel that was rapidly spreading throughout northern Italy – electricity.

When Bellaria was built, electricity was being generated at hydroelectric plants in the Alps, Apennines and anywhere else in Italy where water could be harnessed to power hydroelectric turbines. In 1884, for example, an alternating current power transformer was demonstrated in Turin and by 1889 much of nighttime Rome was lighted by electricity. In the northwest of Italy, Milan and even Piacenza were benefiting from electricity by early 1900. However, very few rural areas benefited from this new technology. Most country homes, like Bellaria when it was first built, relied on kerosene or coal oil lamps for lighting, and remained that way well into the twentieth century.

It was dusk and Emilio was returning from working on a *mulino* at a farm along the river near Roveleto Landi, a small community north of Rivergaro. Usually at this time of day, the entrance to the city was dark and gloomy. However, within the past week workers completed running a cable for electricity from Piacenza to Rivergaro, attaching the power line to already existing telegraph poles. The arrival of electricity at Rivergaro was greeted with great fanfare. Unfortunately, neither Emilio nor any of the family was able to attend that celebration. Now, however, as Emilio entered the city, the *Stazione Tramviaria*, the train station, was awash in light, as though it was daytime. The bright light streamed from electric light bulbs strung along the length of the station's ceiling. Farther down the road to Bobbio, he passed through the Piazza Grande, which also was bathed in light, this time emanating from electric light bulbs hanging beneath circular metal shades affixed to tall wood poles. He was amazed at the sight and already was thinking about what electricity would mean to Bellaria.

When he attended the next public meeting of the city council in Rivergaro, Emilio learned that within the next few weeks electricity would be extended from Rivergaro to Bobbio making use of the existing telegraph poles. There were no plans, though, to extend electricity to the small communities on the Statto side of the river. Nor, would electricity be run to any of the towns or villages between Rivergaro and Bobbio, except for Travo where an electric cable could be easily attached to the bridge that crossed the Trebbia to that comune. However, Emilio was told, the electric line between Rivergaro and Bobbio would pass right by Bellaria. Because there was a telegraph pole on the opposite side of the road from the *trattoria*'s terrace, Bellaria could have electricity if Emilio picked up the cost of running the electric line from that pole to the building. Emilio was ecstatic! He could hardly wait to get home and share the news with Evangelina.

Electricity did come to Bellaria and brought with it many changes. As agreed, Emilio paid to have an electric cable strung from the telegraph pole across the road to the building. All of the rooms were then wired for electricity, with conduit running through a switch next to the doorway up the inside walls to a single light fixture that hung from the center of the ceiling. The younger children were awed that a room could now be lighted by simply flipping a switch, which they would do so often that Evangelina had to threaten discipline in order to stop them. Curiosity got the best of

Luigi, who was now almost fifteen years old. He used one of Emilio's screwdrivers to open a switch case so that he could see how it was wired. Then he probed the inside of the switch with his finger, unwittingly closing the circuit that produced a shock knocking him half way across the room. Emilio was amused, but gave Luigi a cuff in the head for having done such a stupid thing. Then, to no one's surprise, Evangelina announced that she was going to have another baby.

Emilio sat at one Bellaria's outside tables playing cards with three of his friends from Rivergaro: Renato Carmini, Massimo Edini, and Gino Mazoni. Carmini operated a small cheese laboratorio in Scrivellano, a short distance from Emilio's former house in the hills above Statto. Edini was a retired bricklayer while Mazoni brought down timber from the forests of the Alta Val Trebbia for the growing construction needs of the lower valley.

Evangelina, her pregnancy now apparent, served the men their mid-morning caffè and brought them a plate of *cornetti*, croissants filled with apricot, cioccolato, and crème. Although the day was sunny and warm, Emilio was dressed in his trademark clothing: black wool trousers with suspenders, white linen shirt buttoned at the throat, black vest and a well-worn black Fedora hat. Bands of black elastic helped keep the slack in the arms of his shirt in check. An ever present, but unlit cigar, hung limply from the right corner of his mouth. The only time he lit the cigar was in the late afternoon, when it was accompanied by his customary snack of dried cheese and red wine.

The conversation had been animated with much discussion about politics and the state of the Italian economy. Gino Mazoni expressed his opinion about the reason why some of the individuals and families in the area were immigrating to America and other countries.

"Anyone can plainly see that the economy is getting worse," he stated. "Every month I bring less and less timber down here to the lower valley because construction is slowing. Several of the municipal projects in Rivergaro, in fact, have been stalled now for some time. That's why they are leaving – to find jobs in other countries like America or Argentina."

Renato Carmini looked across the table at Emilio and asked, "How about you, *miei cari*?" He referred to Emilio using a local term equivalent to 'our dear friend' that was reserved for only Emilio's closest friends. "Is Bellaria still doing as well as it did last year?"

Emilio shrugged his shoulders and took another sip of the thick, bitter caffè espresso that Italians consumed five or six times each day.

"No, it's not," he admitted. "There was a brief increase in business when we brought electricity into Bellaria and installed an electric light in all of the rooms and outside of the building. People came from quite some distance to see Bellaria lit up and they often stayed for supper or bought something in the store. Now and then someone would also stay overnight in the *locanda*. But, I guess they got tired of the novelty and now once again business is tapering off."

93

Bellaria di Rivergaro

Massimo Edini put down the chocolate-filled croissant that he had been eating and said, "But there is something else that is bothering you, Emilio, isn't there?"

"Perhaps," Emilio responded. "You know, when I built Bellaria just a few years ago it seemed that there would be so much space for all of us in that big house. But, now it seems like the house is shrinking."

Gino Mazoni glanced over at pregnant Evangelina who was standing in the doorway with her arms folded watching the men. "To be sure, *miei cari*, it is obvious that your family is growing," he said with a knowing smile. "Ah, but the real issue is Luigi, isn't it?"

Emilio sighed, "Luigi and Elisa, too," he confided. "Italy is becoming a dangerous place for young men. We lost thousands of our young sons at Adwa," he explained, citing the disaster at Adwa, Ethiopia in 1898 when 7,000 Italian soldiers were killed and another 1,500 were wounded in a key battle that dashed Italy's hopes to colonize Ethiopia.

"After that," he continued, "we sent thousands more to China to help put down the Boxer Rebellion and then what do we do? We send even more thousands to Somalia so we can have our army at the doorstep of the Suez Canal and the Gulf of Aden. What good purpose did all of that serve?"

There was thoughtful silence as the men sipped more caffè and took another bite of the *cornetti*. Evangelina noted that their small demitasse size cups were becoming depleted and quickly brought a pot of caffè to refill them.

"Well, how does this affect Luigi and Elisa?" Carmini asked. "The army conscripts men when they become twenty years old but Luigi is much younger than that. As for Elisa, women do not have to go into the army at all."

"My friends, you might think that these days I just sit around Bellaria reading newspapers and maybe selling a little cheese and wine, but a lot of people pass by here and I speak with many of them," Emilio asserted. "I hear many things. Are you not aware about what is happening in Turkey and Libya?"

The other three men shook their heads indicating that they did not know what Emilio was talking about.

"I believe that there is another war coming soon," Emilio predicted. "And when it happens, Italy will not have enough 20 year olds to conscript into the army and will begin dropping the conscription age. Already in some parts of the country, they are conscripting young men who have just reached their 18th birthday. I do not want my son, Luigi, to be caught up in that carnage just to satisfy the lust of the politicians and generals for more territory."

Emilio was so passionate about what he said that he bit through his cigar. He spat out the wet tobacco and pulled another cigar from his vest pocket, biting off the end and replacing the one now ground into the dirt beneath his feet. Gino Mazoni looked at Emilio quizzically.

"What does Luigi have to say about this?" he asked.

Bellaria di Rivergaro

"Luigi wants to build bridges and tall buildings, not fight colonial wars," Emilio replied. "Unfortunately, it does not look like he will be able to do that here in Italy."

"And Elisa," Mazoni persisted.

"Elisa is approaching marriage age. Who will she marry if the best young men in Rivergaro go off to war?"

Then, having enough of that conversation, Emilio stood up and said that he had to go down to the *stalla* by the river to check on the animals. Understanding that there had been more than enough discussion about the economy, politics and war for one day, the other three men nodded in agreement, thanked Evangelina, and also left.

***

Elisa spotted a piece of stale bread that fallen under the corner table in the smaller dining room of the *trattoria*. She reached under the table with the broom her brother Luigi had made from willow twigs that he cut at the river and swept it away. Then, she continued to sweep the mud and dirt that constantly accumulated on the flat stone floors until with one grand thrust everything was swept out of Bellaria's front door. As she turned to go back into the building, she heard a loud sputtering and banging noise, almost like a gunshot, coming from somewhere up the road that led to Bellaria from Rivergaro. She stood in front of Bellaria straining to see where the noise was coming from. Then, suddenly, there appeared the most incredible sight that she had ever seen.

Something that resembled her father's *calesse* came into sight. Two very nicely dressed men were sitting on top of the single, bench seat, four-wheeled carriage. However, most incredibly, there were no horses or ox pulling it, even though it was moving much faster than a person could walk. At first, Elisa thought that perhaps someone was pushing the carriage down the rise in the road toward Bellaria, but there was nothing behind it. It just continued to move toward her, making terrible sounds and occasionally shooting out puffs of black smoke. In front of the driver and his passenger, where a doubletree usually attaches to the pulling shaft of a carriage, there was nothing, except a black cast iron device that seemed to be the main source of the noise.

Elisa stood dumbfounded as the carriage stopped right in front of her. She was frightened out of her wits. Then, the younger of the two men spoke to her.

"Buongiorno signorina," he said, and then added, "It's a lovely day for a ride, yes?"

At first Elisa was silent, not knowing what to say. Then, she pulled herself together and while staring at the carriage that was shaking, still making loud noises, said that 'yes' it was a nice day.

The older of the two men sat behind something that looked like a pipe stuck out of the bottom of the carriage. There was a lever attached to the top of the 'pipe' that the driver grasped. Two or three smaller levers were attached to the larger one that the driver was grasping. When he turned one of the smaller levers, the noise that was coming from under the carriage stopped, as did its shaking. He laughed as he saw Elisa take a step back and said,

Bellaria di Rivergaro

"Well, signorina, I guess that you have never seen a FIAT," he said. "Some people call it a 'horseless carriage,' however, more accurately it is an automobile that is powered by a gasoline engine located right here," he explained, pointing to the box-like iron device that had been making all of the noise.

Elisa stood rooted where she had been standing and simply shook her head to indicate that she had never seen such a thing. Then the younger man jumped down from the carriage and said,

"It is made in Turin at Fabbrica Italiana Automobili Torino, a very large manufacturing plant that employs 150 people." Then he asked, "What is your name, signorina, and what is this place?"

"Elisa Tagliaferri. This place is called Bellaria. It is the home of my family and it is also our *trattoria* and *locanda*."

"Wonderful," the younger man said. "We could use something to eat. My name is Giovanni Guasconi and my friend here is Signor Angelo Solari. He's the rich one. I could not possibily afford one of these things. Anyway, I prefer a nice two-wheel *calesse* and a young, sprightly horse. They are more reliable, make much less noise, and are fun to drive," he said laughingly.

Elisa liked his smile and casual manner. She felt more comfortable now than when the two first arrived, especially since the beast that masqueraded like a carriage was silent. She also noticed that the younger man was not as old as she had originally guessed. In fact, she opined, he was probably close to her own age. She invited the two men into the

98

trattoria, served them a glass of wine, and ran to get her mother. Evangelina was in the family quarters with Maria making sure that Giuseppe and Antonio, the newest family members, were taking their naps.

"Mamma, the most incredible thing!" she stammered. "Come quick and look outside."

Evangelina went into her and Emilio's bedroom and looked out the front window. "What in the world is that?" she asked in astonishment.

Elisa explained that it was called an automobile, a FIAT - a carriage that did not need to be pulled by a horse. Evangelina had heard about such carriages from Emilio, who was always reading the newspaper and who had read about the new method of transportation called an automobile. However, neither Emilio nor Evangelina had actually seen one – until now.

"What is it doing here?"

"Two men stopped here and said that they were hungry. One of them owns it and the other is his friend."

"Where is your father?" asked Evangelina.

"Down at the *mulino,*" Elisa answered.

"Send Luigi or one of the girls to get him because I know that he will want to see this. Then, let's be off to see what they want to eat. Hurry up, now."

Elisa went down the stairs to the *trattoria* two steps at a time, followed only slightly more slowly by her mother. Evangelina was pleased to see that Elisa had shown the men to a table and already served them a glass of wine. She suggested that they have a plate of *agnoli*, which would take only a few minutes to prepare because the thin-rolled pasta cooks in less than 10 minutes when it is put into boiling water. The men readily agreed, so Evangelina left them and went to the kitchen where a large pot of hot water was always on the stove. It took only a moment or so to bring it to a boil and then she added two generous portions of *agnoli* to the pot. Meanwhile, Elisa put on a clean, blue striped apron over her black skirt and brushed her hair.

In a few minutes, Elisa brought out two plates of the ricotta-spinach pasta covered with melted butter and grated parmesan cheese. Then she brought out a wicker basket with pieces of fresh-baked bread and a bottle of the mineral water that they had also requested. As she placed the bottle of water on their table, she asked where the men were from.

"Il Signor Solari is from Piacenza. He is a merchant and sells furniture to the people who own the large villas. That's why he is rich," he joked.

"And you, Signore Guasconi? I have never seen you in our comune before, either."

"Well, my family is from Castel San Giovanni, about 20 kilometers west of Piacenza. However, right now I am staying in Piacenza to help Signor Solari. He is selling so much furniture that he can't handle it by himself, anymore. That's the price of being successful."

Solari chimed in, "He forgot to tell you, signorina, that he is the nephew of my wife and that if I hired anyone else I would never hear the end of it! However, one of these days I will lose his excellent assistance because he insists on going to America, if he can persuade his mother to go with him. "

"America!" exclaimed Elisa, addressing Guasconi. "You are going to America?"

"I hope to, Signorina Elisa. I want to learn the restaurant business and there is no better place than New York for that – except no doubt here, of course," he added.

The two men bantered back and forth, laughing and joking through the meal, stopping occasionally to comment on how good the *agnoli* was. A few minutes later, Emilio walked through the door, went over to the two men, and introduced himself.

"A carpenter," Solari repeated, after Emilio gave them a brief history of Bellaria. "Well, if I need any furniture repaired or maybe custom built I now know who to call."

"Unfortunately, we still do not have telephones here in the country," Emilio said. "There is a telephone in the Municipio in Rivergaro, the administrative building for the comune. Everyone there knows who I am, so if you need me just leave a message and someone will get it to me."

Emilio accompanied his guests out to the road so he could see their marvelous automobile. He told them that he was aware there was a place in Turin where automobiles called FIAT were made, but that until now he had never seen one. Then he watched in amazement as Angelo Solari put a crank into a hole in the front of the FIAT's engine block, turn it rapidly and engine began to cough and sputter. Solari made some kind of adjustment that smoothed out the engine noise.

Then he pushed another lever on the floor of the carriage and the vehicle pulled away from Bellaria, but not before Emilio caught a glance of young Guasconi turning around to wave at Elisa – and the broad smile on her face as she waved back.

Chapter 10

LUIGI CLAMPED THE RECTANGULAR TOP of the nightstand he was making into the vice on the workbench. He studied the three gougers in his toolbox and selected the largest of the rounded chisels. Then he began to carefully shape the edges of the tabletop so they were concave on all four sides. It was cold and drafty in the workshop behind Bellaria and the lighting was not very good. However, he enjoyed woodworking and building things much more than the farm tasks that his father also directed him to do. His least favorite task was hitching the ox to the heavy cast iron plow and furrowing row after mind numbing row in the fields below the inn.

After a half hour he stood back to examine his work. Not bad, he thought. Papà will be pleased. His father kept telling him that carpentry and cabinet making were the most important skills he could have and someday he would be glad he learned those skills. His thoughts were interrupted when four-year old Giuseppe opened the workshop door hollering, "Gigi, are you in there?"

"Yes, Beppe, I'm right here. Come in and close the door. It's cold outside," Luigi said gently. He loved all of his siblings, but Giuseppe was his favorite. In turn, Giuseppe practically adored his older brother. Luigi was twelve years older than him; from Giuseppe's eyes, Luigi was "all grown up."

"What are you doing?" Giuseppe asked.

"Papà told me to make a new nightstand for one of the guest rooms." Luigi said.

"Why?" Giuseppe persisted.

"You are a curious little one, aren't you?" Luigi replied. "Well, one of the guests put something much too heavy on the old one and broke it," he explained. "Beppe, please hand me that small hammer," Luigi requested. He then praised his little brother for picking out the correct tool.

After a deluge of other questions, Luigi told his younger brother to 'go help mamma.' Giuseppe pouted a little, opened the workshop door, turned and stuck his tongue out at Luigi then quickly scurried away. Luigi took a break from working on the nightstand and sat down on a log chopping block. He was very troubled and needed to think.

Luigi's father had been a good teacher, having taught him as much about carpentry and construction as he could. However, Emilio's own experience was limited to doing the same things: making blades and slats for waterwheels at the *mulini*, building and repairing *stalle*, making chairs, tables and a few other household things, and then working the farm and waiting on customers in the *trattoria*. Luigi was grateful to his father, but this was not what he wanted to do for the rest of his life. However, there was a lot more than just that. The family had continued to grow; this past year his mother had given birth to the eighth member of the family, a boy – Fortunato, little Nino as the family called him. It was getting more difficult for Emilio to support such a large family and it was customary for a son to begin finding his own way in life when he was Luigi's age.

Luigi got up, walked over to the workbench, and unclamped the top of the nightstand from the vice. He set it down next to the bench and replaced it with a rough-cut table leg that he began tapering with a plane. What he really wanted to do was build big buildings, like the huge *grattacieli*, the skyscrapers, that they were building in America. Several young men from Rivergaro about his age had immigrated to America. From the letters they sent back to their parents, many good paying jobs were available to immigrants if they were willing to work hard to earn it. Just recently, Luigi spoke with Carlo Sconti, who returned from America to visit his parents,

"America is a wonderful place," Carlo told Luigi. "Everybody who goes there has a job and many Italians are getting rich. You are wasting your time here," he said.

"So you got rich working for my mother's cousin in the grocery distribution business?" asked Luigi.

"No, I'm not rich yet, but I will be – I promise you," he replied. "In any case, I no longer work for Zanmatti. I left his business a year ago and now I work at a big winery in upstate New York.

"I'm showing them how to grow our good Piacentini grapes."

"And Zanmatti," Luigi inquired. "Does he need anyone else to help him now that you are no longer there?"

"Well, I understand that he hired some *ragazzo* to replace me, but I don't know how that is going," Carlo concluded.

Zanmatti. Luigi thought about that conversation and made a decision. He would write to his mother's cousin Alberto Zanmatti and ask if he needed someone to help him. Perhaps he could follow the same path to America as had Carlo Sconti.

A few weeks later, Luigi was helping his mother in Bellaria's store when the postman stopped to make his mail delivery. As usual, there was a packet of letters and a package or two that Evangelina would sort and place in the appropriate mail cubicle for local residents. Evangelina was sorting the mail when Luigi heard her loudly exclaim, "A letter for you, Luigi! It's from my cousin Alberto Zanmatti. Why is Alberto writing to you?" she demanded.

Luigi knew that he was in trouble. He had not mentioned to anyone that he wrote to Zanmatti and he forgot that most likely his mother would be the first person to see any reply from him. He stammered and said, "Ah, well maybe he just wanted to write me a letter," fully knowing that was a dumb thing to say.

Evangelina gave Luigi the envelope, along with a glare that showed her suspicion about why Zanmatti was writing to him. Luigi excused himself and ran down to the workshop. Giuseppe, who saw the exchange between his mother and Luigi, tagged along to see what was going on. Luigi tore open the envelope and began to read the rather long letter.

Apparently, after Carlo Sconti left to take the job in the winery, Zanmatti hired a local 14-year-old boy to replace him. The boy turned out to be a good worker and for a while, everything went well. Then one day Zanmatti and the boy were making morning deliveries to the small shops and cafes in "Little Italy" when he stopped to drop off an order of groceries at a customer's shop. He gave the boy the reins of the horse and told him to wait in the delivery wagon. While, Zanmatti was in the customer's shop, the boy did something to spook the horse, which kicked the wagon, breaking the young man's left leg. Zanmatti ran out and took the boy to the hospital where they set his leg. Zanmatti paid the boy's hospital bill, but then fired the boy for his carelessness. More unfortunately, the story did not end there.

The boy's parents sued Zanmatti for negligence in not properly securing the horse while he went inside the store. The case went to court and Zanmatti lost. The court ordered him to pay the boy five hundred dollars in damages. Zanmatti was very upset and vowed that in the future he would hire only relatives, whose loyalty he could count on. So, yes, indeed, he could use some help in his business and would be willing to discuss the matter with Luigi's parents. He suggested Luigi ask them to write to him.

Luigi gasped aloud, "I can't believe it! He wants me to go to America." His hands were trembling. When he wrote to Zanmatti he never really expected to receive a positive reply. However, now he held it in his hands and it was frightening. In terms of his physical stature and work skills, Luigi was on the verge of manhood. However, in many ways, he was still a boy. The idea of traveling to America seemed so adventuresome, but the prospect of really doing so was another matter. He also was aware that his parents would be furious that he contacted Zanmatti without consulting them.

Bellaria di Rivergaro

***

There were no patrons in the *trattoria*, so Emilio decided to have the family discussion there. He sat at the table in the back of the dining room where he could look out over the Trebbia and see the Statto Castle and, behind it, the church of Sant'Antonio Abate. Evangelina brought over two cups of caffè, one for her, and one for Emilio. The absence of anything for Luigi, who stood in front of the table, was a sign of her displeasure with him. Emilio broke the silence.

"So, you want to go to America and you did not think that you needed to talk to me or your mother about it, eh?" he grunted.

Evangelina said nothing. She did not have to - her body language told it all. Luigi realized that the conversation was not off to a good start. He knew that he had to do something to acknowledge that he should not have gone behind their backs by writing to Zanmatti without their knowledge.

"Mamma, papà. I am really sorry. I was talking to Carlo Sconti and he said that he was no longer working for Cousin Zanmatti. I just wrote to see what he would say."

"Well, now you know," Emilio said. "You are sixteen and for the most part you are old enough to do as you please. You can join the army, if you want, for that matter." Although the military conscripted young men when they turned twenty, they readily accepted volunteers who were seventeen years old, or even a sixteen year old youth, who lied about his age.

"I do not want to join the army, papà, here in Italy or anywhere else," Luigi said. "I just think that it is time that I made a life for myself and began to use the skills that you taught me."

Emilio's face showed a flicker of pride that his son was acknowledging the importance of the training he had received and also that he was standing up for himself as a man. Evangelina sensed the inevitability of the outcome of the discussion and alternated between holding back tears and biting her knuckles, the signal of anguish typical of all Italian mothers.

"Mamma," Luigi said, turning toward Evangelina, "I love you very much. I love you, too, papà, and all of my brothers and sisters. But, I want to go to America and I want to build things. I want to be as good a builder as papà and I want you both to be proud of me."

That was too much for Evangelina, who put her head in her hands and began to sob. Emilio's eyes became moist with pride, but also sadness as he understood that his oldest son, the once little boy who worked with him to build their beloved Bellaria, would soon leave their home for a very faraway place. Evangelina cried out, "But, we will never see you again!"

"Yes you will mamma. I promise. I will come back often and when I make enough money I will bring you and papà to America too," Luigi protested, now himself almost in tears.

Emilio stood and put his arms on his son's shoulders. "Your mother and I will write to Alberto Zanmatti and tell him that you have our permission and blessing to go to

America if you want. We will see what arrangement we can work out for you."

Luigi thanked them, hugged them both, and left the room. When they were alone, Emilio put his arms around Evangelina to comfort her, but he had little success. Unnoticed by all of them, little Giuseppe sat alone in a corner of the room softly crying. He had heard everything and he, too, was afraid that the big brother he loved so much would go away and never come back.

***

The train was scheduled to depart from Rivergaro at 12:45 PM, so there was a little less than three hours before they had to leave Bellaria for the train station. Luigi came downstairs from the room he shared with Pietro where he was packing the old leather valise his father gave him for the trip. He looked for his younger brother and found him setting tables in the *trattoria*.

"Pierino, would you like to walk with me down to the river?" Luigi asked, using Pietro's nickname.

"Sure, Luigi. Will you show me again how you skip stones all the way across?" Luigi promised he would.

On the road down to the river, Luigi decided to take a shortcut through the north field to check on the *stalla* that served as shelter for the animals when the weather was bad or too hot for them. He spotted a couple of planks beginning to pull away from the siding and did the best he could put them back in place. Then the two brothers continued to the

110

river's edge where Pietro picked up a few flat stones and tried to skip them over the water.

"Not bad, little brother," Luigi said. "Here let me show you how to make a stone skip all the way across to the other side."

He carefully selected the flattest of the stones that fit perfectly in the palm of his hand, grasped one with his thumb and forefinger, twisted his wrist, and threw the stone with a sharp flip at the last second. The stone hit the water, made a long skip and then four shorter skips until it got within a meter of the opposite shore where it dropped beneath the water's surface.

Pietro was delighted and asked Luigi to do it again.

"No, it's your turn now," Luigi told him, as he gave Pietro one of the stones that he selected earlier. "Turn your wrist a little more and now give it a hard flip. Terrific, that's the way!" he exclaimed, as the stone made three good skips before dropping into the river.

"Pierino, you know that I am going away for a while, don't you?" he asked. Pietro nodded that he did. "Well, after I leave you will be the oldest man in the house except for papà. Papà is going to need a lot of help to keep Bellaria looking nice and to make sure that the animals down here in the fields are fed and watered. Beppe and Antonio and baby Nino are still too young to help much, so it is up to you to help him."

"I know, Gigi, but do you really have to go away?"

"I do. I really do. But, I'll be back after a little while. I just want to make sure that you will take care of papà and mamma while I am gone."

"I will, Gigi. I promise."

Luigi gave his brother a hug, took his hand, and led him back up the hill to Bellaria.

Luigi went to the bedroom that he shared with Giuesppe and Pietro. Except for the linen shirt that he wore only to Holy Mass on Sundays, the clothes he would wear were 'hand-me-downs' from his father that were tailored to fit him by his mother. He buttoned his shirt at the top but did not wear a tie; most young men his age did not wear one, unless they were from wealthy families. It was early May; however, he packed a few items that would be useful in cooler weather and one extra set of long john underwear that would supplement the one that he was wearing. He also packed one pair of work shoes because he would be traveling in his 'church' shoes. Then he walked down the stairs to where all of the family waited for him.

Evangelina told Luigi to open the valise. She then rearranged his clothes to accommodate a whole salume, some prosciutto, half-wheel of Grana Padana cheese and a long loaf of pane, all of which he would be glad he had during the transatlantic crossing.

Everyone went outside while Emilio hitched the chestnut mare to the two-wheel *calesse*. Luigi decided to take one last walk around Bellaria. With measured steps, he walked around the entire perimeter of the building. His hand was in almost constant contact with the rough stones and occasional brick of the structure. He stood back, from time to time, looking up the sides of the building, looking at the tiled roof and recalling in every detail how he had helped build it with his father and uncles. In his mind he felt again the pull of the hoe as he mixed the mortar, the weight of every stone or rock that he had lifted to them as they were laying the strata of the walls. He even remembered the time that he chased the intruding squirrel out of the half-built interior of the house. He thought about the day that Bellaria was completed and the day that the family moved in to their new home. He remembered it all. Then, in unison, the church bells of Sant'Agata in Rivergaro and even the bells in Sant'Antonio Abate across the river began ringing the Angelus precisely at noon. It was time to leave.

Luigi's father was waiting for him in the *calesse*, the valise already on the carriage floor. Luigi walked over to each of his siblings and hugged them: Elisa, Elvira, Maria, Pietro, Giuseppe, Antonio, and Nino. Tears were flowing freely from everyone, including Luigi. Then he went over to his mother and the pain and sorrow for both of them was almost too much for either to bear, as they clung tightly together. No words passed between them – none were necessary.

Luigi climbed up on to the *calesse* and Emilio snapped the reins, setting the mare in motion. Although he promised himself that he would not turn back, Luigi could not resist the temptation and immediately regretted that he had done so. His mother and siblings were waving and crying, but it was little Beppe who commanded his attention. Giuseppe was trying to pull away from his mother and then suddenly broke free. He began to run after the *calesse* screaming, "Gigi, don't

113

go! Please don't go!" After a few steps he stumbled, fell to the ground and then lay there sobbing until Elisa reached him, picked him up, and held him over her shoulder, gently patting his back.

At that point, Luigi was on the verge of completely changing his mind, but Emilio cracked the buggy whip harder and the *calesse* with its passengers soon disappeared around the bend, as Bellaria faded from view.

When they arrived at the train station, Emilio made sure that Luigi had the prepaid tickets both for the train and for the transatlantic voyage. Emilio paid for the train tickets but Alberto Zanmatti had paid for Luigi's passage aboard the Steamship La Bretagne sailing out of Le Havre, France on May 13th, in just four days. Zanmatti did not buy Luigi's tickets out of the goodness of his heart. When Zanmatti wrote to Emilio and Evangelina, he offered to sponsor Luigi, pay for his steerage passage to America and he offered him a job in his grocery business. However, in return, Luigi was required to agree that he would work for Zanmatti for at least one year. He also had to agree to have the cost of the transatlantic passage plus room and board at Zanmatti's flat above the store deducted from his pay, the amount of which was yet to be determined.

The travel itinerary called for Luigi to travel from Rivergaro to Milan, passing through Piacenza. In Milan, he would change trains for the long ride to Paris and then another change of trains to Le Havre. It would be a long and tiring journey just to get to Le Havre. Fortunately, while waiting for the train, Emilio recognized a man named Ettore Tramelli who was from Ottavello, not far from Rivergaro.

Emilio had done some business with the man a few years ago. It seemed that Signor Tramelli was traveling to New York to visit his brother who had immigrated to America and who now was very ill. He would be traveling on the same ship as Luigi. Emilio introduced Luigi to Signor Tramelli and asked the older man to keep an eye on Luigi during the voyage.

Moments later, everyone was startled by the train's loud whistle indicating that it was ready to depart from Rivergaro. Emilio and Luigi embraced. There was no need for them to say anything; their feelings had already been expressed back at Bellaria. Without Luigi noticing, Emilio slipped ten American dollars he had obtained from the bank in Rivergaro in exchange for lira into the left pocket of Luigi's jacket. They looked at each other silently and embraced one more time. They Luigi grabbed his valise and jumped aboard the train – this time without looking back.

***

When he saw La Bretagne, the steamship that would take him to America, Luigi was completely astounded. It was the largest manmade object he had ever seen – except, perhaps, for the incredible train station in Milan with its web of girders arching over a network of railroad tracks and platforms. La Bretagne measured almost 500 feet in length, 151 meters. It had five decks topped off by two tall funnels, now belching dark smoke as the coal-fired boilers below began to produce the steam the two huge engines needed to turn the ship's single screw. Remarkably, the loading of La Bretagne's 1,100 passengers took only one hour. In part, that was because there were only 365 first class passengers and sixty in the second class section. The other 675 passengers, who were traveling steerage, including Luigi, were herded rapidly and without fanfare down the hatch leading to the lowest deck of the ship.

Luigi had been advised by Carlo Sconti months earlier what to expect in the steerage passenger compartment. Sconti was correct; conditions were cramped and near chaos governed. Luigi spotted the empty lower bunk that he was assigned and threw his valise on it, claiming it as his private space for the voyage. There was a straw-filled mattress lying over a web of springs on the bunk, one thin and very tattered wool blanket and a life jacket that would have to serve as a pillow. On the mattress was an 'immigrant kit' consisting of a tin plate, tin cup and a knife, fork and spoon. These would be his dining utensils for the entire voyage. No sooner had Luigi stretched out on the bunk when an older man, probably in his late thirties, dropped his valise on the deck next to him. The man looked first at the empty bunk above Luigi to which he had been assigned and then at Luigi and said,

"Kid, get your ass off my bunk. You take the upper one or find some other place to sleep. I'm not going to climb up and down the damn thing."

Ettore Tramelli, who was assigned a bunk not far from Luigi's, glanced over, waiting to see how Luigi would respond. Luigi looked up at the bottom of the upper bunk, barely an arm's height above his face, and decided that he did not want such a confined space anyway. Besides, he did not intend to begin his trip to America getting into a fight with a man twice his age. Deciding to make the best if it, he got out of the lower bunk, placed his valise on the bunk above him then turned to the man and said,

"Of course, signor, I can understand how difficult it must be for someone your age to climb into a bunk that high off the deck." With that, he sprightly leaped up on to the upper bunk and once again stretched out. Tremelli, who had been observing the scene, chuckled to himself and then continued to arrange his own lower bunk.

Five decks above steerage, passengers who were already settled in their compartments assembled to wait for the ship's departure. Luigi joined the crowd and noticed that steerage passengers had access to only part of the deck – the larger section being reserved for first and second-class passengers. The deck was so crowded it was almost impassable. Meanwhile, a light breeze flowed across the Le Havre harbor and was caught by the ship's scuppers, channeling the fresh air to the grateful passengers who were still below deck.

Suddenly, a thunderous roar came from the ship's horn attached to the funnel above the steerage passengers on the aft deck. The long throaty blast signaled that the La Bretagne was ready to leave port. Shortly afterward, the horn sounded again with three short blasts indicating that the ship was backing up. As the ship was pulling away from the dock, hundreds of passengers waved to friends, loved ones, and even strangers who were standing on the dock bidding them a safe voyage. Luigi observed this pageant wordlessly, not fully comprehending the long and uncomfortable voyage ahead. He felt a hand on his shoulder and turned to find Ettore Tremelli standing beside him.

"Well young man," Tremelli said. "You are about to begin a great adventure. Look around you; see all these people? They probably feel like you do. Everything is so incredible, but they wonder if they are doing the right thing. Almost everyone is anxious and uncertain"

"And you, Signor Tremelli, have you been to America before?"

"Once," Tremelli replied. "I was a little older than you and I wanted to make a new life for myself. Ottavello is a very small town and the people there are poor. There was nothing there for me."

"But, you live in Ottavello now," Luigi said in puzzlement.

"I do. I spent five years in America, in Philadelphia where I had an uncle. He had immigrated to America several years earlier, married a local girl and eventually saved enough money to buy a small farm. That's where I learned how to grow some of the best tomatoes that you will ever taste. Then my father died and I returned to Ottavello to take over the family *cascina*. Now, I grow pomodori and sell them to the big processing plant in Rivergaro," he explained.

"Don't you want to live in America, anymore," Luigi asked.

"Beh, I am too old now," Tremelli answered. "Besides, it is hard to leave something that you worked so hard to build," he added, immediately realizing that was the wrong thing to say.

Luigi nodded in understanding, thinking about Bellaria and everything that he left behind. He excused himself and found a space more forward on the deck where he could sit and think. At first, he was very depressed. Perhaps he made

118

the wrong decision and should never have left Rivergaro, his family and Bellaria. However, he remembered what Tremelli said about returning to Italy and using the knowledge that he gained in America to build a better life for himself - right there in Ottavello. Luigi was confident that he could do the same. He could learn how to build large buildings and bridges and even railroad stations. Then he would go back to Italy and perhaps go into business with his brothers, just like his father Emilio had done. Yes, that might be a good plan. He felt much better after that thought; so he stood up and decided that it was time to explore the ship. Afterward he planned to slice some of the salume and formaggio that his mother had packed for him and make a good Bellaria style panini.

The steamship La Bretagne sailed past Sandy Hook, New Jersey at 12:45 PM on Monday, May 22, 1905, nine days after leaving Le Havre. One and a half hours later, it passed the Statue of Liberty. All 1,100 passengers were on deck, occupying every available inch of space. The mood was ecstatic. Family members circled their arms around each other and cried with joy and relief. Strangers hugged strangers. Hats were thrown in the air, many to catch the wind and fall into the sea, people waved at that magnificent gift from the people of France, and the ship's horn once again sounded in salute. Luigi was completely caught up in the exuberance and in that moment, all of the discomfort of the voyage was forgotten. It mattered little now that on one night the ship passed through a terrible squall with waves crashing over the bow and that steerage passengers, including Luigi, were thrown out of their bunks as the ship heaved in heavy seas. The seasickness, bad food, fights among the male passengers, wailing of infants and small children, foul smelling air and sheer boredom were now things of the past. The only thing that mattered was that they arrived in America and their dreams were fulfilled.

Ellis Island was another matter. Tugboats berthed the La Bretagne at a pier on the Hudson River, only a few blocks from the heart of Manhattan. First and second-class passengers debarked there and were swiftly processed through U.S. Immigration. However, steerage passengers were transferred to a ferry that took them across the river to Ellis Island, the U.S. Immigration station that for hundreds of thousands of immigrants each year was the gateway to America. Tragically, for those rejected for admission to the United States, Ellis Island represented the shattering of their dreams and hopes for a better life.

However, Luigi was very fortunate. He had a third grade education so he could read, write, and do basic arithmetic. Because he was bright, he responded well to the examiners' questions and solved their puzzles and skills tests. Further, Ettore Tramelli, who was traveling on a visitor's visa and who spoke passable English, vouched for Luigi, telling Immigration officials that he was accompanying him. The only problem arose when an Immigration officer told Luigi that he had to pay an entry tax of two dollars. Two dollars was all of the money Luigi had and he panicked at the thought that he would be penniless after he paid the tax. However, when he ruffled through his clothing in search of coins, to his astonishment he found a U.S. ten dollar note in his left jacket pocket. The Immigration official marked that he arrived in the United States with a total of twelve dollars in cash and then took two of the dollars for the entry tax. It was not until months later that Luigi learned his father put the money in his jacket pocket.

After paying the entry fee, Luigi breezed through the bureaucracy at Ellis Island and in only three days was back on a ferry that took him to a pier on Manhattan's East River. He stepped off the ferry ramp onto the mainland of America with his valise, the remainder of the food his mother packed for him, Alberto Zanmatti's address and ten U.S. dollars; nine dollars and 85 cents, actually, because he bought a caffè and a pastry after passing through U.S. Immigration. The first thing he spotted when he left the ferry was a cart with a sign with the words "Ice Cream" and the painted image of a chocolate ice cream cone next to it. Luigi walked over to the cart and put to test the few words in English that he learned while on the ship. *"Pleasa, I want uno 'ee chey creamo."* The man behind the cart, himself from northern Italy, responded in Luigi's Piacentino dialect,

"Non è gelato, ragazzo. Tuttavia, ha un sapore piuttosto bene comunque." It ain't gelato, kid. But, it tastes pretty good anyway. Then he handed Luigi a large, double-scoop chocolate ice cream cone. Luigi paid the vendor a nickel and then set off to begin his life in the new world.

Bellaria di Rivergaro

Chapter 11

IN SOME RESPECTS, IT WOULD HAVE BEEN EASIER to take the train between Modena and Genoa. However, the temptation to drive the entire distance in the new 1905 FIAT Brevetti that he purchased only last month was too great for Alfredo to resist. From Modena, Alfredo drove west to Parma and then on to Piacenza, where he turned south for the three-hour leg to Genoa. The car was a dream to drive and he had no problems on the road. If he had run into a problem, his route took him only an hour or so from the FIAT factory in Turin where the car was made. He could easily have obtained help from a factory mechanic there, a factor he considered when planning his route.

Alfredo's business in Genoa was with both the rail and shipping lines. He owned a very successful foundry in Modena that made cast engine components used by both steamships and steam-powered trains. In fact, he was so successful that he was the first person in Modena to own an automobile. His first car was a 1902 FIAT 12 HP that was followed by the 32 HP Brevatti that he now owned. FIAT made good, reliable automobiles, he thought. It helped, of course, that FIAT practically had the automobile market to itself in northern Italy. The Darracq-Italiana plant in Milan owned by a French company gave FIAT only nominal competition.

Alfredo's seven-year old son was sleeping in the back seat of the FIAT. The boy had begged to accompany his father on the trip and Alfredo relented. Even at such a young age, the boy was fascinated by everything that was mechanical – especially automobiles. When they reached Genoa, the boy stayed with his aunt while Alfredo conducted his business. The next day, they left Genoa in late morning, after Alfredo had the FIAT thoroughly checked over by a mechanic. Alfredo decided to take the shorter route home, which would take them to Bobbio and then on to Piacenza. From Piacenza he would retrace his original route to Parma and then home to the hills outside of Modena. However, he had no idea that the twisting roads threading through the Alta Val Trebbia would slow his trip so much.

He reached Bobbio about 6:00 PM, after a tiring and dangerous ride through the upper valley. At Bobbio he decided to push on, at least to Rivergaro or maybe even Piacenza. But, now darkness had fallen and he was anxious to stop for the night anywhere it was safe. For the last several kilometers, the road had been completely deserted, as though the local residents knew that it was silly and unnecessary to be on the road at night. Other than the headlights of his FIAT, the only lights he saw were the dim glow in the window of an occasional *cascina* on a hillside off in the distance. Then ahead of him, he could see a brightly lit building with electric lights hanging from fixtures on either side of a doorway and bright, cheery lights shining in almost every room of the large structure. It was a very welcoming sight; almost a mirage compared with the darkness through which he had been driving.

Alfredo drove up to the building and parked next to two *calesse* with their horses hitched to poles on either side of a watering trough. He noticed an older FIAT parked farther ahead. He woke up his son and went inside, where he found a middle-aged man standing behind a small counter. Through an arched doorway, he could see several diners chatting and enjoying their meals. A woman in her thirties was serving food to the people seated at the tables with the help of two younger women. Everyone was relaxed and was having a good time.

"Good evening. What is this place, sir?" Alfredo asked.

Emilio looked up, smiled, and said, "Good evening, signore. Welcome to the best *trattoria* and *locanda* in Rivergaro. This is Bellaria – Bellaria di Rivergaro."

The next morning, Alfredo and his son had a tasty breakfast of cold meat, bread, cheese, and pastry. Alfredo savored the fresh-brewed caffè, while his son, Enzo, drank milk so fresh that it was still warm. After he finished a second cup of caffè, Alfredo asked Emilio for the latest road information between Rivergaro and Piacenza. Meanwhile, Enzo played on the floor of the dining room with his newfound friend Giuseppe. Emilio and Alfredo were amused at how intensely Enzo and Giuseppe were playing with Enzo's favorite toy, a model of a FIAT 24 HP Corsa, one of the fastest racing cars in Northern Italy.

"Your son obviously enjoys the Corsa," Emilio observed.

"Ah, that's all that he seems he wants to do," replied Alfredo. "He thinks that when he grows up he'll be a great racing car driver."

"Why not?" Emilio said. "Every day I see automobiles passing Bellaria on the road between Rivergaro and Bobbio or crossing the Statto Bridge. Almost all of the drivers think that they are on the Circuit di Bologna," he said, referring to the famous automobile racing event. "Perhaps someday your son can race there."

Alfredo paid his bill and went outside to start the Brevetti. He called to his son to come along. Enzo was having so much fun playing with Giuseppe that he did not want to leave. But, when his father called a second time he got up, said goodbye to Giuseppe and jumped into the front seat of the FIAT. Just before they pulled away, Emilio noticed that his guest had forgotten to take his receipt for the night's stay. He took the receipt out to Alfredo and said,

"I hope that you enjoyed your stay at Bellaria, Signor Ferrari. You too, Enzo. Come back and visit us again."

***

Two months passed since Luigi left for America without any word from him - nothing at all. Evangelina could not stop worrying. Was he all right? Did something happen to him aboard the ship? Did he get lost? Where is he? The questions did not cease. The constant questions from Giuseppe did not help either. When was Luigi coming home? When could Giuseppe see him? The girls seemed to be more patient, though not less curious or concerned. Emilio alone maintained his calm. What else could he do? He tried to reassure Evangelina and the rest of the family that surely everything was fine; that they could not expect to hear from Luigi this early. Then the long awaited letter arrived.

Elisa had taken over most of her mother's duties in the store and the postal substation so that Evangelina could deal with the growing business of the inn and the restaurant. The afternoon that the letter arrived, Elisa was busy stocking the shelves of the store with jars of homemade blackberry, currant, and fig jam. The young postman brought a bundle of letters and packages into the store and placed them on top of the counter. He flirted briefly with Elisa, who pretended to ignore his attention. The postman winked at Elisa and then left, telling her to save a jar of peach preserves for him the next time she and her mother made a batch. It was only when Elisa was putting the mail into the cubbyholes that she found the envelope Luigi had addressed to his father.

Elisa was so excited that ran into the main entrance of Bellaria screaming for her mother.

"Mamma, mamma!" she cried out. "It's Luigi, we got a letter from Luigi!"

Evangelina was in the kitchen with Elvira rolling and cutting the tagliatelle pasta that she would be serving Bellaria's guests that evening. She ran out of the kitchen wiping her hands on her apron, ridding them of the clinging pasta dough. Elvira followed close on her mother's heels. Maria was holding baby Nino and also followed. Evangelina tore the letter from Elisa's hands and then saw that it was addressed to Emilio, who was in the stable shoeing a horse. When she shouted that there was a letter from Luigi, Emilio moved as quickly as a man with arthritis in his hip could, and in a moment was standing beside her. Pietro and Giuseppe had been cooling off from the July heat by sucking on chips of ice from the ice shed in the corner of the workshop. However, they also heard Evangelina call to Emilio and raced into Bellaria.

Emilio tore open the envelope and began reading the somewhat stilted letter. With only three years of formal education, Luigi had learned only the basics of reading, writing and arithmetic.

Dear Papà,

I am here. In New York. The boat was not too bad but I did not like it. Signor Tremelli helped me. New York is big and the buildings are very tall. Almost everyone here is Italian. Or Irish or German. Cousin Alberto put me in a room with four other men. I have a bed. One man sleeps on the floor. Cousin Alberto pays me 20 cents an hour to help him deliver groceries. But, he takes most of that to pay for the room and my food. At the end of a week I have maybe $2.00 left.

The streets have names like Mulberry, Baxter, Mott and Canal. I live at 132 Bleecker Street. Mulberry Street is very dirty and crowded. This part of the city is not very pretty. But, there are nicer places. I miss you and mamma and all of my brothers and sisters very much. Please tell Beppe that I love him. I also miss Bellaria.

With much affection,

Your son, Luigi

When Emilio finished reading the letter, there was silence. Emilio, himself, looked crestfallen. Evangelina had tears in her eyes and stared off into the distance. The children were quiet and somber, except for Giuseppe who asked when Luigi was coming home. This was not what any of them expected. America had been portrayed as a wonderful place where anyone could go, get a good paying job, and begin a new life.

However, that was not the picture Luigi painted in his letter. According to Luigi, living conditions for immigrants were very not good. In fact, the section in New York where most Italian immigrants lived was dirty, crowded and the pay they received was barely livable. Mentally, Emilio berated himself for allowing Luigi to leave Bellaria.

Time passed quickly during the rest of that year. The restaurant and inn business of Bellaria continued to improve, though it never really prospered. The holidays passed and several other letters were exchanged between Emilio and Evangelina and Luigi. Elisa also wrote to Luigi to give him special notes from each of his siblings, except for baby Antonio for whom she drew a childlike picture to include with the letter. Unlike his first letter, which was downbeat, each new letter from Luigi indicated that he was slowly but surely acclimating to the New World way of life. He was learning to speak English and his self-confidence seemed to be growing. Still, he missed his family very much and he missed the open, rolling countryside of the Val Trebbia and the comforting familiarity of Statto and Rivergaro and of his home – Bellaria.

***

In the period around 1900, Italy was the most overpopulated country in Europe. The majority of Italians who immigrated to other countries (not only to the United States) were from Southern Italy, where living conditions were abysmal, especially for those who lived in Sicily and the area around Naples. Although conditions were somewhat better in Northern Italy, jobs were scarce, as they were throughout the country (especially among the vast uneducated and unskilled population). Taxes were very high and compulsory military service for young Italian men combined to make emigration highly desirable. It is said that Southern Italians left Italy because they had to while Northern Italians left because they wanted to.

When most Italian immigrants arrived in America, they were shocked to discover that conditions were not at all what they had expected. For many, living conditions in cities like New York, Philadelphia, Boston, and Chicago were just as crowded, dirty, and oppressive as what they had left behind in the old country. In addition, they were often confronted with discrimination from other ethnic groups that had immigrated much earlier and were now better established in the social, economic, and political structure of the new world. Remarkably, the Italians – most of whom were Catholic – were even discriminated by their own church that at the time was run largely by Irish priests and Irish bishops who held little regard for Italian immigrants.

Until Pope Leo personally intervened, Italians in New York City were not allowed to celebrate Mass together with Irish or German Catholics. Instead, they were forced to attend Mass in the basement of the churches or in buildings like warehouses. Also, in many cases they were relegated to the most menial and low-paying jobs. The exception was those Italian immigrants who had a craft or trade. This is exactly where the training and experience that Luigi received under his father's guidance paid off. As young as he was, he had excellent job skills. It was time to put them to use.

Over the past year Luigi had worked hard and diligently for Alberto Zanmatti, who was a very distant cousin to

Evangelina on the Piergiorgi side of the family. Luigi was grateful to Zanmatti for making the arrangement to bring him over to America and for helping him get started with a job, room and board. Nonetheless, he had no intention of continuing to work in the grocery distribution business any longer than necessary, in this case for the agreed term of one year from his date of arrival in New York.

When Luigi arrived in New York, the tallest commercial structure was the 138 foot Flatiron Building completed in 1903. But now, much larger commercial buildings were either under construction or in the planning stage. One of the structures under construction was the Singer Tower at Broadway and Liberty Streets. When completed it would be 612 feet tall, a true skyscraper. As his time in the grocery business grew short, Luigi visited that construction site as often as possible. He spoke with the men working on the foundation, many of them Italian immigrants, and learned who he had to see to get a job.

The day after his term with Zanmatti ended, he made a beeline down to the Singer Tower construction site and asked to see a man named Angelo Marcuzzi. Marcuzzi was a tough, burly Northern Italian from Milan about the age of Luigi's father, who had worked on the famous Galleria Vittorio Emanuele II, a four-story double arcade shopping mall built by Giuseppe Mengoni in 1877. As with all foremen of that time, his word on the job was the law.

"Signor Marcuzzi," Emilio said, speaking in Italian. "They said that you are hiring men to work here."

Bellaria di Rivergaro

"I'm hiring men," Marcuzzi said, as he chomped on a well-chewed Tampa cigar. "Not boys. Get the hell out of here."

Luigi was almost 18-years old. He stood 5' 10" tall and weighed 155 pounds. He took off his jacket and rolled up his sleeves, ready to work if given the opportunity.

"I am from Rivergaro, Signor Marcuzzi, south of Piacenza" Luigi said. "He pulled out his Italian passport, opened the booklet, and offered it to Marcuzzi. I am a carpenter. Look here," he pointed to the last line of the booklet where it showed that his occupation was *falegname*.

"I have built many things, including many *stalle* and *mulini* and I worked with my father, also a carpenter, building our family home, *trattoria*, and *locanda* – Bellaria di Rivergaro. Is that not the work of a man?" He asked.

Marcuzzi waved the passport away and seemed to ignore Luigi as he looked at a group of laborers working on a column of the building's foundation.

"Do you know how to use a shovel?" He asked.

"*Si, signore*, I know how to use one very well!" Luigi exclaimed.

"You will be paid thirty cents an hour. You start work at 7:00 AM every day and you stop when I tell you. If you are ever late, you'll be fired. Now, get your ass down into that hole and help those paisani clear out the footer trench."

With that, Marcuzzi threw down his chewed out cigar, ground it into the mud and stomped away. Luigi did not waste a moment. He grabbed a shovel, jumped into the trench, said "*ciao*' to the other men and joined them clearing mud from the footer. His construction career had unceremoniously begun.

At first, Luigi continued to live on Bleecker Street, paying his cousin Zanmatti one dollar a week for rent. Getting to the Singer Tower job site was no problem. The New York City Interborough Rapid Transit stopped at Bleecker and Broadway, not far from where he lived. Then, after a ten-minute subway ride, Luigi could get off at either Broadway and Fulton or Broadway and Wall Street, both only a three-block walk to the job site. Work was very hard and the hours were long; he usually worked a fifty to fifty-five hour week. However, he was accustomed to hard work and long hours because back at Bellaria, his father was no less a taskmaster than Angelo Marcuzzi. Then one day, Marcuzzi came storming down into the "pit," as the area where the building foundation was called, hollering at the top of his lungs,

"Do any of you sons of bitches know how to build a shanty?" Marcuzzi's boss had told him to put up a construction shanty where the engineers could layout their blueprints and be sheltered from the weather.

Luigi shouted, "I do, Signor Marcuzzi! I am a carpenter." In truth, Luigi had never built a shanty, as such, in his life and was not exactly sure what one was. However, he was confident that he would figure it out – it couldn't be more difficult than a *stalla*.

Marcuzzi vaguely remembered something about Luigi having carpenter experience.

"You, Tagliaferri – the carpenter – pick a couple of men and follow me."

Luigi selected two of the more capable of the men working with him and followed Marcuzzi to a spot some distance away from where he had been working. Marcuzzi gave him a one-sheet blueprint with the details of the shanty he wanted built, told Luigi where to get the material he needed and abruptly left. Luigi had never seen a blueprint in his life, but he recognized that the outline was similar to the sketches that his father made for the buildings they constructed. He immediately recognized the floor plan, elevations, the spacing of studs, wiring, and other details. He instinctively knew how he was going to build this shanty. He also knew quite a lot about the tools and material needed to build small wood structures. With this confidence, he turned to the men and said,

"*Bene, avete sentito l'uomo. Andiamo!*" OK, you heard the man. Let's go! He then led his small team to get what they would need to begin his first construction project in America.

***

Another night had fallen at Bellaria, more than 4,000 miles from where Luigi was beginning to build the construction shanty. Evangelina and Elisa were getting the children ready for bed. Elvira and Maria shared one bed while Pietro and Giuseppe shared another. Elisa placed baby Antonio in her bed. Emilio and Evangelina had the privacy of their own bedroom. A wood crucifix hung over the beds in each room. Giuseppe no longer asked when Luigi was coming home. Instead, every night, as this night, he knelt at the foot of his bed to say his prayers. He prayed to God for his mother and father and sisters and brothers. And then, he said a short, poignant prayer for his big brother Luigi,

"And, Dear Jesus, please give my big brother Luigi a big hug and tell him that I love him and that I miss him very much. Amen."

Then, he jumped into bed, closed his eyes and was soon dreaming about the wonderful times that he had spent with his brother Luigi running and playing in the fields below their beloved Bellaria.

Bellaria di Rivergaro

Chapter 12

EMILIO SAT AT ONE OF THE TABLES outside Bellaria
enjoying his customary cigar, wine and cheese. His four-year
old grandson, Andrea, was playing nearby under the
watchful eyes of his grandmother, Evangelina. Emilio seldom
lit his cigars, but today he decided to do so. He would not, of
course, inhale. Cigar smoke was far too strong for that.
However, he enjoyed the aroma of smoldering rolled
Egyptian tobacco and he found great amusement in blowing
smoke rings to the continuous amazement of his grandson.

"Grandpapà, do that again," Andrea pleaded. "Do a big
one and then a little one."

Andrea laughed and laughed as Emilio puckered his lips
and puffed, sending perfectly round rings of smoke sailing
away in the light breeze. Emilio snorted and also laughed
and Evangelina, who was watching, shook her head in
amazement at the string of smoke rings that now stretched
away from Emilio.

Eventually, Andrea became bored and wandered off to
find some other amusement. Evangelina followed him
closely, leaving Emilio to his own thoughts. Emilio blew
another couple of smoke rings for his own entertainment, set
the cigar on the edge of the wood table, already scarred by
dozens of other cigars that had rested there, and poured
himself another glass of locally made red wine. He nursed
the wine, sipping slowly, and then leaned back in his chair
and reached once more for the stogie that had now lost its

glow. No matter. He put the unlit cigar in his mouth, anyway, and thought about all that had happened in the ten years since Luigi had left for America.

Emilio remembered that the first few letters Luigi sent him and Evangelina from New York were disappointing. Luigi missed his family and Bellaria very much; the conditions in which immigrants lived and worked were depressing; and, there was much discrimination against immigrants, Italians in particular. For many, there was no escape from the low-paying jobs, long hours, and overcrowded tenements that characterized the 17 square block section of Lower Manhattan called "Little Italy." However, for Luigi, the big break came when he got the construction job at the Singer Tower.

After that, Luigi's letters took on an increasingly positive tone. He moved out of the boarding house owned by Alberto Zanmatti and rented a small apartment on East 101st. Street. He also bought new clothes and was actually able to save a little money. Because he eventually wanted to move out of Little Italy, where practically everyone still spoke Italian in one dialect or another, he did his best to learn English – essential if he had any hope to get a better job in the future. Then, less than two years after he got the job at the Singer Tower in New York, Luigi's boss made him his assistant foreman. All of this fascinated Elisa who decided to travel to New York to visit her brother. Luigi was delighted and invited Elisa to share the apartment with him during her stay in New York.

Because of the difficulty of transatlantic travel, very few people would endure two weeks or more of travel by rail and then steamship only to spend a short visit with a friend or relative in America. Elisa was no different. She intended to stay with Luigi for at least several months before returning to Italy. However, that meant that she would need an income. Luckily, she was able to get a job at a lower Manhattan factory that prepared the feathers that were used in fancy ladies' hats. She soon became friends with a coworker named Giuseppina Guasconi from Castel San Giovanni, a small town west of Piacenza. The name Guasconi and the town of Castel San Giovanni seemed to be familiar to Elisa but she could not recall why. Then, one day at work the two women were talking…

"Now I know why we Italians have supper so late at night," Giuseppina declared. "We have to begin work at 7:00 in the morning and we work until 7:00 at night. How could we possibly have supper before 9:00 or 10:00?"

"*D'accordo*," Elisa said in agreement. "And, staying with Luigi is just like being married. I have to go to the market or street vendors to shop for food. Then, I have to prepare the meals, wash the clothes, clean the flat and all of the other chores a housewife would do," she complained.

"Me, too," Giuseppina said. "Don't forget that I share an apartment with my brother, as well."

"Yes, and we get none of the benefits a married woman would get," Elisa giggled. "Anyway, tonight Luigi is working late so I have only myself to worry about."

"Why don't you come over to our apartment?" Giuseppina asked. "You can help me make risotto and I'll introduce you to my brother."

"Thank you," Elisa said. "That's a wonderful idea!"

After work, Elisa and Giuseppina stopped by Luigi's apartment so that Elisa could leave him a note telling him where she was going to be that evening; otherwise, Luigi would be frantic wondering where she was. Then, the two women took the subway and got off at Broadway and 137th Street, which was only a short distance from Giuseppina's flat. Giuseppina's brother was in the kitchen of the small apartment when they arrived.

"Giovanni worked as a waiter when he first came to New York," Giuseppina explained, as they walked into the kitchen. "But, last year he bought his own café around the corner on 137th Street. It's open only for breakfast and lunch so he usually has supper started by the time I get home."

"Giovanni, I want you to meet a friend of mine, Elisa Tagliaferri," she said, as he began to turn toward them.

Giovanni looked directly at Elisa, triggering a flash of instant recognition between them.

"My God," she said. "You're the…"

"Ragazzo riding in his uncle's FIAT," he continued for her. "And, you are the beautiful signorina from…"

"Bellaria," Elisa said. "I simply cannot believe it," she added.

Giuseppina was totally confused. "You two actually know each other?" she asked.

Almost in unison, both Elisa and Giovanni said, "Not exactly." Then Elisa explained that several years ago Giovanni and his cousin stopped by Bellaria, her family's inn and restaurant and her home and had a light *pranzo*.

"I was riding with our cousin Angelo in his new FIAT," Giovanni said. "We were hungry and we came across this most delightful *trattoria* that the proprietor, Elisa's father, told us was called Bellaria di Rivergaro. We decided to have lunch. Your friend Elisa and her mother served us the best *agnoli* in all of Piacenza. Then sadly we had to leave because it was a long drive back to Castel San Giovanni."

"But, you did turn to wave goodbye," Elisa said.

"Ah, you remember. Well, of course," he laughed. "I wave to all pretty girls! I also remember that you smiled and waved back. I always meant to return to see you again, but it is such a long distance between Bellaria and Castel San Giovanni."

"Tell me, Giovanni. Do you miss Italy much?" Elisa asked.

"Sometimes," he said. "However, if I stayed in Italy it is unlikely that I would have my own café – at least this early in my life. How about you; do you miss it?"

"I have only been here a few months," she said. "But, even though my brother is here, I miss the rest of my family very much. And I truly miss Bellaria."

141

"Well, I can understand that," Giovanni said. "Giuseppina and I miss our family, also. However, Castel San Giovanni and Bellaria are there and we are here. In any case, this time I would very much like to get to know you better."

***

Emilio glanced around the patio outside the main dining room of Bellaria and spotted something wrong. In order to provide shade for his patrons from the hot summer sun, he built a trellis over the patio that was now covered with rapidly spreading grape vines. In one section of the trellis, vines had apparently escaped their tether and looked rather straggly. Emilio retrieved a pair of clippers from the workshop and went to work trimming the errant vines and making sure that they were properly tied to the trellis. He could not stop thinking about Luigi and Elisa, however. After Elisa went to America, so many things happened so fast that it was hard to keep up with events or to really comprehend them.

About a year after Elisa arrived in New York, Luigi met a beautiful, petite young woman named Ines Bocchi, who was originally from Campomorone, a small town northwest of Genoa. They soon fell in love and decided to marry. As Catholics, both Luigi and Ines wanted to get married in a Catholic church. However, Luigi had a run-in with the Irish priest who was the parish pastor. Luigi balked at paying the steep "donation" that the priest said was customary for people who wanted to marry in the main part of the church. When Luigi protested the amount of the "donation," the priest told Luigi that he would have to get married elsewhere

142

– which he did. On November 2, 1909, Luigi and Ines were married in the City Hall of New York City. Elisa and Giovanni, who were now seeing each other as often as possible, attended the brief civil ceremony. After their wedding ceremony, Luigi moved into Ines' apartment leaving Elisa with her own flat.

A few months later, Emilio and Evangelina received a letter from Elisa announcing that she and Giovanni were in love and wanted to get married. Giovanni sent Emilio a letter formally requesting his permission to marry Elisa and apologizing for not being to make his request in person. Emilio gave the couple his blessing; however, both he and Evangelina were very upset. It now seemed that the move to America for both Luigi and Elisa was becoming more permanent than either Emilio or Evangelina had envisioned. This was not what they intended for their two oldest children. Nor did the passing of time make any of this easier. The promised return visits to Rivergaro kept getting differed, but they never materialized.

Just before Christmas in 1909, Elisa and Giovanni were married in St. Ann's Catholic Church on 110th Street in New York City. This time it was Luigi and Ines who attended the small but festive wedding. In January, 1911 Ines gave birth to Angelina, the first grandchild of Emilio and Evangelina. Elisa and Giovanni announced the birth of their son Andrea Camillo in October of the same year and two years later Emilio and Evangelina were grandparents again when Luigi and Ines presented them with Emilio's eight pound two ounce namesake, Emilio Luigi Tagliaferri. However, the thrill and joy of having three grandchildren was diminished by the sadness of not being able to see any of them. Then one day, Elisa sent Evangelina a letter saying that her sister-in-law Giuseppina was taking Andrea to Italy so that both sets of grandparents could at last see their grandson.

***

Elisa and Giovanni accompanied Giuseppina to the East River piers where she and 4-year old Andrea boarded the Transatlantic Italiana line's Dante Alighieri for the long voyage to Genoa. Before Giuseppina boarded the ship, Elisa gave her a packet of six envelopes, each containing a personal letter and an American One Dollar bill, that Luigi requested be distributed to his siblings when Giuseppina visited Bellaria with Andrea. Elisa tearfully hugged her little son, barely able to control her emotions at the thought that it would be several months before she saw him again. More Bon Voyage hugs were exchanged and then Giuseppina and Andrea climbed the gangplank, becoming lost to view among the hundreds of other passengers crowding the main deck of the ship.

The Dante Alighieri was a much newer ship than either the La Bretagne or the La Lorraine, the ships in which Luigi and Elisa crossed the Atlantic, respectively. Built in 1914, it was 504 feet in length and had a beam of sixty feet. Its passenger accommodations were larger and more comfortable than those in ships built before 1900. Third-class passengers (equivalent to steerage class), for example, were assigned to cabins that had from four to six berths, rather than the cavernous open compartments of earlier immigrant ships. On this particular crossing, the ship was not full, so and Giuseppina shared her cabin with only one other woman. That left plenty of extra space for her and Andrea. At first,

144

Andrea was awed at the size of the ship, but the novelty of it soon wore off and he resumed behaving just like any other four-year old. Although the weather was good, the sailing was not without incident.

Once again the world was a dangerous place. The year before Giuseppina returned to Italy with Andrea, Archduke Ferdinand of Austria was assassinated. Tensions among European powers escalated following that incident, leading to the 1915 breakout of hostilities between Germany, the Ottoman Empire and Austria-Hungary (the Central Powers) and Great Britain, France, Russia and later Japan and Italy (the Allies). The United States formally entered the war as part of the Allies in 1917; however, it had been supporting the Allies' war effort by shipping arms, badly needed supplies, industrial goods, and material to them earlier.

This "Great War" was characterized by incredible carnage on both sides with over nine million military personnel killed and millions more maimed and injured. The extent and scope of the carnage was largely due to the introduction of new warfare technology such as airplanes, mechanized vehicles, tanks, poison gas and submarines.

Both Germany and Great Britain depended on extensive imports of goods and materials to maintain their respective economies during World War I. Great Britain's powerful naval forces posed a significant threat to Germany's ability to import the goods and material it needed to sustain its economy and the war effort. Germany countered by building a massive fleet of U-Boats – submarines designed to sink not only British warships but also commercial shipping that was supplying Great Britain. It was in this environment that

145

Bellaria di Rivergaro

Giuseppina and Andrea were sailing from New York on their way to Genoa, Italy.

Two hundred fifteen nautical miles east of the Straits of Gibraltar, the sun had just begun to set. The sea was mostly calm with gentle, rolling swells. Speeding at almost twenty-one knots, the Dante Alighieri's sharp bow cut through the sea as smoothly as the dozen or so porpoise keeping pace with the sleek passenger liner. But, this was not a routine transatlantic crossing. Heavy German U-Boat activity had been reported in the northern transatlantic lanes. Only two days earlier, a British freighter had been sunk with a single torpedo shot that hit it amidships, sending the freighter to a watery grave in less than ten minutes with the loss of twenty-six seamen. Therefore, it was no surprise to the passengers of the Dante Alighieri that lookouts had been posted fore and aft and on both beams of the ship to watch for any sign of U-Boats.

In addition, once dusk turned to darkness, smoking was prohibited on deck and all external ship lights, plus any interior lights that could be seen through a porthole or open hatch, were doused for the night. On the open sea, the glow of a cigarette could be seen as far away as a quarter of a mile and the light from a pocket torch usually was visible for up to three miles. Even more dangerous, on a clear night cabin lights could be seen for many miles. The last thing that the captain, crew, and passengers of the Dante Alighieri wanted was to provide a beacon for roaming U-Boats.

Aboard the German submarine U-38, the commanding officer, Kapitänleutnant Otto Schmidt, peered through the lens of the periscope and fixed his gaze on the silhouette of a

146

large passenger ship steaming at a bearing of twenty-three degrees off his boat's port bow. Schmidt identified the ship as the Dante Alighieri, an Italian passenger liner en route from New York to Genoa. The U-38 was a Class 31 long-distance submarine with a crew of thirty-five. It had a displacement of 971 tons, a length of 211 feet and a range of almost 9,000 nautical miles. Today it was on its way back to the Germaniawerft shipyards in Kiel, Germany, southeast of the Jutland Peninsula. Schmidt had only one torpedo left at his disposal and had been saving it for any tanker or freighter that might have the misfortune to cross his path.

However, within the past twenty-four hours Schmidt received a radio message from the German Naval Command in Kiel instructing all U-Boat commanders to sink any allied shipping they encountered - even passenger liners. Schmidt was repelled at the thought of killing civilians, especially women and children. He was duty-bound, however, to follow orders. Still, if he used his 105 mm deck gun to disable the passenger ship's steering gear he could allow the captain of the Dante Alighieri to abandon ship, thus saving as many passengers as possible. Schmidt would then use his last torpedo to sink the Dante Alighieri with minimum loss of life.

In her cabin far below the main deck, Giuseppina tucked Andrea into his bunk and began patting him to sleep. There would still be several more days at sea and then a stop at Palermo, Sicily before the ship reached Genoa. But, at least the hardest part was almost over. At supper, a ship's officer told the passengers that tomorrow they would pass through the straits of Gibraltar, the landmark that meant that they would soon be home. Andrea was almost asleep and

Giuseppina's cabin mate Lucia Cabrini was being as quiet as she could to help the boy doze off.

A crew member standing on the lookout platform on the starboard side of Dante Alighieri's bridge saw an ominous dark object arise from the sea about 1500 yards off the ship's starboard beam. He shouted "submarine!" into the voice tube that ran to the bridge. The first officer, who was manning the bridge, ran to the lookout station and focused his binoculars on the terrifying sight now clearly visible. He barked "full speed ahead" and "hard-a-port" to the bosun, who immediately rang the engine room with the command and swung the ship's wheel to port causing the Dante Alighieri to heel heavily to starboard as the 10,000 ton ship began to respond to the change of course.

As soon as the U-38 broke water, Kapitänleutnant Schmidt ordered the gun crew on deck to make ready for battle. Schmidt and Oberleutnant Zur See Fritz Bern stood on the conning tower bridge issuing orders as the gun crew took the waterproof cover off the deck gun and prepared to load it with 105 mm shells. They observed the Dante Alighieri increase speed and heel to the outside as it began a turn to port and immediately knew that they had been spotted. As the passenger ship turned, the two officers were stunned as they saw that the bulk of the Dante Alighieri had shielded what appeared to be a tramp steamer off its port side. In horror, they saw the tramp steamer come alive as panels on its bow and stern dropped, exposing heavy naval guns that were quickly being trained on the U-38. Schmidt realized that what seemed to be a tramp steamer was actually a "Q-Boat," a decoy that the British Navy used to lure unsuspecting

German submarines to the surface and then shell them with hidden armaments. He shouted the order to dive, as he and the gun crew frantically scrambled to get below decks. But, even as he was reaching to close the hatch, Kapitänleutnant Otto Schmidt heard shells screaming overhead and felt a tremendous concussion as the conning tower over his head exploded.

In Giuseppina's cabin below deck in the Dante Alighieri, the women felt the vibration of straining engines and the sudden heeling of the ship that threw them against the bunks on the opposite side of the cabin. Terrified, Giuseppina braced herself and reached over to Andrea, who sleepily asked what was happening.

"Why are we leaning over like this, Zia Giuseppina?"

Trying to overcome her own fear, Giuseppina said, "Don't worry, darling. The captain is just trying to steer the ship around a big fish."

"Silly captain," Andrea mumbled, as he slipped back in to a peaceful sleep.

The rest of the voyage was uneventful; although everyone was on edge after learning about the submarine attack. Four days later the Dante Alighieri docked at Genoa, Italy. It was only then that the passengers also learned that on the same day they were attacked, another German submarine had sunk the luxury passenger liner Lusitania off the coast of Ireland with the loss of almost 1,200 lives.

***

Bellaria di Rivergaro

Emilio lit up another 'stogie" to replace the one that he now discarded. He shifted in his chair and decided he was thirsty. He bellowed for a cup of caffè espresso. Soon Elvira came from Bellaria's kitchen bearing not only a cup of espresso but also a plate of almond cookies that Evangelina always kept available for Bellaria's guests. Emilio became quite pensive as he thought about the danger that confronted his young grandson and his aunt, Giuseppina when the Dante Alighieri encountered the German U-Boat. Then there was the sinking of the Lusitania with heavy loss of life. Back in the United States, Elisa and Giovanni were well aware of the danger and had sent a letter to Emilio and Evangelina, telling them that they were very fearful of the danger that Giuseppina and Andrea might face if they returned to New York before the holidays as they had planned. Both Emilio and Evangelina shared the concern of their daughter and son-in-law, as did the child's Guasconi grandparents in Castel San Giovanni. So, it seemed that Andrea might have a longer visit with his grandparents than anyone had intended.

***

It was late in the afternoon and the sun had circled half way around Bellaria casting its shadow across the road in front of the table where Evangelina had now joined Emilio. Elvira and Maria stepped outside, taking a break from preparing the evening's meal. There were no guests at the inn and Tuesdays were not good nights to expect guests for the *trattoria*. Tonight's dinner would be for the family only. Elvira kept looking up the road from Bellaria in the direction of Rivergaro, expectantly. Then, she and Maria walked over to the table where their parents were seated.

"You two seem to be deep in thought," Elvira said. "Are we interrupting something?"

"No, nothing at all," Evangelina replied. "We were just talking about the letter that we received from Elisa about Andrea. She misses him terribly but she is afraid what might happen if Giuseppina takes him back to New York when there is such terrible danger to even passenger ships."

"It's getting worse," Maria said. "I understand that our own military has launched an attack on the Austro-Hungarians in the Trentino region, north of Venice. I'm so afraid that soon there will be another terrible war."

Evangelina was about to reply when a figure on a bicycle appeared coming down the road from Rivergaro. A young man in his mid-to late twenties rode toward them, stopped and got off the bicycle laying it against the building. Elvira stood up and as though she was completely surprised.

"Hello Severino. What brings you here?" she said, as though she had no idea that he was coming. Before he could reply, she turned to her parents and said, "Mamma, papà, this is Severino Angiporti. He lives on Via Motta."

"Nice to meet you, Severino," Emilio said.

"*Piacere*," Evangelina added.

"*Piacere*, it is my pleasure, Signor *e* Signora Tagliaferri," Severino replied. He then said, "*Ciao, Maria.*"

"*Ciao, Severino*," Maria responded with a smile.

"Angiporti," Emilio said. "I think that I have met your father. Does he work at Acuti?" he asked, referring to the factory with the tall smokestack just outside of Rivergaro that produced concentrated tomato sauce.

"*Si*, Signor Tagliaferri. I work there, too."

"*Bene*," Emilio said. "And, what can we do for you today, Severino?"

"Ah, actually," he stammered, "I thought that perhaps I might speak with Elvira for a few minutes."

"Why don't you two go in where you can have some privacy?" Evangelina said. "Maria, go with them and then please bring you father another cup of caffè."

Maria ushered her older sister and Severino into Bellaria while Evangelina and Emilio looked at each other.

"Well, what did you expect?" asked Evangelina. "She's twenty-four years old. Do you want her to be an old maid?"

Maria returned and served her father another cup of caffè espresso as well as a refill of the almond cookies. She thoughtfully brought a cup of caffè for her mother, as well. As she turned to go back inside Bellaria, Evangelina said,

"No, Maria. Leave them be for a while and come and sit with us." After Maria joined them at the table, Evangelina asked, "Tell me. What do you think about Severino?"

Chapter 13

SEVERAL INCHES OF SNOW had fallen overnight, giving Bellaria the appearance of a gingerbread house topped with fluffy white icing. Maria opened the front door of Bellaria and looked out at the beauty of untouched snow all around her. She pulled the wool shawl closer around her shoulders and head to shield her from the cold wind blowing down from the Alta Val Trebbia. Maria knew this was going to be a magical day. She had an urge to run through the snow as she did when she was a child – perhaps even laying down, spreading her arms in the white fluff, and making a snow angel. Instead, she trudged through the snow to the attached stable at the south end of the building where the horses and ox waited to be fed.

Maria chose to take care of the *stallazzo* because she loved animals. Her brothers did the hard manual work in the fields and the *mulino* and Elvira and she helped their mother tend to the guests of the *trattoria* and *locanda* and perform regular household duties. When the inn was built, the *stallazzo* was used to shelter saddle horses for the family and inn guests and the mare that Emilio hitched to the *calesse*. However, as time passed, fewer and fewer of Bellaria's guests arrived in horse-drawn carriages. Automobiles, although still very expensive, were becoming more common. Emilio, on the other hand, disdained the use of an automobile and rode his bicycle to town every day to play cards with his friends in the Piazza Grande. Pietro, however, had acquired a motorcycle that was the envy of his younger brothers. In any event, the *stallazzo* was now home to the draft animals that were used to plow the fields and haul the work carts. It also housed Pietro's motorcycle, Emilio's bicycle, and the little mare that was used to pull the *calesse*.

Maria opened the large, heavy door of the *stallazzo* and quickly slipped inside, closing the door after her. As she walked into the stable, the stalls for the animals were on the left side. Her father's bicycle leaned against the wall on the opposite side of the stable, just behind Pietro's motorcycle, standing upright supported by its metal kickstand. The body heat from the animals took a little of the chill out of the air; but more importantly, the *stallazzo* shielded Maria from the cold wind. She fed the horses and the ox their usual diet of hay, willow sprigs, dried weeds and thistle and gave the little mare a special treat – an apple that she carried in her apron pocket. Then, she did her best to clean the stalls; replacing the manure with a fresh layer of hay.

Nino bounced into the *stallazzo* just as Maria was completing her daily task.

"Mamma said that we should go to the workshop and bring her the *ceppo* and the *presepio*," he said excitedly.

Maria smiled and gave Nino a sisterly hug. Then, she opened the *stallazzo* door and disregarding the cold and wind outside said, "Come on, little brother. We have a lot to get ready. Tonight is Christmas Eve!"

The two most important religious feast days of the year for most Italians are Christmas and Easter. Arguably, Christmas is the more festive of the two holidays. Emilio, Evangelina, and their family celebrated Christmas the traditional way. For them, the holiday began on December 24th, Christmas Eve day, and continued through the feast of the Epiphany (the feast of the Three Kings) on January 6th. Christmas Eve day would be a day of fasting and abstinence. Only one full, meatless meal could be taken. Eating or snacking between meals was strictly forbidden – unless no one was watching. The highlight of the day would come after a light supper of spinach and ricotta ravioli in butter and cheese sauce. That is when the family gathered to setup the *ceppo* and the *presepio*.

The *ceppo* is a triangular wood-framed object in the shape of a pyramid, about two meters tall. Four or five shelves divide its height and serve as a platform for candies, cookies, dried fruit, and nuts and sometimes small gifts for members of the family. A garland of pine, decorated with colorful bows of ribbon, traces its way up the sloping sides of the frame and brings the scent of a snow-covered forest indoors. Sometimes the *presepio*, a Christmas crèche representing the stable in which Jesus was born, is placed on the lower shelf of the *ceppo*. However, often, as with the *presepio* at Bellaria, it has its own special place.

Andrea's two sets of grandparents agreed that he would stay at Bellaria this Christmas and in Castel San Giovanni with the Guasconi family for Easter the next year. Everyone at Bellaria was happy with that arrangement because it had been several years since the family celebrated Christmas with a child as young as Andrea. Nino, the next youngest and family "baby" was now almost thirteen.

In addition to Andrea, there was another guest at Bellaria for *la cena*, supper that Christmas Eve. For several months,

Bellaria di Rivergaro

Elvira had been seeing Severino Angiporti and the two were obviously getting serious about each other. Elvira had invited Severino to join them to celebrate the beginning of Christmas. Shortly after Severino arrived, the family took their seats at the double table that Emilio and Pietro set up in Bellaria's main dining room. Emilio welcomed Severino, said grace as usual, and the family enjoyed a sparse, albeit tasty meal. There was no antipasto before supper or *dolce*, pastry, afterward. Everyone was fasting in order to be worthy to receive Holy Communion the next morning on Christmas Day. Even Andrea was denied snacks, although he was officially exempt from fasting because of his age. This was a special hardship for the young lad because all day Evangelina and the girls had been busy making several types of biscotti, panettone, sweet cakes, and other delicacies for the family to enjoy on Christmas Day.

Andrea could hardly wait to set up the *ceppo* and presepio. As the evening dragged on he kept asking, "Is it time yet?" Or, "When can we set up the *ceppo*?" Giuseppe and Antonio would look at each other and laugh each time Andrea repeated his mantra. But, finally the table was cleared and it was indeed time to set up the decorations. There were no guests at the inn on that Christmas Eve, though they would have been welcome to join in the fun had any been there.

Emilio peeled off the butcher paper that was wrapped around the *ceppo* to protect it from damage while it was stored. He stood back and looked at the six-foot tall, three panel, fold-out wood frame that was painted white on the flat surfaces with red paint down the spine of each vertical frame.

156

Even folded you could see that the frame was in the shape of a tree – just like the fir trees surrounding Bellaria with the flowing boughs now covered with snow. Most commonly, a *ceppo* was made simply of tent-like poles or long, thin wood slats. But, Luigi made this *ceppo* for the last Christmas that he was home at Bellaria. It was far more elaborate than most of them and showed how well he had learned his craft from Emilio.

That is what struck Emilio now. He thought about his oldest son, about the wonderful times that they enjoyed together in Statto, about how Luigi helped him, Silvio and Giuseppe build Bellaria, about how much he missed Luigi and about how much he missed Andrea's mother, Emilio's oldest daughter Elisa. Emilio was sixty-two years old, now. He was no longer a young man. Sometimes, like now, he became melancholy and felt his emotions more strongly. He continued to stand looking at the *ceppo* in silence; then his eyes began to glisten with tears. Pietro walked over to Emilio, put his hand on his father's shoulder and said,

"It's OK, papà. We understand. We miss them, too."

Emilio nodded and said, "What's everybody waiting for? It's Christmas Eve," as he wiped his eyes with the thumb and forefinger of his right hand. Then, in deference to Andrea, who still believed in the fantasy of Christmas, he said, "Let's put up the *ceppo* and *presepio* so Babbo Natale and La Befana can bring everyone presents!"

Evangelina decided that the *ceppo* should be put up next to the fireplace in Bellaria's larger dining room. That way, when Babbo Natale came to visit Bellaria later that night by sliding down the fireplace chimney or sneaking in through the door leading to the terrace, he would find delightful treats waiting for him on the *ceppo* shelves. Andrea kept pestering the adults with questions.

"How did Babbo Natale get up on top of the roof?"

"How can Babbo Natale come down the chimney when there is a fire in the fireplace?"

"Why doesn't Babbo Natale just come in through the front door like everyone else?"

Elvira and Maria did their best to answer Andrea's questions. Then, just when it seemed that he was satisfied with their explanations, he asked,

"If Babbo Natale is tired when he gets here can he stay in one of the rooms upstairs for the night?"

Emilio shared glances with Evangelina and shook his head in astonishment.

Emilio and Evangelina let the young people set up and decorate the *ceppo*. The garland with its colorful ribbons and bows were fastened to the outline of the tree and a blown glass angel from Murano capped its apex. Before going to bed for the night, Elvira and Maria made sure that there were partially eaten snacks placed on one of the shelves of the *ceppo*. When Andrea awoke the next morning, it would be obvious that Babbo Natale enjoyed the treats set out for him when delivered the family's Christmas presents.

The next task was to look for a good spot to erect the *presepio*. In any Italian home, the crèche was the most important religious symbol to display, second only to a crucifix. Maria suggested that it should be placed near the front entrance so that in addition to being seen by the family, it would be one of the first things that a guest saw upon entering Bellaria. Antonio brought a small table and placed it against the front entrance wall. The family then knelt before the creche and Emilio led them in a short prayer. He noticed that during the prayer, Elvira and Severino were holding hands and were looking at each other. When they had finished the prayer, everyone stood, silently reflecting on their own thoughts. Suddenly, Severino spoke up.

"Signor Tagliaferri," he said nervously, "I ask your permission to marry your daughter Elvira, who I love very much."

Evangelina stared at Severino wide-eyed. The boys gaped. Maria lowered her head as though she had been part of a conspiracy. Elvira looked at her father with hopeful, almost pleading eyes. Andrea ignored everyone and continued to play with the figurines of cows, sheep, and shepherds that surrounded the crèche. Emilio sighed and said, "Son, let's have a little chat."

Andrea piped up, "When is La Befana going to come to bring us presents?"

Maria caught her mother's glance and knew that it was time to put Andrea to bed, so she quickly ushered him upstairs.

Emilio took a near panicking Severino into another room where they could speak in private.

"Severino," he said. "I think that you are a fine young man. However, you and Elvira have only known each other for a few months. How can you be sure that you are ready for marriage? And further, you work in the *pomodoro* factory. How can you afford a wife and perhaps children?"

"Signor Tagliaferri..." Emilio interrupted. "Call me Emilio."

Severino cleared his throat and started to make a speech that he had rehearsed countless times, first in front of a mirror and then in front of Elivra.

"Ah, Emilio," But then halted and said, "I cannot call you Emilio. It does not seem right. May I please continue to call you Signor Tagliaferri – at least for now," he pleaded.

"*Come vuoi*," replied Emilio. "As you wish."

Severino told Emilio that it was not the length of time that he and Elvira had known each other but rather the depth of their feelings. However, he pointed out that even though he and Elvira had been seeing each other romantically for only several months, they had gone to school together at Sant'Agata and had seen each other frequently at church. As for his work, Severino said that he had recently been appointed a supervisor and that meant an accompanying increase in pay.

"Where would you live?" Emilio inquired.

Severino told him that for a while they would live in the same house as his parents, but it would only be a little while before they could afford their own apartment. In the end, Emilio knew that he had no reason to withhold his permission. He rose from where he was sitting at the table, walked over to a shelf behind the counter of the *trattoria* and took out a bottle of his best wine, a 1903 Gutturnio. He opened the bottle, poured three fingers of the ruby red wine into two tumblers, and handed one to Severino. Emilio raised his tumbler to Severino, said, *"Salute!"* and downed half the wine. Severino waited for something more; however, Emilio simply said, "Good man," and smiled at him.

Severino was perspiring, but he assumed that Emilio's gesture meant that he approved of him and of the marriage. He raised his own tumbler, returned the toast, and then, in great relief, downed his entire glass without pause. Emilio smiled again, finished the wine remaining in his glass, and poured another three fingers of Gutturnio for both of them. When that was consumed, he gave a familial hug to Severino, welcoming him into the family, and said, "Let's go tell the others."

By now Maria had returned from putting Andrea to bed and had joined her mother and siblings in the kitchen – Evangelina's enclave of peace and security when she was under stress. Everyone was waiting for Emilio and Severino to return from their discussion.

"We can't all fit in there," Emilio barked, and everyone filed out into the small dining room adjacent to the kitchen.

Elvira immediately spotted the smile on Severino's face. She hugged him and gave him a soft kiss. Emilio smiled approvingly and said, "Well, I guess that says it all. It seems that our Bellaria family will soon have a new member."

***

Bellaria di Rivergaro

Over 4,000 miles away in New York, Elisa and Giovanni waited patiently as the last lunch patron of the afternoon left the new restaurant they had opened at 137th St. and Broadway. It was Christmas Eve Day and the restaurant was closed that evening. After the patron left, Giovanni locked the restaurant door and pulled down the shade over its window. He placed a CLOSED sign on the window ledge next to the door and went back into the kitchen to help Elisa clean up.

About an hour later they slipped out the front door, locked it once again, and walked hand-in-hand to their flat a few blocks away. They checked the mailbox in the lobby of the apartment building, finding one or two advertisements and a letter from Italy postmarked four weeks earlier. Then, they climbed the stairs leading to the three and one-half room apartment, unlocked the door, and entered the small parlor. Elisa sat on the sofa and tore open the letter.

As they had hoped, the letter was from Maria, who seemed to have taken on the role of correspondent for the family. The letter told them that except for an occasional cold or case of lumbago everything was *"al solito,"* as usual, with the family. Maria reported that Elvira was seeing Severino Angiporti and that the two were getting "serious." She said that Pietro was riding his motorcycle all over the province and that Antonio was becoming a whiz at repairing bicycles. She said that Papà still rode his bicycle to Rivergaro every day to play cards with his friends on the Piazza Grande and that Mamma was OK but seemed to be getting a little frail. She saved the news that Elisa was looking for most for the last – the news about her son Andrea.

Bellaria di Rivergaro

Andrea was doing just fine. He stayed with the family at Bellaria every other week or so and loved to play in the fields with his uncles Antonio and Nino, who treated him more like a younger brother than a nephew. Maria said that Andrea missed his mother and father very much and kept asking when he could go home to his "Mamma." But, best of all, Maria enclosed a photo of Andrea framed in the front door of Bellaria waving to his Mamma and Papà who were so far away.

Elisa handed the letter and photo to Giovanni and looked around the room at the small Christmas tree with its bright ornaments and gold-colored garland. She glanced at the table in the kitchen that was set for only her and Giovanni and at the empty child's seat that occupied one of the other chairs. Then she burst into tears and sobbed as Giovanni tried unsuccessfully to console her.

***

This was the first Christmas that Luigi and Ines were celebrating in their own home. Luigi never liked New York, which to him was a dirty, overcrowded city – the exact opposite of the beautiful, open country of the Val Trebbia that had been his childhood home. Even more, he felt confined and restricted in lower Manhattan's Little Italy that in his eyes was nothing more than a ghetto holding down Italian immigrants from fulfilling the dreams they had when they left the hardships of their homeland for the opportunities that America held out to them. Meeting and marrying Ines was the most wonderful thing that had ever happened to Luigi and he was determined to provide the best America had to offer for his family. So, when his boss, Angelo Marcuzzi, offered him the chance to join him at a fledgling construction company in Ohio, Luigi jumped at the opportunity and moved to the Midwest with Ines and baby Angelina.

After a one-year stint working on a project in Bolivar, Ohio some fifty miles south of Lake Erie, Luigi relocated to the company's headquarters in Cleveland where he worked as a foreman supervising the construction of exactly the kinds of structures that he had dreamed of as a youth – tall buildings, bridges, industrial plants and factories and more. Ten years after arriving in America, he had saved enough money to buy his own house, a single family, four-bedroom home on a nice brick-paved street in Lakewood, Ohio, a suburb of Cleveland. It was while they were in Bolivar that Ines gave birth to a son, who they named Emilio Luigi after Luigi's father.

Luigi and Ines kept many of the Christmas traditions that they had grown up with in Italy. Luigi made a new *ceppo*, a virtual duplicate of the one that he had made the last Christmas that he was at Bellaria. They set up a crèche under the picture window in the parlor but they also put up a real pine Christmas tree, in the corner next to Luigi's favorite chair, against the stairway leading to the bedrooms on the second floor.

Christmas Eve supper was almost identical to the customary *cena* that his mother and sisters prepared at Bellaria – spinach and ricotta *agnoli* or ravioli in a light butter and cheese sauce. After supper, the children were allowed to open one present each from under the Christmas tree before they went to bed. But, when they came down in the morning, they would see that Babbo Natale – now called Santa Claus –

had left many more presents for them when he came down the unlit chimney during the night. Of course, the cookies that the children had put on a plate for Santa Clause and his reindeers the night before would be gone and in their place there was hard candy, torrone nougats and other delights.

After the children were put to bed, Ines and Luigi sat in the parlor looking at the bright lights glowing on the Christmas tree. The phonograph was playing Christmas music and they enjoyed the quiet time of being alone together. It was a very long way to Bellaria and to Campomorone where the rest of their family lived. They missed their families in Italy, but there was no turning back. The future of their lives, those of their children and eventually their grandchildren was here in America. They snuggled a little closer and thanked God for having brought them here.

***

It was a wonderful Christmas that year at Bellaria. The sun came out and glistened on new fallen snow as Emilio, Evangelina and their family walked across the Piazza San Rocco to attend Christmas Mass at Sant'Agata. After Mass they returned to Bellaria, which looked like a snow fairy palace sheathed in fluffy snow and decorated with ice cycles acting as prisms in the reflected rays of the sun. The boys made a very big snowman and pelted each other with snowballs. Andrea tried to make a little snowman but succeeded only in getting snow in his gloves and boots and finally he ran back into the house because he was so cold.

Bellaria di Rivergaro

Christmas *pranzo* was incredible, as usual, and lasted a full three hours. Then the entire family sang Christmas carols until their voices gave out. It was such a magical day that Bellaria even seemed to come alive to join in the celebration. But, Evangelina knew that soon there would be an even more magical day at Bellaria. It would happen in the spring and it would be the wedding of her beloved daughter Elvira.

Chapter 14

IT WAS ANOTHER BEAUTIFUL early spring day in the Val Trebbia. Evangelina joined Emilio at the table outside Bellaria where he had been enjoying his afternoon caffè.

"Where is Andrea," Emilio asked.

"Pietro took him and Antonio down to the Trebbia to teach them how to skip stones over the river," she replied.

"He's a good boy," Emilio stated. "Still, I would love to see Luigi's children, too. We have three grandchildren but we have seen only one of them. Luigi and Ines' Angelina is several months older than Andrea, but we have never seen her. Then there is two-year old Emilio and, of course, we have not seen him, either."

"At least we have their photographs," Evangelina said. "But, think about this. All three of our grandchildren are American citizens, while their parents are Italian. That seems so strange."

"I have thought of that, also," Emilio said. "The language they speak is still another matter. Do they speak Italian, the language of their parents, or do they speak English, the language of the country of which they are citizens - or both?"

"Well, Andrea might be a good example," Evangelina replied. "He speaks Italian quite well but he also speaks English. Perhaps that is a good thing – being able to speak both languages."

Bellaria di Rivergaro

"Amazing," Emilio said. "None of this was on anyone's mind when Elisa and Giovanni and Luigi and Ines got married. However, what can you expect? They were married in America and naturally their children are American. As recently as a few years ago, who could have imagined that our grandchildren would not be Italian? At least Elvira and Severino were married here so any children they have will be Italian and more importantly, Piacentini!"

"Ah, Elvira's wedding," recalled Evangelina. "Now, that was indeed a wonderful event."

***

After consulting with her mother and Padre Don Pier Luigi Veneziani, the parish pastor, Elvira scheduled the wedding for a Sunday morning in early June, a particularly beautiful time in northern Italy, at the church of Sant'Agata in Rivergaro. Traditionally, it brought good luck to be married on a Sunday. There were many preparations that had to be made for the wedding and Elvira and Evangelina had less than two months to make them.

Naturally, the wedding banquet would be held at Bellaria. Now, with the wedding date and church also being settled, the next order of business was Elvira's wedding dress. Unfortunately, Evangelina's wedding dress, which she lovingly kept over the years in a cedar chest, was not suitable for Elvira. Evangelina was somewhat more petite and slender than Elvira when she and Emilio were married. Besides, wedding fashions changed greatly in Italy during the past thirty years. The trend was now more toward formal wedding dresses rather than the older practice of the bride wearing her best "church" dress.

Rivergaro was a small town with a population of less than 3,000, including outlying communities like Niviano. However, it was the center of commercial, social, and religious activities for the entire comune or county. It was one of those places where everyone knew everyone else, especially if the person was prominent, as was Emilio and, of course, Evangelina. Luisa Cassinera was the only dressmaker in Rivergaro. She had a small shop on Vicolo Curioni, a short, blind alley that ran between the Piazza Grande and Via San Rocco, not far from the church of Sant'Agata. Evangelina had known Luisa for years, so it would have been inconceivable not to ask Luisa to make Elvira's wedding dress; although in Piacenza – not that far away – there were several dressmakers who were arguably more skilled than Luisa.

However, Luisa was a traditionalist. She favored the older, traditional styles of wedding gowns. Elvira, on the other hand, was part of the new generation of women who were more assertive of their rights and who did not hesitate to break away from tradition when it suited their purpose. She read fashion magazines and she liked the "new look" in the wedding gowns that she saw in those magazines. She dismayed Luisa when she picked an off-white long, high-waist "empire" style dress with a high collar and full length sleeves. The skirt had pleats with a narrow band of wedding bows around the cinched waist.

At first, Luisa insisted that she could not make the kind of dress Elvira wanted and she kept trying to steer Elvira back to a more traditional style. This was causing everyone much stress until Elvira bluntly told Luisa that if she could not make the dress she would have it made in Piacenza. Luisa did not want to face the gossip that would create. So, she agreed to use the patterns Elvira wanted – provided Elvira, in turn, kept some semblance of tradition by making the length of the wedding veil one meter for each year the couple was engaged. Elvira and Severino were engaged for only one year. The length of the wedding veil, therefore, would be only one meter, so Elvira agreed.

The second stress-causing situation that Luisa presented to Elvira occurred two weeks before the wedding. Luisa said that she needed an additional three weeks to complete the dress. Elvira was in tears when she heard that news and Evangelina was livid with anger. Then, that crisis suddenly disappeared when Luisa unexpectedly announced that the dress would be completed easily within the required time. Neither Elvira nor her mother ever learned why Luisa reversed herself. However, they did recall that a couple of days earlier Emilio mentioned that he, Silvio and Giuseppe had a pleasant and constructive *pranzo* with Luisa's husband at a café in the Piazza Grande.

***

Maria came out of Bellaria and walked over to where her parents were sitting. "Papà, there is a telephone call for you."

"Who is it?" Emilio asked.

"I'm not sure, but it sounds like your friend Signor Edini."

Emilio rose from his chair and said, "Thank you Maria. Please tell him that I will be there in a minute." Then, he turned to Evangelina and said,

"You know, when they finally ran telephone service down here to Bellaria, I thought that other than electricity it was the best thing that had every happened. Now, anyone can call you and interrupt whatever you are doing. I'm not so sure, anymore."

Evangelina chuckled. "I know what you mean. But, even worse, any party on our line can listen in on what we are saying to anyone else. Privacy seems to be a thing of the past."

Emilio returned in a few minutes and rejoined Evangelina at the table.

"By the way," she said. "Did you have anything to do with Luisa Cassinera changing her mind about how long it would take to finish Elvira's wedding dress?"

Emilio shifted slightly in his chair, replaced the cigar in his mouth, and said, "Now, why would I do that?"

"Hmm," Evangelina responded.

***

The wedding was everything that Evangelina hoped for her daughter. Following tradition, on Sunday morning Severino arrived at Bellaria early and gave Elvira his final gift as a single man, a beautiful wedding bouquet of white roses surrounded by a spray of Baby's Breath. Emilio gave Severino a small piece of iron scrap from the workshop at Bellaria that he put into his suit pocket to ward off evil spirits

171

during the wedding. Then Severino and his parents left for the church, soon to be followed by Elvira, her parents and two sisters. Maria was her maid of honor and Severino's sister and two friends of Elvira served as bridesmaids. Severino's best man was his brother Carlo. There were three other members to his wedding party including a very proud and nervous Pietro.

The wedding Mass at Sant'Agata was set for eleven o'clock in the morning in order to avoid a conflict with the regular nine o'clock Sunday Mass. As the guests arrived at the church, they were immediately seated. Severino and his best man were already in the church standing in front of the altar. Elvira, Evangelina, Emilio and Elvira's maid of honor and bridesmaids stood outside the church in the cobblestone San Rocco Piazza waiting for the signal to begin the bridal procession. Evangelina looked lovely. She wore a red silk dress with a short feathered off-white hat and matching gloves reminiscent of the dress that she wore when she and Emilio were married. The younger women of the bridal party wore Old Rose colored, full-length dresses with wide brim hats and gloves of matching color. Emilio looked distinguished in the new black Italian wool suit that Evangelina insisted he buy for the occasion.

The wedding party waited impatiently in the small piazza outside the church. Flanking the church to the left of its towering campanile was the imposing Villa Anguissola-Scotti, one of the residences of a very wealthy merchant family in the province whose commercial power extended from Genoa to the Far East. Then, precisely at eleven o'clock, the church bells in the magnificent campanile began to ring and Evangelina was escorted into the church by her son, Pietro. As soon as she was seated, the bridal party began its slowly paced march into Sant'Agata with Elvira and her father trailing behind the maid of honor and bridesmaids with their escorts.

They noted the 15th century bust of Sant'Agata as they passed under the facade of the church and walked through its heavy double wooden doors. Sant'Agata was designed in the form of a crucifix, like all Catholic churches. A long nave ran up the center of the church forming the main aisle with the apse and main altar at its head. Two lateral transepts crossed the nave, each with a lesser altar at its end. Hanging from the domed crossing was a great chandelier in the form of a golden crown. The ornate pulpit, tabernacle, and wooden choir had originally been in the church of San Vincenzo in Piacenza, but were transferred to Sant'Agata in 1819. The marble tabernacle had been sculptured by Severino Roncoroni in 1881 and the organ, now playing the familiar wedding march, was built by Bossi in 1866. Frescos adorned the domed ceiling and walls of the church. In the eyes of Elvira, Sant'Agata was the most beautiful church that she had ever seen.

Severino waited for Elvira at the altar together with his best man Ernesto and Padre Veneziani. He wore a new pinstriped suit, white shirt, and black bow tie. As Elvira glided toward the altar, Severino could not take his gaze from her and thought that at that moment she was the most beautiful woman who ever walked this Earth. Following the words of the priest, Emilio, now himself with tears forming in his eyes, gave his daughter to Severino Angiporti and

173

returned to sit next to his wife, Evangelina. Vivid flashbacks of a similar scene twenty-five years earlier passed through his mind.

The Mass proceeded according the rites of the Roman Catholic Church and came to the final moment when the priest proclaimed Severino and Elvira man and wife. They kissed at the altar and turned to leave the church to the smiles, tears, and applause of their relatives, friends, and guests. As they left the church, a line of well-wishers threw rice over them following an ancient practice calling upon the married couple fertility, prosperity and a lifetime of blessings. As soon as the couple could escape the crowd, they headed back to Bellaria where a grand feast awaited.

***

The sun was setting and the air had definitely turned cool. Evangelina pulled her shawl more closely around her shoulders. Why is it, she wondered, that beautiful events like a wedding take so long to plan and then in a flash they are over? Here it was already almost a year after the wedding and now they were left with just memories. Emilio agreed, somewhat melancholically. However, they perked up again as they recalled how festive the banquet was and how everyone ate, drank and danced for hours.

They remembered when Elvira threw her wedding bouquet over her shoulders to all of the single women, each one hoping to catch the bouquet so that she could be the next bride. But, her aim was off and it was poor Uncle Giuseppe who caught the bouquet and then just stood there not knowing what to do while everyone roared with laughter.

Then there was the ceremony where the groom slowly removed the garter from the bride. But, before Severino could throw it to the groomsmen, young Antonio snatched it from Severino's hands and ran off with it – again to roaring laughter.

They also recalled that after such a full day, it was a relief when the evening finally closed and the bride and groom sliced a Crostata di Frutta, a delicacy made of fruit, pound cake, and vanilla cream and shared it with their guests, after serving each other the first two slices. Then, the newly marrieds gave each guest a small gift packet of sugar coated almonds made in Cremona, not far from Piacenza, and amid shouts, hoots and well-wishes from their families and friends, they left to spend the night at the Grand Hotel in the Piazza Grande in Rivergaro.

The two looked at each other and smiled with satisfaction at the love, joy, and happiness that had been shared that day at Bellaria. There was no way that they could know that it would be a very long time before Bellaria saw another day as happy as this one.

Bellaria di Rivergaro

Chapter 15

SHOPPING IN PIACENZA WAS A SPECIAL EVENT. On
the infrequent occasions Evangelina went there, she
determined to look her best. For this trip, she wore a plain
light rose-colored Battenberg blouse that had a high neck
with a band collar. The blouse tucked loosely into a black
circular skirt, giving it a "pigeon breast" look, matching in
fullness the bishop shape of the blouse's sleeves. A deep V
leather-dip waist belt circled her slim waist. The back of the
skirt was in a habit style with a six-inch sweep. Maria
thought her mother looked very attractive. In contrast, Maria
chose to wear a plain wine-colored jumper with an off-white
blouse. Her dark brown hair was pulled back and fastened
with a matching wine-colored bow.

The purpose of this trip was to shop for linens to replace
the aging bedspreads in the four guest rooms of Bellaria. It
was amazing and disturbing that guests could damage bed
linens in a room so quickly. The same kind of linens that
usually lasted family members several years might last only a
fraction of that time when abused by guests of the *locanda*.

The train arrived on time in Piacenza at Binario 2. Track
number two was the usual terminus for the tram that went
from Rivergaro through Grazzano Visconti to Piacenza. The
two women stepped down from the train, passed through the
brick railway station and walked across the Via La
Primogenita. They walked one block to Viale Piacentino and
entered the beautiful Giardini Margherita. They had all day
to shop so they decided to stroll through the gardens that

featured an ancient temple and bronze busts of notable Piacentini. It was landscaped with a variety of old cedar, poplar and pine trees as well as flowering shrubs and flower beds. From there it was a leisurely walk to the Piazza Duomo and its many cafés and shops that lined the large square.

Approaching Piazza Duomo, they heard the noise of shouting and the mechanical noise of motor vehicles. As they turned in to the Piazza from Via Legnano, they were startled to see several military trucks lined up in front of the shops and cafes on Vicolo Pazzarelli. A group of soldiers was marching in the center of the piazza led by a strutting squad leader. People began crowding into the piazza to see what was happening. *Carabinieri*, para-military police, were pushing the crowd back and were trying to clear a path for the marching soldiers.

Evangelina spotted an empty table outside a café and quickly led Maria over to it. While they were waiting for a *cameriera* to take their order, a boy waving newspapers passed by. Maria gasped at the headlines that read "Terrible Defeat at Caporetto!" She reached in her purse, gave the boy five centesimi, and began reading the shocking news to her mother.

In the years leading up to World War I, Italy was part of the Triple Alliance, a so-called defense treaty with Germany and Italy's longtime foe Austria that it ratified in 1883. In the following decades, Italy engaged in hostilities in Ethiopia, Turkey and in the Balkans – in some cases disastrously - in an attempt to reestablish itself a colonial power. However, as Germany and Austria began to expand their military adventurism against Russia, Serbia, Montenegro, Albania and

178

other countries, Italy maintained a cautious neutral stance. Then, in 1915 Italy declared war on Germany and Austria, launching a conflict that would result in Italy joining with the Allied forces of Great Britain, France, and later the United States in a conflagration that would sweep throughout almost all of Europe.

Italy's principal theater of war was in the northeast part of the country as it attempted to counter an attack by Austria that threatened to drive south through the Trentino region. Initially, Italy repulsed the attack and drove the Austrians back north of the Isonzo River. However, in 1917 the Germans and Austrians together launched a massive counterattack at Caporetto on the Isonzo line. Italy was caught by surprise and suffered a terrible defeat, losing 40,000 men killed or wounded, 280,000 men captured, and another 350,000 who deserted. In addition, Italy lost most of its artillery weapons and countless military vehicles and small arms and munitions.

"Oh mamma," Maria said. "This is so awful. What a terrible loss of life!"

Her words were drowned out by the loud angry voices from the crowd demanding retribution and revenge for the humiliating defeat.

"We have to remain calm, but we must return to Rivergaro right away," Evangelina replied. "This is not a day for us to be here. It is all so frightening!"

They got up from the table but decided not to cross the piazza where the largest crowd was. In front of them, some of the military trucks were beginning to leave, while others with more soldiers had just arrived. They quickly slipped around the corner on to Via Francesco Daveri and headed back to the train station. This time they did not tarry in the Giardini Margherita. When they got back to the train station, they found that a train loaded with injured soldiers had just arrived from Bologna; some were being sent to Milan while others were debarking in Piacenza. It was a pathetic sight distressing both women; however, there was nothing they could do to help any of the soldiers.

The next train to Rivergaro was scheduled to leave in in another hour, so they had no choice except to endure the wait. Maria was able to make a telephone call to Bellaria and speak with her father, who said that he would meet them at the train station. Then she sat down next to her mother and took the older woman's hands in her own.

"It's going to be OK, mamma. Papà will know what to do."

An anxious Maria and her mother sat next to the window of the train that was taking them back to Rivergaro. Instead of a carefree day of shopping in Piacenza, the day was turning into one of sadness. Maria closed her eyes and tried to shut the sights that she and her mother had seen earlier out of her mind.

***

A half hour later, the train passed through Niviano, only a few minutes from arriving at Rivergaro. Maria glanced out the window at the fields where the contadini were now spreading manure they collected over the winter in the *stalle*

180

that sheltered hundreds, if not thousands, of dairy cows. In only a few weeks, the same *contadini* would fill the fields with literally thousands of tomato plants that by July or August would be harvested, packed and shipped as plump vine-ripened *pomodori pelati*, peeled tomatoes, to markets far from where they were grown. However, the tomato crop was so large that there was more than enough for the local markets, as well.

Even to this day, Maria and her mother went to the farmers market in Rivergaro every Friday to buy tomatoes and other produce they were unable to grow at Bellaria. The *trattoria* patrons at Bellaria were served only the very freshest vegetables and fruit. Still, it was strange, she thought, that with all of the tomatoes grown in this region one might expect that Piacentini housewives would prefer to use a tomato-based sauce when serving pasta dishes – like the Bolognese sauce so popular in nearby Parma, Modena and Bologna. But no, throughout the province of Piacenza, most pasta dishes were served in a melted butter and cheese sauce. In their region, tomatoes were used for salads and other dishes, but not so much for pasta. Maria found this to be very curious.

***

Evangelina nudged Maria, saying that they would soon arrive in Rivergaro. Ten minutes later, the train, really more like a commuter tram, pulled into the wrought iron framed station at the north end of Rivergaro almost exactly on time. Italian trains, even locals like the one that brought them to Rivergaro, were rarely late.

Bellaria di Rivergaro

The moment that Evangelina saw Emilio she knew that something was wrong. He was a man who did not wear his emotions well. Worry was all over his face. They briefly embraced and then he led her and Maria to the 1912 FIAT that was another of his concessions to modern technology; although his preferred mode of transportation was still his bicycle. Pietro was waiting in the driver's seat. He looked solemnly at his mother and sister, and then turned his head as though he was holding something back.

"Pietro, what is it? I know you like a book," Evangelina said. "I can tell that something is not right."

Pietro remained silent and handed her a letter. She read it and paled at its contents. It was a notice from the Military District of Piacenza informing Pietro that he was required to report for military service within two weeks. Her eyes filled with tears as she passed the notice to Maria. Her son was going off to war.

They drove back to Bellaria in silence. There was nothing to say; they all felt the same emotions. Luigi left Italy before he was 18 years old, violating the law that prohibited single males under the age of 18 from emigrating from the country. That is why Luigi traveled all the way to Le Havre, France to take a ship to America. The authorities would not know that he was immigrating to America, rather than simply visiting another European country. But now, if Luigi came back to Rivergaro he could be arrested for draft evasion, imprisoned, and then required to serve in the military. There was no statute of limitations for draft evasion. That is why so many young Italian men never returned to their native country after they immigrated to the New World.

A couple of years later, their oldest daughter Elisa traveled to America to visit Luigi. Everyone expected her to return to Rivergaro after a few months. Instead, she met and married Giovanni Guasconi and the two had a child. Now, it seemed that both Luigi and Elisa were building a new life in America and Evangelina had no idea when she would see either of them again. Meanwhile, within two weeks their second oldest son, Pietro, would be sent to war to face unspeakable danger. It was almost too much to bear. But, there was even more to come.

When they returned to Bellaria, Emilio's brother Giuseppe was waiting for them. Emilio could see the concern on his face so he ushered the women into the house and then guided Giuseppe and Pietro to a table in the dining room near the terrace at the north end of the building. Emilio grabbed a bottle of wine and three glasses and returned to the table.

"You heard the news, Giuseppe?" He asked.

"Yes, Antonio told me. I am afraid that I have some bad news of my own"

The mood was grim and Emilio and Pietro waited for him to continue.

"My son, Giovanni, has decided to volunteer to serve in the army," he said.

Emilio pounded his hand against the top of the table.

"Dear God!" He exclaimed. "Where is this madness going?"

"He did not want to wait until he was drafted, and that was inevitable considering the incredible loss of manpower that our army has just incurred up on the Isonzo," Giuseppe said, referring to the losses at the battle of Caporetto. "Do you know that in addition to losing 300,000 men killed, wounded, and captured by the Austrians and Germans, and another 350,000 who deserted, we lost 500 airplanes, 1500 cannons, 1500 trucks and thousands of machine guns and other weapons? They practically wiped us out. That's why there is a big drive now to draft and recruit as many replacements as possible."

"I hope they get rid of that son-of-a-bitch Cardorna, who lost the battle," Emilio said. "He is hated by every one of his soldiers. He has no regard for them and does not hesitate to march them out in front of the other troops and shoot them for the slightest infraction."

"They did get rid of Marshal Cardorna," Giuseppe replied. "I hear that General Armando Diaz is being appointed Army Chief of Staff."

"So, what is my cousin Giovanni going to do?" asked Pietro.

"Apparently the army is forming an Alpine Artillery regiment to participate in what they call the Italian Far East Expeditionary Corps. That unit will be sent to Manchuria and Siberia to fight the Bolsheviks," he said. "If you can imagine, Giovanni is actually excited about it. He even said that he intends to keep a diary of his entire experience."

"Well," Pietro interjected, "It does make some sense. If you have to serve in the military you might as well sign up for something that is exciting. Perhaps I should have done the same thing. Maybe it's not too late to volunteer for the Alpine Artillery regiment."

Emilio and Giuseppe just looked at each other and shook their heads, not believing what they just heard. Then Emilio reached for the wine bottle and filled their glasses.

Bellaria di Rivergaro

Chapter 16

THE ENTIRE NORTHERN PART OF ITALY was in great turmoil. Riots broke out in Milan as many people protested Italy's continued participation in the war. There was great fear that the Austrians would soon push farther south and occupy several of Italy's most important cities including Venice, Bologna, Verona, and Padua. However, even though Austria, with the help of Germany, had defeated Italy at the battle of Caporetto, it had exhausted its own military resources and its ability to carry the battle further.

The two cousins, Pietro and Giovanni, reported for military duty as ordered, leaving their parents and siblings to worry about their safety. The army sent Pietro to Vittorio Veneto in Treviso Province where he served as a lorry driver ferrying troops to the front lines. Giovanni proudly wore the green-gray service uniform of the Alpine Corps with its distinctive green collar patch and a Capello Alpino, the grey felt hat with a black raven's feather fastened to the left side. In July 1918, he boarded a ship and began his incredible journey to exotic places like Tientsin, China and Krasnojarsk, Siberia. He kept a detailed diary of his entire military experience. Many years later, his diary served as the basis for a book titled *From the Val Trebbia to Krasnojarsk*.

In the ensuing months, Italy recovered from its defeat at Caporetto and with the help of France launched a series of successful counterattacks against Austria. Suffering several battlefield defeats, as well as political crisis and rebellion on the domestic front, Austria sued for peace with Italy and an

187

armistice between the two countries was signed on October 29, 1918. In November, 1918, representatives of Britain, France, and Germany signed an armistice ending hostilities in World War I. The Treaty of Versailles, the actual peace treaty, was signed six months later on a railroad carriage in the Forest of Compiègne about 30 miles north of Paris.

In the meanwhile, a different kind of danger would soon confront the families that the war left behind.

***

The "crush season" is a very busy time in the Colli Piacentini, the wine making hills of Piacenza. Months earlier, buds began appearing on the grapevines that covered the Emilia Romagna hill slopes as they responded to the warmth of the late spring sun. Another summer had passed, and by September millions of bunches of plump blue and green grapes overflowed the region's vineyards, waiting impatiently to be harvested. If grapes are not harvested at just the right time, when the sugar content is perfectly balanced, the quality of the wine for which they were grown will suffer.

Emilio knew the wine making process well; he had been making wine for as long as he could remember. He had a small vineyard behind the Statto house when he lived across the river. Then, after building Bellaria, he planted a larger vineyard on the slope of Bellaria's south field – enough to produce two barrels, or about 500 bottles, of wine each year. Emilio preferred red wine, so he chose to grow Barbera and Bonarda grapes that he blended (65% to 35%) to produce his version of a wine called Gutturnio. This blend of wine was

188

known to the ancient Romans, who poured it from narrow-necked Gutturnium jugs from which the wine derived its name. However, not all of Bellaria's guests shared Emilio's preference for red wine. So, each wine season Emilio first ensured that he had a sufficient amount of Gutturnio for Bellaria's use. He then traded some of the red wine that he produced for a few dozen bottles of the white Trebbiano wine made by his friends in Statto across the river.

At this time of year, everyone in the family had a role to play in harvesting the grapes and making the wine. Giuseppe, Antonio, and Nino helped their father carefully snip each bunch of grapes from its vine and put the cut bunches into a metal pail, making sure the skin of the grapes was not damaged. After they filled a bucket, they emptied it into a wood bin fitted on a *barra*, the two-wheeled cart pulled by an ox that was Maria's job to drive. Later, they transferred the grapes to a large wooden tub located under the vine-covered pergola that Emilio had built alongside Bellaria.

Crushing the grapes was another family affair. Usually, everyone gathered for the fun event in which the younger members of the family took turns stomping the grapes in the tub until their feet and lower legs were purple with grape juice. When the children were younger, the event was especially comical as they often slipped and slid on the mashed grapes, falling inside the shallow tub and then emerging covered with purple grape pulp. This year, Elvira and Severino were invited to help crush the grapes, but Elvira came down with the flu and Severino feared that he was getting it, also. For that matter, Evangelina did not feel that well and she noticed that Nino seemed to be getting the

189

sniffles. Young Andrea would have loved to jump in the tub and squish the grapes but he was staying with his Guasconi grandparents in Castel San Giovanni this weekend.

In any case, over a three-hour period several hundred kilos of grapes were thoroughly stomped and mashed until the tub was full of a purple slurry and there were five pairs of very tired, purple legs and feet! Next, the mash, called "must" for red grapes, was allowed to ferment naturally in the covered tub for two weeks. The tub was then drained and the wine was filtered and poured into dark, narrow-necked bottles that were put in the Bellaria's wine cellar where they would age for at least six months, until the spring or summer of 1920.

A very weary Bellaria family sat in the shade of the pergola drinking cool lemonade Maria brought in a large pitcher from the kitchen. Antonio saw that his mother was perspiring rather heavily.

"Mamma, are you alright," he asked. "You look like you don't feel very well."

Emilio looked up with concern and Maria went over to Evangelina and put her hand to her mother's forehead.

"Mamma, you have a fever," she said urgently. "I want you to come into the house with me right now!"

"It's nothing," Evangelina protested. "It's just hot under here and there isn't a breath of air."

"Evangelina, I think that Maria is right. You look awfully pale. Please go with her now," Emilio said sternly.

"Nino," he said, using Nino's nickname, "go with them. It looks to me like you are coming down with something also."

Giuseppe saw a look of concern in his father's eyes, but he waited until his mother, Maria and Nino went back inside Bellaria to say anything.

"What's the matter, papà? Mamma and Nino will be OK."

Emilio looked directly at both Giuseppe and Antonio and said,

"I want you both to listen to what I am going to tell you. Yesterday I rode to Rivergaro, as I usually do almost every day, to play cards with my amici. Renato and Giacomo were not there because they are sick with the flu. So, Gino, Massimo, and I sat in the piazza and chatted. We smoked a stogie and had a couple of cups of caffè. A ragazzo walked by selling newspapers. When I saw the headline, I bought one of them.

"The headline was 'FLU EPIDEMIC GETTING WORSE!' Then I read the article. That damn Spanish Flu keeps sweeping through Europe. In Italy, it seemed at first to be worse in the southern regions. Now, it is all over our region, as well. In fact, the paper said that even America has been hit hard by it. It is everywhere, and the worst problem is that so many people are dying from it – millions of people.

"I don't like the looks of this at all. We need to keep a close eye on mamma and Nino. If they get sick we might need to send for the doctor."

Bellaria di Rivergaro

***

By the time it ran its course, the 1917-1919 influenza pandemic killed over 50 million people throughout the world. It was even more devastating than the Black Plague of the Middle Ages. Wartime censorship restricted newspapers from reporting the extent of the influenza pandemic in the United States, Great Britain, France, and Germany, preventing their populations from knowing the devastating global impact the disease was causing. However, Spanish newspapers were not similarly restricted and widely reported news about the effect the flu was having in Spain and throughout the world. In addition, the Spanish King Alfonso XIII became gravely ill with the flu and so the pandemic acquired the misnomer Spanish Flu.

Italy suffered a terrible mortality rate from the disease with 10.7 out of every 1,000 people dying from it, second only to Spain where the mortality rate from the flu was as high as 12.1 out of every 1000 people. There was no cure; it simply had to run its course. It took its greatest toll on the younger people – those between the ages of 20 to 40 – although the very old and the very young suffered too. At Bellaria, along with Evangelina and Nino, Antonio also contracted the illness. Emilio tried to send for a doctor (there were now two in Rivergaro) but they were so busy that it was impossible for them to make all of the requested house calls. The nearest hospital was in Travo and all of those afflicted in the family were too ill to be transported there.

While available doctors were scarce due to the incredible large number of flu victims, the newspaper published medical bulletins designed to help the public cope with the emergency. Following those suggestions, Emilio decided to temporarily close the *trattoria* and *locanda* to help prevent the spread of the disease. Whenever they were in direct contact with the family members who were ill, Emilio, Giuseppe, and Maria wore masks to filter out germs. They also kept the patients hydrated, fed them chicken-based broth and gave them aspirin to help reduce their fever. Still, it was a miracle that the three of them escaped contracting the disease themselves.

The fever broke first for Evangelina and then for Nino and Antonio; they slowly began to recover. However, late one morning Emilio's friend Gino Mazoni stopped by Bellaria to give him the sad news that Giacomo Sconti had died the previous night from pneumonia that was brought on by the flu. Two days later, Emilio and his son Giuseppe attended a funeral Mass for Emilio's old friend and patrono Giacomo at Sant'Agata in Rivergaro and paid their respects to his grieving widow, Maria. By the time that the pandemic finally subsided, there would be many more funeral Masses in Rivergaro.

***

As late fall approached, two events helped to lift the gloom that had descended on everyone at Bellaria over the past two years. First, Emilio received a letter from Pietro stating that he was being released from the military and that he would be home by Christmas. The joy and relief that was seen on Evangelina's face when he told her the good news boosted everyone's spirits. The second event left the family with mixed feelings. Giuseppina Guasconi, Elisa's sister-in-law, visited Bellaria and told the family that she received a

193

letter from Elisa and Giovanni saying that because the danger of war was over, they believed transatlantic travel was now safe for Andrea. Giuseppina said that as soon as she received that information, she booked passage for her and Andrea aboard the Duca Degli Abruzzi. Andrea would soon be going home to America.

"Oh, I am going to miss him so much," Evangelina said. "He has become such an important part of our lives. What are we going to do without him being here with us at Bellaria?"

"The same thing we did when Luigi, Elisa, and Pierino left," said Emilio, referring to Pietro by his childhood name. "We'll be sad for a while – maybe a long while – but we'll get over it."

"That's easy for you to say, papà," Maria said. "I still miss Luigi and Elisa every day and I don't think that Giuseppe has every gotten over his big brother being away for so long."

"You know," Evangelina commented, "it's a strange thing, but when you think about it Antonio was only three years old when Luigi left and Nino was just a baby. Those two never really knew Luigi and they barely remember Elisa."

"What's your point," Emilio asked Evangelina.

"I'm not sure," she replied. "However, Andrea was not even four years old when Giuseppina brought him here. He is almost nine, now. I wonder how well he actually remembers his parents."

"He has seen photos of them," Maria said. "He reads their letters and writes his own to them. So, perhaps it's not the same. Anyway, sometimes when he is over here all he does is talk about his 'mamma,' and how much he wants to be with her. The last time he was here he told me that when he gets home the first thing that he is going to do is to give her a big hug."

Emilio nodded his head in understanding. Then he asked, "By the way, where are the boys?"

"They went fishing down at the river," Maria answered. "They said that they were in the mood for some trout for supper."

"I hope that they have better luck than I do," Emilio quipped. "The fish must sense when I go down to the river and sound some sort of alert. It's been months since I caught anything."

Emilio had barely finished speaking when Nino and Antonio burst through the back door by the kitchen, each holding up several brown trout. Giuseppe trailed a moment later with only one fish, but it was a six-kilo barbel, large enough to feed the entire family.

Emilio shook his head and sighed.

Bellaria di Rivergaro

Chapter 17

ELISA ASKED GIOVANNI ONCE AGAIN, "Gianni, are you sure that we can afford the call? The operator said that the cost would be one dollar if we called after 5:00 PM. That is half the price if we called before then."

Giovanni waved his hand in the air and said, "My love, he is your brother and it has been a long time since you talked to him. Yes, we can afford a three-minute telephone call."

Elisa picked up the black rotary dial telephone that was fastened to the kitchen wall of their apartment and dialed "O" for the operator. She explained that she wanted to make a call to Lakewood, Ohio, which was a suburb of Cleveland. The number was Academy 1-6254. The operator wrote down the calling information provided by Elisa, and then told her that she would call her back once the other party was on the line. The operator passed the information to another operator, who looked up the route the call should take, and then that operator built up the circuit one link at a time by connecting to operators at switchboards along the route. A typical call took seven minutes to set up; however, because of line problems this one took almost 15 minutes. Once the operator established the circuit, it would be dedicated to that conversation until the end of the call.

Luigi loved his job as foreman for the Hunkin-Conkey Construction Company in Cleveland, Ohio. He was proud to work for the company whose founder had the primary responsibility of rebuilding San Francisco after the disastrous

1905 earthquake. Just last year, Luigi played an important role building the High Level Bridge over the Cuyahoga River connecting Detroit Road on the West Side with Superior Road on the east side of the river. After the High Level Bridge was completed, he was assigned to supervise building a plant for Republic Steel in the area of the Cuyahoga Valley known as the Flats.

Luigi usually did not get home from work much earlier than 7:00 PM. However, today was a Friday and his thirty-first birthday. His boss, Angelo Marcuzzi insisted that he go home an hour earlier.

"Hey paesan," Marcuzzi shouted as Luigi left the superintendent's shack. "Tell your wife to give you a special birthday treat tonight!" He said wickedly.

"One can only hope!" Luigi answered.

Luigi lugged his lunch pail over to the 1917 Ford Model T that he bought new two years ago for less than five hundred dollars. He left the window curtains down because it looked like it might rain. Then he cranked the Model T's 34 horsepower engine trying to avoid the crank snapping back and hitting him in the wrist when the engine came to life. The engine caught and Luigi jumped back, once again avoiding a bruised wrist.

He climbed into the car, adjusted the choke, shifted to the first of the two forward gears, and drove off. When the "Tin Lizzy" accelerated to almost twenty miles per hour, he shifted to the second forward gear. At the same time, he turned off the gravel road leading into his job site and took Detroit Road for the short twenty-five-minute ride home. Traffic was light;

his worse concern was dodging passengers jumping aboard or alighting from the frequent electric trolley cars that ran on parallel tracks up the center of the street. Almost a half-hour later, he turned left onto Orchard Grove and drove up the incline of the street, his tires singing on the brick pavement. The apple orchard, after which the street was named, was now only a distant memory.

Luigi made another left turn onto the split concrete driveway of his house that consisted of two concrete strips spaced apart to accommodate the wheel spread of a car. They were separated by grass designed to catch the inevitable oil leaks of the automobiles of that time. He left the engine running, got out of the car, and opened the double doors of the garage. In another moment, the car was safely parked for the night. Luigi walked past the tall walnut tree next to the driveway and up the back stairs of the house to be greeted by two neatly dressed children jumping up and down shouting "Happy Birthday, Daddy."

"Buon Compleanno, mi amore," Ines said as she warmly embraced Luigi and gave him a passionate birthday kiss. She looked absolutely beautiful. Her full, dark brown hair was parted in the center, pulled back, and fastened in the back in a short bun. She wore a plain white blouse, accented with a navy blue bow at the V of her neckline, a full-length, navy blue skirt, and a white, freshly pressed apron. Her smile melted Luigi's heart. At that moment, he remembered what Marcuzzi said earlier, and he smiled.

"Grazie, Tesoro," Luigi said, still speaking Italian as he called her Sweetheart. Angelina and Emil were waiting for their turn to hug their father, so he sat down and pulled both

of them to him. Switching to English, he thanked them for
looking so nice for his birthday; winking to Ines in
acknowledgment of the work she did getting them ready.

   When Luigi and Ines moved to the Cleveland area, they
decided not to live in the city's Little Italy. They were proud
of their heritage; however, they lived in America – not Italy –
and they fully intended that their children would be brought
up to be American in all respects. That also meant speaking
English when they were around the children, although for
many years they would continue to speak their native
language to each other.

   Ines told Luigi to relax while she finished preparing
dinner. That usually meant pouring himself a glass of Haig &
Haig Pinched Bottle Scotch and lighting up a Tampa cigar.
Before he could do so, however, the telephone on the kitchen
wall rang. He walked over to the phone, picked up the
receiver, and said "Hello."

   "Ciao, Luigi," the voice said. *"Buon compleanno e tanti
auguri."*

   "Elisa!" Luigi's voice was filled with excitement hearing
his sister wish him a happy birthday.

   "How are you, little brother?" She asked. "Are you
having a nice time on your birthday?"

   In the background, Luigi could hear Giovanni tell Elisa to
wish Luigi a happy birthday from him, as well.

   "Oh, Sis. It's so good to hear your voice. I miss you very
much. How are you and Giovanni?"

"Tired, but OK, and I miss you, too, Luigi. It has been too long since we were together."

"Little Lina was two-years old when we left New York," Luigi said. "Now she is eight. The problem is that this is such a big country. It is as far from here to Queens, New York as it is from Milan to Naples. I am afraid that my poor "Tin Lizzy" could never make it."

"I understand, Luigi. It is as great a problem for us and we do not have a car, so we would have to take a train. But also, we cannot afford to shut down the restaurant for a couple of weeks or more. How are Ines and the bambini?"

"Great," Luigi answered. "Do you have any news about Andrea?"

"Yes, and in addition to wishing you a happy birthday, that is one of the reasons that I called. We have great news. Giovanni and I have decided that it is safe for Andrea to return, so we asked Giuseppina to bring him back. He's coming home, Luigi!" she said, her voice filled with emotion. "He will be home before Christmas."

"That's wonderful news, Elisa. I'll tell Ines. Listen, I am planning on buying a new car next spring. The one we have now is not big enough for the four of us. Maybe next April or May I can take a couple of weeks off work and bring Ines and the children to see you, Giovanni, and my nephew."

"Wonderful idea," Elisa replied. "By the way, have you ever thought about going back to Italy – just for a visit?"

"Of course," Luigi answered. "But, I don't see how it's possible. Even though the war is over, they would probably

201

arrest me for emigrating from Italy. If that is not enough, with a wife and two children I can't afford to leave a good-paying job for six or eight weeks to go back there. I feel terrible but what can I do?"

"I understand, Luigi. Mamma and papà do, too."

"Elisa, how is the restaurant doing?"

"Not bad, but it is so much work. Most days Gianni and I are there ten to twelve hours, if not more. I must confess, it's very tiring and at times, like now, I really feel run down.

"Listen, I have to go now. Lots of love and once again have a happy birthday."

"Thank you so much for calling, Elisa. I love you."

"I love you, too, little brother. *Ciao.*"

Luigi hung up the telephone, walked in to the living room and sat down in his chair next to the fireplace. He was filled with emotion, happy that Elisa had called but feeling morose about being so far away from his sister and from the rest of his family in Italy.

Ines came over to where he was sitting and placed her arm around his shoulder.

"I know what you are feeling, Luigi. My father Augusto and my brother Nelson are here in America but all of the rest of my family, my dear cousins, aunts and uncles, are back in Italy. I miss all of them, too."

"I love you and the children so much, Ines. As long as we have each other everything will be fine."

Then, he looked up, grinned at her, and with his left hand gave her a "love pat" on the fanny.

"Now, my love, how about that birthday dinner that you have been telling me about? I hope that you made me a cake!"

"You know I did," she said in Italian as she walked back in to the kitchen. "But, be surprised when Lina and Emil bring it out to you after dinner."

***

The Italian passenger ship Duca Degli Abruzzi was scheduled to depart from Genoa at 5:00 PM on Saturday, November 15th. The train to Genoa would leave Piacenza at 9:00 AM and take three hours and forty-two minutes to reach its destination. Giuseppina and Andrea would have no problem reaching the steamship passenger terminal on time. However, the week before their departure would be very busy and it would not be practical for Andrea to be with his "other" grandparents at Bellaria during that time. So, Evangelina, Maria, and Elvira set up a small family farewell party for Andrea and Giuseppina at Bellaria the weekend before they were to leave for New York.

Andrea stayed at Bellaria Saturday night, November 8th and the next morning he attended Holy Mass at Sant'Agata with his grandparents, aunts, uncles and cousins. After Mass, Padre Don Luigi Veneziani gave Andrea and Giuseppina a special blessing, praying that they would have a safe voyage to New York. Then the family returned to Bellaria where they enjoyed another fantastic *pranzo* that was finished off by a big ricotta cheesecake that was both one of Bellaria's signature desserts and also a favorite of Andrea. Like his father Giovanni, Andrea loved horses. So, as one of Andrea's farewell gifts, he received a wooden horse and *calesse* set that had been hand carved, polished, and varnished by Emilio and Andrea's uncles. His grandmother and aunts gave him wool mittens, a wool cap and wool scarf that they had knitted in the hope that they would keep Andrea warm during the coming winter in America. Then, after a tearful "good-bye," Pietro drove Giuseppina and Andrea back to Castel San Giovanni.

It was four years since Giuseppina and Andrea were on a large ship. The change in the treatment of third-class passengers was quite noticeable. The most notable change was that on this voyage passengers were treated with greater courtesy and respect by the ship's crew. There were now more cabins with four to six berths as opposed to the large, overcrowded dormitory-like facilities of ships built between 1880 and 1910. Although still somewhat restricted, third-class passengers were allowed much greater access to deck space where they could enjoy the fresh ocean air, relax, and even play shuffle ball. The dining facilities were very much improved. Third-class passengers now sat at tables for eight or ten that had linen tablecloths and real chinaware. The dining selection was improved and meals were brought to the passengers at their tables.

The entire voyage from Castel San Giovanni to New York was mostly uneventful. Mid-afternoon on Tuesday, December 2, 1919, tugboats nudged the Duca Degli Abruzzi into its berth at the Chelsea piers on Manhattan's west side, not far from Greenwich Village. A very excited Elisa and

Giovanni Guasconi were among the hundreds of family members and friends who were waiting for the ship to arrive. They strained to spot Giuseppina and Andrea as passengers lined the crowded railings of the upper decks.

"There they are!" Elisa shouted, pointing to two tiny figures on the boat deck high above the wharf.

"I see them," Giovanni said. Both he and Elisa waved and shouted, hoping that either Giuseppina or Andrea would see them. Finally, Andrea's sharp eyes found his parents in the crowd below. From that moment, the four of them blew kisses to each other, made hugging motions, waved, and cried.

Passengers usually began disembarking within a half-hour to one-hour of a ship's arrival. However, one hour turned into two before a small trickle of people began to walk down the gangplank – first-class passengers, it seemed, if judged by their apparent affluence.

Elisa felt that telltale tickle at the back of her throat that is often the precursor of a cold. Now is not the time to be catching cold, she thought. If one did break out she would have to be very careful that Andrea did not catch it. Besides, no one wanted to be sick for Christmas, now only four-weeks away.

Then, the trickle of passengers who were disembarking stopped. The passengers on the decks were ushered back inside of the ship and several United States Immigration Officers gathered at the ship's railing with megaphones. A bewildered Andrea quickly waved to his mother and blew her another kiss before disappearing into the crowd returning to the interior of the ship. When the deck was cleared of all passengers, one of the immigration officers put a megaphone to his mouth and said,

"Upon inspection by officers of the United States Department of Health, several cases of scarlet fever were discovered among the passengers of this ship. Therefore, all passengers who might have been exposed to those who were infected are being transported to Ellis Island where they will be quarantined until further notice."

"My God, what does this mean?" Elisa asked frantically.

"I'm not sure, my love," Giovanni replied.

"Do you think that Andrea has scarlet fever?" She was almost hysterical now.

"No, no, of course not," Giovanni said, trying to be reassuring. "It's just a precaution. I am sure that he will be released from Ellis Island soon. They just want to make sure that he is not infected. He will be home soon and we will have a lovely Christmas together."

***

Less than a week before Christmas, a letter arrived from Giuseppina informing everyone at Bellaria that she and Andrea were being held in quarantine on Ellis Island. She said that medical officials were not sure how long they would have to remain in quarantine, but it was unlikely that they would be released before Christmas. Giuseppina explained the problem was that scarlet fever had been detected among a few passengers, but neither she nor Andrea had contracted the disease. The quarantine was strictly precautionary. She also said that she had spoken with Elisa over the telephone and that Elisa had not been feeling well.

Giuseppina's letter did little to brighten the Christmas mood at Bellaria. This year, Elvira and Severino planned to spend the holiday with Severino's family. Pietro had already left for Milan to spend Christmas with the family of one of his friends from the Army. Of course, Luigi, Elisa, and now Andrea were gone, so that left only Emilio, Evangelina, Maria and the three ragazzi to celebrate Natale together. However, Giuseppe was now twenty years old, Antonio was eighteen, and Nino was fifteen. In previous Christmas celebrations, the exuberance of younger children had always made the holiday seem to come alive. This year, Andrea's absence was particularly missed.

***

Things were not much better among the family in America. It seemed that the Spanish Flu was making some sort of resurgence, as though the disease was not yet satisfied with the amount of human suffering that it had caused. People who caught it during its earlier sweep seemed to have developed a resistance to it this time. However, it was particularly brutal among those who escaped the flu's first wave. Luigi and Ines were especially concerned about the children.

"I think that we should do everything we can to avoid crowded places," Luigi said. "That includes not going to Mass on Christmas day and also on this next Sunday."

"How could we possibly do that?" Ines demanded. "My God, Luigi that would be a mortal sin."

"Nonsense. It's not a sin to miss Mass when you are sick. So, it is hardly a sin to avoid becoming sick, especially with something this serious going around."

"Well, if we do that then you had better not have Vito Congemi, Luigi Colosimo and your other amici over here on Christmas Eve. That would be almost sacrilegious!"

Most of these men were subcontractors who Luigi, first in his capacity as a foreman and now as a superintendent, hired to do masonry, plumbing and electrical work at his various construction projects. Ines knew that they made a practice of making a visit on Christmas Eve to pay their respects to her husband by dropping off a few boxes of his favorite Tampa cigars, baskets of fruit from Florida and, perhaps, a few bottles of his favorite Haig & Haig Scotch. In turn, Luigi made sure that there was plenty of Grappa, Amaretto, and Galliano, plus espresso and Christmas pastries, available for his visitors – all of which broke the Christmas Eve fast set by the Church. This bothered Ines; however, Luigi never paid much attention to fasting on any occasion.

"Umm," Luigi grunted. "We'll see." Being a *patrono* was one of the benefits of his position. He did not abuse it, but at the same time, it had its advantages.

As it turned out, six of Luigi's subcontractors showed up on Christmas Eve for their usual visit. In addition, the doorbell rang several times that evening with deliveries of beautifully wrapped baskets of foodstuffs ranging from biscotti and citrus fruit to salami, cheese and bottles of good Italian wine from his other paesani. There was hardly room for the children's gifts that Ines would place under the

Christmas tree after the little ones were asleep. The next morning, however, Luigi relented and they did attend Christmas Mass at St. James.

***

It was Wednesday afternoon on Christmas Eve day. Giovanni and Elisa were closing their restaurant that was located in a section of Manhattan heavily populated by Northern Italian immigrants – many of them Piacentini, like Giovanni and Elisa. It was obvious to Giovanni that Elisa did not feel well. The long hours and hard work at the restaurant were beginning to take their toll on her health. Her face was flushed and she seemed to perspire easily. Giovanni was very concerned; at the same time he did not feel that well, himself.

"My love," he said, "I think that we need to close the restaurant for a few days. There is not going to be much purpose in keeping it open until next week. This is family time and very few people will be going out for breakfast or lunch over the long weekend. Besides, you need some rest. You look very tired and even a bit feverish."

"I do feel exhausted, Gianni, and I am very disappointed that our Andrea is so close yet so far away," she replied. "We can see Ellis Island from Chelsea and it's only a twenty minute ferry ride from the Battery. I miss him so much."

All Giovanni could say was, "I do, too."

"Perhaps you are right," she said. "I need to rest. I feel congestion in my chest and I think that I may have a slight fever. At least we know that both Andrea and Giuseppina are safe and healthy. From what I understand, the medical staff on Ellis Island is doing the best that they can to make sure that the people who have not been cleared to leave the island have as nice a Christmas as possible."

"I can't believe that this is happening," Giovanni said. "However, if you are coming down with something we wouldn't want Andrea to catch it, especially on his first days back home."

"*D'accordo*," Elisa said in agreement. "Let's go home and I will make you a nice bowl of tortellini in brodo. A little chicken broth will be good for me, too."

***

Darkness had fallen early and the lights of Manhattan across the Hudson River sparkled in the crisp, cold air like a field of fireflies. Andrea tugged at the scarf that Zia Maria and Zia Elvira had made for him, adjusting it around his neck and chest. He pulled up the collar of his woolen jacket as a further shield against the chill and decided to put on the mittens that Nonna Evangelina had lovingly knitted for him. He knew that his mother and father were not far away – just over there, across the river. I bet that I could swim there, he thought. Or, maybe I can find a boat and row across. When I get there all I have to do is ask someone where Giovanni and Elisa Guasconi live and I will simply walk to our apartment, he reasoned. Won't mamma and papà be surprised when I knock at the door and they open it! I'll give them such a big hug. Such was the logic of an eight-year-old boy who missed being with his mother and father more than anything else in the world on this Christmas Eve.

210

"Andrea," Giuseppina called. "Ah, there you are. Come on now, hurry up. They are going to start the celebration in the Great Hall."

Reluctantly, Andrea turned away from the river and accompanied his aunt into the Great Hall of the Immigration Building at Ellis Island. He could hear music and singing and even laughter. They climbed the steps and entered the building through its two large doors. Andrea could hardly believe what he saw. Hundreds of people, almost all of them immigrants, were milling about the Great Hall, gazing at nine brilliantly lighted and decorated Christmas trees. Groups of people were singing traditional Christmas carols in their native language. Russian here, German over there, Italian and Bulgarian and so many more. Volunteers from the Immigration staff joined missionaries from various Christian (and non-Christian) denominations handing out gifts to everyone: candy, oranges, toys, soap, and handkerchiefs.

It might not have been possible for the Immigration and Health Inspectors to screen all of those people so that they could be with the friends and loved ones that they came to join in America by the holiday; but they tried very hard and compassionately to brighten their spirits this Christmas Eve.

Andrea looked up at Giuseppina and the two smiled. He squeezed her hand and ran to get in a line where a pretty, young nurse in a while uniform was handing out red and white striped candy cane.

Bellaria di Rivergaro

Chapter 18

THE NEWS THAT GIUSEPPINA WAS WAITING for finally came one afternoon in early January. U.S. Government Health Inspectors at last cleared all of the remaining passengers from the Duca Degli Abrucci and released them from quarantine. Further, the following morning, Giuseppina, Andrea and the other passengers would be transported by ferry back to the Battery in lower Manhattan where they were free to debark, meet their friends or relatives and to continue their journey. Andrea was ecstatic!

Giuseppina waited in a long line to access one of the few telephones available to immigrants so she could convey the good news to Giovanni and Elisa. It was late in the afternoon. Giuseppina knew that the restaurant closed after lunch, so she called their apartment. After a few rings, Giovanni answered the phone.

"I have great news," Giuseppina said. "They finally cleared us. You can meet us tomorrow at the Battery."

There was a pause as Giovanni tried to clear his throat. He coughed a few times, and then responded.

"Thank God, Giuseppina. It will be wonderful to see you again. Are you both OK?"

"We're fine, but it doesn't sound like you are. Is something wrong?"

"Elisa has the flu. She's very sick. I think that I might be coming down with it, too; but, if you let me know what time

213

the ferry gets to the Battery I'll meet you and bring you back here."

"No, Giovanni. I'm familiar with New York. We will have no trouble taking a trolley or subway. You stay out of the cold and take care of Elisa. We will see you sometime tomorrow. *Ciao.*"

"*Ciao*, Sis, *a domani*, I'll see you tomorrow" Giovanni replied. He was relieved he did not have to go all the way down to the Battery feeling as he did, but he was also concerned about Giuseppina and Andrea coming home to an apartment where they could be exposed to the flu. Before he could think much more about it, he heard Elisa coughing and hurried to see if he could make her more comfortable.

The Thomas C. Millard was as close to being a derelict as a ferry could be. Its steel sides were streaked with rust. A ring of algae circled the ferry at its waterline. However, in the eyes of Giuseppina, it was the most beautiful boat that ever existed. Shortly after Giuseppina and Andrea boarded, the ferry pulled away from the Ellis Island Ferry Building and curved past the north side of Liberty Island toward the South Ferry pier at the Battery. Giuseppina and Andrea watched in silence as the ferry passed behind Lady Liberty, whose uplifted torch of freedom and impassive gaze was a beacon to millions of immigrants, past and future, who left their faraway homes to seek a better life in the new world.

In less than a half-hour, the ferry docked at the Battery. Within minutes, Giuseppina and Andrea followed the scores of other passengers who were struggling down the gangplank with their luggage. Slung over Andrea's shoulder was a

214

smaller canvas bag that held the carved wooden horse and *calesse* set that was his farewell gift from his uncles. From the ferry dock it was only a short walk from the ferry terminal to the South Ferry Station of the IRT subway where they took the 3rd Avenue "el" to the 106th Street stop. Another ten minutes and they were looking up at the five-story red brick tenement building where Giovanni and Elisa lived and that was Andrea's home before Giuseppina took him to Italy four years earlier.

Andrea ran up the stairs to his parents' apartment and pounded on the door, Giuseppina trailing with the luggage. There was no response. Andrea pounded on the door again and shouted, "Mamma, Papà, it's me!" Finally, the door opened. An obviously ill Giovanni stood in the doorway and threw his arms around Andrea, hugging him and patting his back. Giuseppina looked at her brother with alarm.

"Where's mamma," Andrea asked.

"Oh, Andrea. You have grown so big," Giovanni said, as he continued to hug Andrea. "We have missed you terribly."

"I've missed you, too, papà. Is mamma home? Where is she?"

They stepped into the apartment but before Giovanni could reply, heavy coughing could be heard in the bedroom in the rear of the apartment.

"Is mamma sick?" Andrea asked, and then he ran into the bedroom where he saw his mother lying in bed, wheezing, coughing and clearly in great distress. Elisa tried to wave Andrea back, but she was too weak. Andrea went over to the

215

bed and threw his arms around his mother. He began to cry as he realized that she was very ill.

"Mamma, what's wrong?" he asked. "Papà, Zia Giuseppina, why is mamma so sick?

Giovanni walked over to Andrea and gently took him by the shoulders.

"Mamma has the Spanish Flu, Andrea," was all he could manage to say.

Elisa looked up at Andrea. Her brow was perspiring from the fever and she looked pale and very weak.

"I love you, Andrea. I am so happy to see you," she managed to say. "You are such a big boy now. I don't want you to worry. I'll be better soon. But right now, please go with your father. I don't want you to catch the flu, too."

Giuseppina was completely dismayed by the scene before her. However, she knew that Elisa was correct and that they had to protect Andrea from contracting the flu. It seemed that Giovanni had already come down with it. Giuseppina thought about the quarantine that they had just experienced on Ellis Island and realized that it was necessary for both her and Andrea to avoid as much direct contact with either Giovanni or Elisa as was possible.

"Giovanni, has a doctor seen either you or Elisa?" she asked.

"I called Doctor Lauzetta; however, so many people are ill with the flu that he hasn't been able to get here yet. He said that he would be here as soon as possible."

While Giuseppina and Andrea were on Ellis Island the medical staff held several briefings about the Spanish Flu during which they said the disease was highly contagious; however, there were preventative measures people could take to avoid catching it. The health officials recommended avoiding physical contact with people who were ill with the disease. They urged people to wear gauze masks when in the presence of ill persons and wash their hands frequently and thoroughly. They told them how to disinfect bedding, towels, and even clothes worn by ill people with a carbolic acid solution and they emphasized the need to maintain proper nutrition and avoid physical and emotional stress, which could lower a person's immune system.

The medical staff on Ellis Island candidly said that there was not much that could be done once a person contracted the disease except to let it run its course. They said that the ill person should be given aspirin to relieve pain, plenty of fluids to maintain hydration, dry crackers with light soup or broth, and whatever soft food the patient could tolerate. In addition to aspirin, cold packs helped to reduce the fever. In some cases, patients received enemas to cleanse the colon as often as twice a day. With this knowledge, Giuseppina immediately took charge and began doing what she could to care for Elisa and Giovanni, while at the same time protecting her and Andrea from catching the disease.

A few days later, Doctor Lauzetta made a visit to the apartment. He examined both Giovanni and Elisa thoroughly and then checked Giuseppina and Andrea. Doctor Lauzetta said that there was nothing more that he could do than what Giuseppina was already doing. He promised to make another visit in a couple of days. As he left the apartment he looked at Giuseppina and shook his head sadly.

Several times each day, Andrea went to the doorway of his parent's bedroom. He watched his mother's labored breathing and winced each time she had a coughing spell – ever more frequently, now. The doctor strictly forbade Andrea from entering the room. However, when his mother was awake, he would blow her kisses and she would weakly wave to him. It was such a terrible sadness for an eight-year old boy to bear.

***

Luigi trudged back to the construction shanty that served as his job site office and poured himself another cup of hot coffee from the thermos Ines had packed. Then he took an almond biscotti out of his lunch bucket and enjoyed a morning snack. That morning, after Ines sent the children off to school, she and her neighbor from across the street hurried to catch the Hilliard Road trolley. They were on their way to Fazzio's market to buy a fresh perch or pike for the night's supper and freshly killed chickens that they planned to pluck and singe for Sunday's *pranzo*.

In Rivergaro, it was already late afternoon. Evangelina and Maria were washing dishes, quite pleased that almost a dozen patrons had stopped by Bellaria for *pranzo*. If the *trattoria* had a good weekend, there might be enough extra money to buy the new tablecloths that Evangelina wanted for the main dining room. Emilio and Pietro were down at the *mulino* where Silvio was cutting planks that he needed to repair a customer's *stalla*. Giuseppe was helping his younger

218

brother repair bicycles for Rivergaro's race team in the workshop and Nino had gone off with his friends to explore the ruins of the Statto Castle on the other side of the Trebbia.

In New York, Giuseppina kissed the forehead of her beloved sister-in-law, walked over to the bedroom dresser, and stopped the clock. Then she went into the parlor and hugged a sobbing Andrea and his grieving father.

***

Ines heard the clattering of the engine of Luigi's Ford as it pulled into the back yard. She peeked out the rear window of the kitchen and waved as he closed the garage door and climbed the three steps of the back stoop. She knew what he was going to say the moment he opened the door.

"Ines, we have to do something about that damn walnut tree. I swear that it is possessed and is hell-bent on destroying my car."

"Yes, dear," Ines replied. "But, don't forget how much you like the shade it gives in the summer and you don't seem to mind when I make walnut liquor in the fall."

"Umm," Luigi grunted, in his typical response when he really did not know how better to reply.

"Where are the *ragazzi*?" he asked.

Ines went to the hallway door and hollered, "Lina, Emilio, your father is home."

The two came bounding into the kitchen, gave Luigi their customary hug, and just as quickly ran back in to the parlor

219

where they were running up and down the stairs leading to the second floor, making all kinds of a ruckus.

Luigi opened a cupboard above the kitchen counter and reached for a bottle of Haig & Haig. The telephone rang and Ines answered it. She looked at Luigi and said, "It's Giuseppina and she's crying."

Luigi grabbed the phone from Ines and in rapid Italian asked, "Giuseppina, *perché piangi*? Why are you crying?"

His face turned white and he clutched the counter as she said, "*Se n'è andata, Luigi. La nostra amata Elisa è morta.* She is gone, Luigi. Our beloved Elisa is dead."

"Oh my God," he said, as he handed the phone back to Ines. "She's dead, she's dead," he cried out in English. Then he walked over to the kitchen table, sat down in his chair and began to cry like a baby.

Ines could barely control her own emotions. She understood that Elisa had died and she did her best to learn the details. Both Luigi and she had known that Elisa was suffering from the flu, but neither had known how serious her illness was. Giuseppina was barely able to tell her about Elisa's final hours and how all during the preceding night, she struggled until she was so weak that her heart could beat no longer.

The children came into the kitchen sensing that something was terribly wrong. Giovanni was unable to speak with anyone, so Ines told Giuseppina that she would call her in the morning. She hung up the phone and told the children as gently as possible that their aunt had gone to heaven. Then, she went over to Luigi, put her arm around his shoulder and held is hand, doing her best to hold back her own tears. She had never before seen him cry and felt helpless to ease his inconsolable pain.

It was fortunate that the next day was Saturday; Luigi was still not in an emotional state where he could have gone to work. However, the family at Bellaria had to be informed about Elisa's death. This was January, 1920. Transatlantic telephone lines were still in the experimental stage. The only way to contact the family was by letter, even though it would take several weeks to reach them. After Luigi wrote the short letter, he addressed it to his father only, knowing that Emilio would break the tragic news as gently as possible to Luigi's mother and siblings.

In New York, the effects of the Spanish Flu were so devastating that cemeteries were overloaded and burials were rushed. A wake was held for Elisa in her and Giovanni's apartment and was attended by many friends and restaurant patrons. After a hurried funeral Mass at Saint Ann's Church, Elisa was buried at Calvary Cemetery in Queens, New York on Monday, February 2, 1920. Only Giuseppina, Andrea, and friends of the family were able to attend her funeral. Giovanni was too sick with the Spanish Flu to attend and it was impossible for Luigi to make the necessary travel arrangements in the short period between Elisa's death and her burial.

***

The weather was particularly unpleasant in Rivergaro this February. Snow alternated with periods of freezing rain to make each day seemingly more miserable than the previous one. It was impossible to do any work outdoors. Even feeding the livestock that was sheltered in the *stalla* down by the river was a difficult challenge. Because of this, everyone in the family at Bellaria stayed indoors as much as possible. There were no guests at the inn or restaurant in this weather, so Emilio and his sons were doing some much needed interior maintenance. Evangelina and Maria were busy pressing bed linens and tablecloths.

The front door of Bellaria opened and Marcello, the mail carrier from Rivergaro, walked in with a bundle of mail Evangelina would later have to sort and place in the store's mail cubicles. Evangelina offered to make him a cup of hot caffè, but he declined saying he still had to go to Travo and wanted to get there before the weather turned even worse.

After Marcello left, Evangelina noticed a letter from Luigi that was addressed to Emilio. The postmark was Saturday, January 30. She took it to Emilio, who wondered aloud why Luigi would address a letter to him alone. Emilio opened the envelope and took out the letter. By this time, his comment had aroused the curiosity of Maria and her brothers, who all gathered around their father as he read Luigi's letter in silence.

My Dearest Papà,

I have the most terrible news that I must tell you. A few weeks ago, our beloved Elisa, became ill with the Spanish Flu. She struggled bravely to resist the disease, but yesterday morning, Friday, January 30, at 9:00 she died in the presence of Giovanni, who also is seriously ill with the flu, Andrea and Giuseppina.

According to Giuseppina, who called yesterday to inform me about Elisa's death, the doctor did everything possible to bring her back to health, but to no avail.

Ines and I join you, mamma, and all of our family at Bellaria in grieving for Elisa and we pray that she now rests in peace with Almighty God.

I will write to you again as soon as I have more information about her death and burial. I love you all very much.

Your son,

Luigi

As he read the letter, Emilio felt a knot tighten in the pit of his stomach. A wave of nausea briefly swept over him and his legs almost buckled. Then, as calmly and gently as he could, his voice cracking with emotion, he broke the news to the rest of his family. Maria uttered a cry so mournful that you knew it came from the depth of her soul. Evangelina sobbed, tottered, and would have collapsed if it were not for Pietro and Giuseppe who rushed over to steady her. Emilio clutched his wife tenderly, trying to console her while at the same time grappling with his own grief. Antonio and Nino did their best to console Maria.

Pietro saw how distraught his father was and sent Giuseppe to Statto to inform Silvio and his brother about the tragedy, and Antonio to Rivergaro to find Elvira. He asked Nino to remain at Bellaria to help as might be needed. Although Pietro and his brothers were stunned by the news, they were able to deal with it a little better than Maria or their parents. They were all much younger than Elisa was and had not shared as much of their lives with her as had their parents, Maria and Elvira.

An hour later, a shocked Elvira burst into Bellaria with her husband Severino and Antonio. Tears flowed once again as the three women shared their grief and disbelief. When Emilio saw that the women were all right, he stepped outside of Bellaria unnoticed into the light rain and gloom. He walked over to his favorite table on the terrace where on a clear day he could easily see his old Statto house, the house of Elisa's birth and early childhood. He sat down in the drizzle, unmindful about the cold that was beginning to penetrate to his skin. He put his head in his hands and remembered the treasured moments that he had with his beautiful daughter; how happy and full of life she was. It was as though any moment she would come bounding out from Bellaria and this would be nothing more than a bad dream. Then his stoic facade broke and for one of the few times in his life, he gave in to his grief and sobbed uncontrollably. Above him, rain steadily dripped off the weathered tile roof, as though Bellaria, itself, sensed the loss of a loved member of its family and was sharing in his grief. Elisa would never come home.

Inside Bellaria, Pietro abruptly noticed Emilio's absence. He and his brothers made a hasty search of the house and then Pietro ran outside. He found Emilio, now completely drenched from the cold rain, just as his uncles Silvio and Giuseppe arrived. Together, they got Emilio back inside Bellaria, seated him in front of the fireplace, and wrapped a warm blanket around him.

Chapter 19

ONE OF THE REASONS BELLARIA was successful as a business was a clear and efficient division of labor with respect to serving Bellaria's *trattoria* patrons. For the most part, Evangelina and Maria prepared food in the kitchen, cleared tables, and washed the dishes and silverware. Nino was the waiter. He took patrons' orders and served them their meals and beverages. Pietro and Giuseppe alternated as backups; Pietro was now married and both he and Giuseppe worked elsewhere most of the time. Antonio was busy with the bicycle shop so he was not directly involved in the *trattoria* or *locanda*. Emilio's role was that of a typical proprietor. He greeted patrons at the reception counter, showed the patrons to their tables, strolled through the dining areas, chatted with patrons and handled the money. He also frequently gazed at the beautiful, portrait photograph of his daughter Elisa mounted on the wall immediately behind his chair at the reception counter.

Five years had passed since Elisa's tragic death. Although the formal period of mourning was long past, her memory would never be forgotten. A very dejected Giovanni Guasconi had given the photograph to Emilio and Evangelina when he brought Andrea back to Italy only months after Elisa's passing. Giovanni gave up his interest in the restaurant that he and Elisa had owned and instead considered opening one in Italy. However, for the next few years he seemed to flounder, unable to put his grief behind him. Then, about a year ago, a friend from New York contacted Giovanni and strongly urged him to return there to open a new restaurant.

At first, Giovanni was unenthusiastic about the idea. However, Italy's economy was in shambles. The country emerged from World War I heavily in debt. Unemployment was staggering and riots and strikes were occurring in most major cities – especially in Milan. These disastrous conditions gave rise to a new social concept called Fascism, in which the state controlled most aspects of individual life, but where free enterprise and the right to own property was still allowed. This concept was sharply in conflict with another new social concept in Italy called Communism. It was clear to Giovanni that under these conditions there was no way he could open a business and remain in Italy, so he decided to accept his friend's suggestion and return to America. Evangelina tried to persuade Giovanni to allow Andrea to stay with them at Bellaria, but Giovanni insisted that Andrea accompany him back to New York.

At Bellaria, the afternoon was proceeding as usual. Several *trattoria* patrons and *locanda* guests were enjoying *pranzo*. Evangelina, Maria, and Nino were going about their normal routine. Emilio was sitting outside of Bellaria enjoying the July sun and, as usual, one of his favorite stogies. Unexpectedly, two motorcycles, accompanying the most magnificent, deep maroon limousine Emilio had ever seen pulled up in front of Bellaria. The nameplate on the grill of the automobile identified it as an Isotta-Fraschini, a luxury, custom-built vehicle only the wealthiest – or most powerful – could afford.

It was a convertible with the top in the up and locked position and with real glass side windows. A wide running board extended fully between the front and rear wheel wells on both sides of the automobile. On each side of the vehicle, immediately behind the front wheel well, was a large spare tire seated in a black metal tire boot. However, what made Emilio truly take notice were the two oversized headlights to which were affixed flags displaying the gold "Fasces," a bundle of rods around an axe. Originally an ancient Roman symbol of authority, it had now been adopted by the Fascisti (Fascists) as their authority symbol. Only someone of great importance in the Fascist movement – perhaps even Mussolini, himself – would be allowed the status of that automobile.

The two motorcyclists wore black helmets and black shirts with grey trousers. Two other men got out of the front seat of the limousine; one, who also wore a black shirt, was apparently the driver. The other was a man in his forties. He wore a light-weight tan suit with buttoned collar and a narrow tie, and a dark brown, checkered Berteil driving cap. The two "Black Shirts," who had ridden the motorcycles, came over to Emilio, told him to get up, put his hands over his head and then they frisked him. They demanded his identification card and his Fascist Party Card. Emilio had no idea about what they were asking and simply told them his name and that he was the proprietor of Bellaria. The man wearing the Berteil driving cap looked on with amusement.

The driver said something to the occupants within the vehicle and opened the passenger-side rear door. A beautiful, very elegantly dressed woman, who was likely in her mid-thirties, stepped out. She looked around, taking in the scene of Bellaria set against the hills across the Trebbia. The driver quickly walked to the drivers-side of the limousine, opened the other rear door and stood at attention as a distinguished looking man, perhaps ten years older than the woman, exited the luxurious motor vehicle. He was dressed in a grey, pinstriped suit, black shirt and a red and grey patterned tie. A gold pin with diamond studs protruded through the rounded collars of his shirt.

The same "Black Shirt" who had frisked Emilio ordered him into the *trattoria* in full view of the gaping diners. The "Black Shirt" looked around and saw that the *trattoria* had two dining rooms plus a terrace. He told Emilio to set a table on the terrace for three people and a second table in the main dining room for another three. Then he went back outside and he and the second "Black Shirt" motorcyclist escorted the lady, the man of obvious importance and the man with the Berteil cap into Bellaria and through the dining rooms to their now set table on the terrace. When the three were seated, the "Black Shirts" took a set table inside the main dining room with a full view of the terrace for themselves.

Emilio asked his unexpected guests if they would like something to drink. The man wearing the Berteil cap spoke first,

"I heard you tell Decimo, referring to the "Black Shirt who had frisked Emilio, "that your name is Emilio. Is that correct?"

"Yes, signore, my name is Emilio Tagliaferri."

"Do you know the Families Barilla, Lanzano, and Ferruci?"

Emilio nodded that he knew them, wondering why he was being asked that question.

"Yes, of course you do," said the man with the Berteil Cap. "They are all loyal fascists, known to our people in Rivergaro. That is why we stopped here today. They were asked where we might find a quiet *trattoria* that had good food and service and also a pleasant panorama. They recommended Bellaria, a place operated by an Emilio Tagliaferri and his family.

"Tell me, Emilio, are you and your family loyal fascists?"

Emilio did not know what to say. He was obviously uncomfortable, and was fumbling to say something when the other man said,

"Later, Costante. We will talk about that later. Right now let the man bring us a bottle of his finest wine and a nice antipasto of cold meats and local cheese."

Then, he turned toward Emilio and said,

"Go, Emilio, be about your business. And do so quickly."

Emilio said, "*Si, signore,* immediately," and he rushed to the kitchen. He alerted Evangelina and Maria to what was happening and told them that whatever the guests ordered, they should make sure it was made to perfection. Then, he told Nino to serve the three "Black Shirts" now seated in the dining room adjacent to the terrace whatever they wanted – no questions asked. Pietro came in to the kitchen from the rear of the building and asked what was going on.

Evangelina told him to "clean up" immediately, help serve the other diners and to be on stand-by for whatever else might arise. The family was now fully mobilized for this unusual event.

Emilio returned to the terrace, bearing two bottles of his best wine. One was a sparkling red Gutturnio Frizzante, a favorite of northern Italians, especially of the Milanese, who Emilio suspected were his guests because Milan was a major center of fascism. The second bottle was a white Malvasia varietal that was a blend of Malvasia and Trebbiano wines. The man called Costante tasted the wines and indicated satisfaction with both, much to Emilio's relief. Emilio poured a glass of the Malvasia for each of the three people and then went back to the kitchen to retrieve an exquisite plate of antipasto that he quickly served to the guests on the terrace. As he turned to leave, the older man spoke.

"Do you know who I am, Emilio?"

"Forgive me, signore, but, no, I do not."

"My name is Arturo Bocchini. The gentleman to my left is Doctor Costante Leopardi, an attorney and an old friend of mine. We studied law together at the University of Naples. The three men in your dining room have been assigned to make sure that nothing unpleasant happens to me or my friends. The beautiful lady to my right shall remain unnamed. However, she is from Piacenza, which is why we are passing through this area. My close friend Benito Mussolini has just appointed me Prefect of Genoa, where we are now going. The drive through the Val Trebbia to Genoa is much more relaxing than going through Milan, wouldn't you say?"

Emilio's heart practically stopped when he heard who his guest was. Arturo Bocchini was reported to be one of Mussolini's most trusted lieutenants, and one of the most ruthless. He had previously been Prefect of Bologna and before that Prefect of Brescia. It was said that he played a major role in the rise of the Fascist Party and had accompanied Mussolini on his March on Rome in 1922, the uprising that resulted in Mussolini being appointed the head of the Italian government.

"The Val Trebbia is very beautiful," Emilio said, carefully wording his response in a way that he hoped would preclude further conversation.

"Yes, well, we are ready to order," Doctor Leopardi said. He then ordered the same *pranzo* selection for all three, the house special that began with potato gnocchi in marinara sauce and continued on to roast pork with locally grown vegetables. And, more wine, of course.

By this time most of the other patrons of the *trattoria* had quickly finished their meals and departed the restaurant; some had even left their meals unfinished and had simply exited Bellaria as rapidly as they could. In the main dining room, the three "Black Shirts" ate their meals in near silence, while out on the terrace Arturo Bocchini and his two guests were engaged in a lively conversation about politics and were enjoying their meals to the fullest.

Emilio stood attentively near the terrace ready to respond to any request that his guests might make. Nino stood by the quiet, nearly sullen, "Black Shirts" as they finished their meals. The driver went back out to the Isotta-Fraschini to make sure that no one was tampering with it. One of the other "Black Shirts" stood guard next to the doorway leading to the terrace while the third found the kitchen where he stood arms folded staring at the women, his eyes mostly on Maria – intimidating, but not threatening.

When Emilio saw that Arturo Bocchini and the other two terrace guests had finished their meals, he cleared their table and informed them that the dessert selection for the day was ricotta cheesecake with fresh whipped cream. Bocchini looked at his female guest with wide eyes, she smiled and nodded, and he immediately ordered the cheesecake and espresso for all three of them.

Emilio hoped that when the three guests on the terrace finished their dessert and caffè his family's ordeal would end. He could not have been more mistaken. Doctor Leopardi ordered another round of caffè for all three and when Emilio brought it out he said,

"Now, Emilio, please bring all of your family here."

Every nerve in Emilio's body tensed, however, he thought it best to comply with this order – at least for now.

When Evangelina, Maria, Pietro, and Nino were assembled on the terrace with Emilio, Leopardi asked where Giuseppe and Antonio were. Emilio could not believe that Leopardi knew so much about his family. He explained that both of the boys were in Rivalta helping their uncles repair a *mulino* near the Castello di Rivalta.

232

"Ah, that would be their uncles Silvio and Giuseppe," Leopardi said.

A cold chill ran through Emilio as he realized that these people knew far more about his family than he could have imagined. And, for what purpose, he wondered? This was intimidating and frightening.

"Very well," Doctor Leopardi continued, as Arturo Bocchini watched every move and every body language expression that Emilio and his family made. All he saw was fear and apprehension.

"You read the newspapers and talk with your amici in Piazza Grande as you sip your caffè and enjoy your cigars," he said. "What do you think about the economic and social conditions here in Italy right now?"

Emilio strained to think how to respond in a way that would not jeopardize his family.

"I am not a politician, *signore*, just a…"

Leopardi cut him off impatiently.

"Yes, yes, but you are someone of importance in this comune, so I want to hear your views and I want you to be clear and unambiguous about them. So, again, how do you feel about the conditions in Italy now- today?"

"They are better than they were even three years ago," Emilio said. "For several years after the war, no one could find a job. There was a shortage of everything, including food. Everyone here in Rivergaro knows about the terrible riots in Milan, Bologna, and even Rome. There were gangs everywhere, looting, and robbing, even here in Rivergaro."

Arturo Bocchini spoke up.

"Do you know why things are better now, Emilio?"

"Ah, well, I guess that the government is doing a better job now," Emilio replied, stumbling for words.

"Not the government," Bocchini declared emphatically. "Things are better now because Il Duce (the title meaning 'Chief' that Mussolini had adopted) is in command and because we fascists are getting rid of corruption, waste, and inefficiency in the government. Many more people have jobs today than in 1922. Modern roads, highways, and railroad lines are being built. The economy is improving, people have enough to eat, and lawlessness is no longer tolerated - all because of fascism, Emilio. I want you to remember that - all of you."

Emilio and his family stood speechless at the lecture that they had just received.

"Now, there is one more thing," Arturo Bocchini said. He beckoned to the "Black Shirt" standing in the doorway. When the man came over, he whispered something in his ear. The "Black Shirt" briskly left the terrace, returning a few moments later with one of the fascist flags that had been attached to the headlight of the limousine.

"Earlier this year, the Italian Parliament proclaimed Il Duce, Dictator of Italy. Now, many things are going to happen and they will happen fast. It is necessary that all community leaders become members of the Fascist Party and support fascism completely. However, there will be mistakes, as some things might be done in haste.

"My guests and I have had a very delightful afternoon here in your Bellaria. Your food and service was exceptional. In lieu of payment for all of this, which I know you would refuse, I am giving you this flag." He took a pen out of his jacket pocket, wrote an inscription in the gold field of the lictors, the axe-headed bundle of rods, set against a solid black background and handed the flag to Emilio.

"A time may come when you will need this," he said. "If so, you will know what to do with it."

Then, without further fanfare, Arturo Bocchini, Doctor Costante Leopardi, and the unnamed lady stood up from the table and walked directly to their waiting limousine. A moment later, the automobile sped off in the direction of Bobbio.

Emilio and those of his family who were present were completely shaken by the experience.

"Papà," said Maria, "What should I do with the flag? We are not fascists?"

"Do nothing with it now, except put it somewhere where we can get it if needed," Emilio said. "I don't know what Signor Bocchini is talking about, but I am sure that he knows much more about what is to come than we do."

Maria stared once again at the flag and at the inscription that Arturo Bocchini wrote on it. She folded the flag and placed it under the reception counter, wondering what fascism had to do with any of them at Bellaria. It would not be long before she found out.

Bellaria di Rivergaro

Chapter 20

IT WAS 1:00 AM IN THE MORNING. Maria was having trouble sleeping. So was almost everyone else at Bellaria. The previous day was one of the hottest days of the summer. Temperatures were well up in the forties (centigrade) and stubbornly refused to cool down, even as night fell. Adding to the discomfort, the usual cool evening breeze coming down from the Alta Val Trebbia failed to materialize. The air was very still.

Maria turned restlessly in her bed and then decided to get up and write a letter to Luigi, or more accurately to Ines. Luigi was not much of a letter writer. She went downstairs to the kitchen, made herself a cup of caffè, and cut an apricot-filled cornetto in half. Next, she went out to Bellaria's lobby where she found a quill pen, jar of ink and sheet of letter paper in a drawer behind the counter. Then, she returned to the kitchen, sat down at the heavy wood table and began to write, occasionally nibbling at the cornetto, and sipping the caffè.

Maria wrote about all of the family happenings in Rivergaro – the homey things that the women of the family talk about when they get together. She informed Ines that in the fall, Luigi's brother Giuseppe planned to marry a lovely local girl named Natalina Ruffi and that Elvira's son Armando just made his first Holy Communion. She mentioned that Pietro and Paola's daughter Elisa was now twelve years old and was becoming a very lovely young lady. Maria wrote that on Ferragosto, August 15, the family planned to attend Holy Mass and then, after Mass, they would go back down to the Piazza Grande to enjoy the festival. She had just finished the letter when her mother entered the kitchen, not being able to catch much sleep in the heat, herself.

"Mamma, you worry me," Maria said. "You look like you haven't slept in a week. You are working too much, again. Maybe we should hire someone to help us with the *trattoria* and *locanda* so you don't have to do as much."

"I'm fine, darling. Nobody can sleep in this heat. Anyway, what is there to worry about? You take such good care of papà and me."

Earlier in the year, Maria celebrated her fortieth birthday. She was still single, not that she would have hesitated to marry if the right man came along; but none did - not yet. She was very devoted to her parents and was concerned that both of them had begun to show their age. Emilio was now seventy-nine and Evangelina was sixty-five years old, but she seemed to look even older. She had always been petite, however now she seemed to be not so much petite as frail.

Emilio was definitely slowing down. However, he still rode his bicycle into Rivergaro every day to play cards with his friends. He occasionally did some carpentry work, building or repairing a *mulino* here or there, and kept active fussing about Bellaria's *trattoria* and *locanda*. However, more frequently he could be found just sitting outside Bellaria at his favorite table, snoozing with the ashes from his cigar dropping down to burn small holes in his vest.

Maria loved both of her parents very much and was happy that fate left it to her to take care of them – a role, she knew, would become even more important in the future.

"Mamma, we need to get some sleep. It is after two in the morning and we have a big day ahead. There is church, then the Ferragosto festival and then we must be back here to get everything ready for the Zangrandi birthday party in the evening."

"I almost forgot about the Zangrandi's party," Evangelina said. "How old will Carmela be?"

"Fifty-five," Maria answered. "They made a reservation for twenty-three, including grandchildren, so we will have to use the main dining room."

Evangelina nodded sleepily and the two women climbed the stairs to their bedrooms, hoping to catch a little sleep before sunrise.

***

After Mussolini came to power, the fascist regime in Italy instituted various policy changes and programs designed to capture the loyalty of the country's labor force. Many of these programs failed, however one that achieved considerable success was the Opera Nazionale Dopolavoro or OND, the Italian national recreation and leisure organization. The OND sponsored heavily subsidized vacation trips and tours to spas and tourists attractions in the mountains and along the seashore that would otherwise have been unaffordable for the average Italian worker. Customarily, the OND also organized elaborate festivals throughout Italy on the holiday of Ferragosto. They used the occasion as a means to promote both national unity and the propaganda goals of the Fascist Party.

In Rivergaro, Ferragosto 1933 was planned to be a spectacular event. The holiday evolved from a festival introduced in 18 BC by the Roman Emperor Augustus. Originally intended as a secular holiday, the Catholic Church eventually claimed the date as a Holy Day to celebrate the Assumption of the Virgin Mary to Heaven. Because of this, Ferragosto always began with the faithful attending Holy Mass, either at Sant'Agata or at the Santuario della Madonna delle Grazie del Castello, The Sanctuary of Our Lady of Grace of the Castle. This year, Emilio and his family intended to meet at the Piazza Grande in Rivergaro and walk the half kilometer up Via Castello to attend the 10:00 AM Mass at the Santuario. Then they would return down the hill and attend the holiday celebration in the Piazza Grande.

The Santuario is located on top of the hill overlooking Rivergaro and the Trebbia. It was originally a private chapel in the tenth century castle of San Giacomo, upon the ruins of which it stands. There were still traces of the original chapel, although the actual structure of the building was reconstructed in the late 1800s to give the bell tower and façade a neoclassical look. The interior of the Santuario was attractive, but not as beautiful as the interior of Sant'Agata. On each side of a center aisle, there were ten pews. Together they could accommodate less than one hundred parishioners. There was standing room in the back of the church for perhaps another twenty people.

Bellaria di Rivergaro

A twelfth century statue of the Madonna was on a
pedestal in front and to the left of the main altar. Farther to
the left, in a niche in the wall of the short nave, was a statue of
San Giacomo, the patron saint of the castle that originally
stood on the site. An ornate reredos above the tabernacle in
the center of the altar housed a gold monstrance, which was a
receptacle for the Sacred Host. A marble Communion rail
guarded the altar itself.

The walk up the steep slope of Via Castello was difficult
for Emilio and Evangelina. Therefore, neither had a problem
with the younger members of the family taking the lead up
the hill while they brought up the rear. When they reached
the top of the hill, the family paused for breath on the flat
stone terrace of the church, admiring the view of the town
and river below. Then, they climbed the last two stone steps
and entered the small, narrow sanctuary that because of its
diminutive size might better have been called a chapel, like
the original structure.

The order of the rite of the Holy Mass is standard
throughout the world: Procession to the altar including
greeting, opening, and penitential prayers; Liturgy of the
Word with scripture readings; Liturgy of the Eucharist;
Communion Rite; and Concluding Rite. The offertory
collection is part of the Liturgy of the Eucharist. Antonio was
one of the ushers passing the baskets for the offertory
collection. When he completed passing the basket to his side
of the aisle, and to a handful of standing people, he saw that
he collected only 325 lire. His fellow usher did a little better
and collected 365 lire. The fascist government had fixed the
value of Italian currency at 19 lire to one American dollar.

That feast day's collection, therefore, yielded the equivalent of about thirty-six American dollars – not very much to operate a church until next week's collection.

However, the paltry collection that day fazed neither Antonio, nor the parish priest nor even his bishop. Italian Catholic churches did not rely on contributions from parishioners for their subsistence. Mussolini and the Vatican had reached an accord by which the Church would keep out of Italian politics (except for those concerning the Vatican City, which Italy and most of the Western World recognized as an independent city-state). In turn, Mussolini gave the Catholic Church a monopoly on religion in Italy. In other words, Catholicism was the officially recognized state religion with the exclusive right to teach religious classes in all state schools. Further, a percentage of the tax revenue collected by the Italian government was allocated to the support of the Catholic Church, including the salaries of its clergy and the support and maintenance of the physical infrastructure of the Church.

Antonio returned to his seat and the Mass continued. The parishioners sat, rose, or knelt in accordance with the rite of the Mass. Everyone carried a prayer book to church; however, none was needed. The diligent nuns at Sant'Agata Catholic School had long ago drilled the prescribed prayers into the memories of the faithful. At Holy Communion, all but five people went up to the altar railing, knelt and received the Sacred Host. As the faithful returned to their seats, many wondered why those five people had not received Holy Communion. Had they broken their fast or perhaps committed a mortal sin? It was quite awkward not to receive Holy Communion with everyone else.

After church, the family made its way back down Via Castello, into Piazza Grande. Some type of event was happening everywhere they looked. As they passed through the piazza, they saw files of Balilla youth, ages eight to fourteen, neatly dressed in black shirts, black cap, grey shorts, and grey socks marching to patriotic music under fascist banners and flags.

Piazza Grande was restricted to pedestrian traffic only and the various cafés had set extra tables and chairs to accommodate the many festivalgoers. In the center of the piazza was a large speaker's platform covered with banners in the green, white, and red colors of the Italian flag with the fascist symbol of bundled axe-headed rods in the center. Large photographs of Il Duce with patriotic sayings were displayed everywhere. In front of the platform, a group of Avanguardisti, the fascist youth group that all young people ages fourteen to eighteen were required to join, were playing tug of war under the supervision of an adult fascist leader dressed in his black cap and grey uniform with knickers and black boots.

Emilio and Evangelina looked at each other and then at the rest of the family. No one was smiling. Pietro whispered something to Emilio, who suggested the family grab a few tables outside of the Café Italia. Everyone readily agreed; they were all hungry and ready for caffè and pastry. A young woman came out to take their order. They recognized her as Pina Mezzardi, a former schoolmate of Giuseppe. Pina was dressed in a typical fascist young adult uniform consisting of a white blouse, black cap, grey and black tie, black skirt and black low-heel shoes. Emilio again looked at Evangelina and simply shook his head. Giuseppe, who was with his fiancé Natalina Ruffi, did his best to avoid his father's gaze. Elvira and Severino looked out at the crowd.

Emilio ordered colazione for everyone and then sat back and lit up a stogie. A few minutes later, Pina returned with enough pastry and coffee to ensure that no one would be hungry again until the late afternoon. When everyone had eaten his or her fill, Emilio said that Evangelina had a slight headache and that he was going to take her back to Bellaria. As for everyone else, he said *"Come vuoi,"* or "Do what you want." Emilio paid the café bill, helped Evangelina get up and together with Maria began to leave the festival. It was abundantly clear that he did not approve what he saw earlier. Emilio spotted Silvio and Giuseppe and their families, spoke with them for a few minutes and then walked back to where he left his car, with Evangelina and Maria.

Giuseppe and Natalina decided to stick around and observe some of the athletic events planned for the early afternoon. Pietro, Severino and their families went their own ways. However, Antonio and Nino said that they were going back to Bellaria to help set up for the evening birthday event. Antonio retrieved his Moto Guzzi motorcycle from where he had parked it, told Nino to hop on the back and the two sped off in the direction of Bellaria. They were only a few hundred meters outside of Rivergaro when they saw two black shirts in their late teens beating a young man they recognized as Ernesto Bessi, who lived in Statto. They jumped off the motorcycle and ran to Bessi's aid.

244

"This is none of your business," one of the black shirts said. "This scum is anti-fascist and we're going to teach him a lesson."

"Like hell, you are," shouted Antonio, as both he and Nino pulled the young punks off Bessi. The second black shirt was about to throw a punch at Antonio when Bessi, now on his feet, tackled him from the rear. Antonio grabbed the wrist of the other black shirt with his powerful hand, twisting it behind the young man's back. Then he put his foot on the hapless black shirt's rear end and sent him sprawling in the dirt.

"Now, get out of here and go back to whatever hole you crawled out of," Nino said.

The two black shirts stood up and staggered away, but not before one of them turned and said, "I know who you are. You are from Bellaria. You will regret this, I swear." Then they ran off.

"What happened, Ernesto?" Antonio asked.

"I was on my way home from the festival when the *bastardi* stopped me and demanded to see my Fascist Party registration card. I told them to piss off. That's when they jumped me. My God, thanks for helping."

"This is getting pretty damn bad," Nino said. "I heard that last week a gang of the black shirts got some poor fellow from Pieve Dugliara, right outside of Rivergaro, and when he did not show them a Fascist Party card they tied him to a tree and forced castor oil down his throat."

Forcing someone, who was thought to be actively anti-fascist, to swallow castor oil was a favorite tactic of the black shirts. The castor oil quickly loosened the victim's bowels and resulted in the person uncontrollably soiling himself – a humiliating condition, as intended.

"Well, we better be prepared for something unpleasant," Antonio said. "They won't forget that we live at Bellaria."

***

With the help of Antonio and Nino, Maria and Evangelina did a splendid job of decorating the main dining room at Bellaria for the Zangrandi birthday party. Brightly colored paper streamers hung from the ceiling and on the wall was a large banner that read: *"Buon compleanno!"* wishing Carmela a Happy Birthday. Paper cutouts of the number "55" were on all of the tables. It was very festive.

About 8:00 PM, the birthday guests began arriving. Soon the main dining room filled with chatter and laughter. Earlier in the day, everyone in the birthday party had stuffed themselves at a *pranzo* held at the house of Carmela's sister. Consequently, tonight's supper would consist only of Bellaria's special pizza and bruschetta, followed by two types of dessert: a lemon, ricotta torta layered with mascarpone and topped with powdered sugar and a traditional tiramisu. As always, there would be an ample supply of wine, birra, and caffè.

Everyone was having a great time. Evangelina and Maria had just brought out more pizza and bruschetta, Nino was clearing the tables of those guests who had finished their meals, and Antonio was in the kitchen cleaning up as much as he could. Emilio sat at his chair behind the reception counter. Suddenly, the front door was kicked in with a crashing sound and a half-dozen black shirts in their mid-twenties stormed into Bellaria armed with clubs, an ax, and a jar of castor oil. Everyone in Bellaria froze in shock and terror at the intrusion. A few small children began to whimper, but their mothers did their best to calm them. Emilio stood up but remained behind the counter, the anger on his face more than palpable. Evangelina, Maria, and Nino stood silently waiting for what would come next.

A tall man in his late thirties, dressed in the uniform of a fascist officer, strutted into Bellaria, a leather riding stick in his right hand, slapping it against his cupped left hand. On his head was a grey wool fez with a thick black tassel made of silk threads. An insignia on both sides of his grey collar indicated that he held the rank of captain. He looked scornfully around the crowd until his gaze fixed on Nino, who was still holding a tray of plates that he had cleared from one of the tables. It was clear to everyone that something terrible was about to happen.

"I am captain Petrucci," the fascist officer said. Then, he turned to one of the black shirts, pointed at Nino and said, "Is he one of them?"

"Yes sir. His name is Nino and he was identified as one of the two men who interfered with the Avanguardisti who were administering discipline to a man who is disloyal to the regime."

"Where is the other man?" Petrucci asked.

Bellaria di Rivergaro

Antonio stepped out from the kitchen into the main dining room. His right hand clutching a butcher knife he kept concealed behind his back.

"I am that man," Antonio said, his eyes on the snickering black shirts impatiently waiting for orders to take their vengeance on Bellaria and its guests. Antonio knew that he might get himself killed; however, at the first move these *bastardi* made to harm anyone, he fully intended to go after the officer with the butcher knife he grasped.

Tension filled the room. The fascist officer again pointed at Nino and said, "Bring him here."

The black shirt standing closest to Nino grabbed his arm and jerked him forward, causing Nino to drop the tray of dishes that fell to the floor with a crash, adding to the tension. Antonio began to move to aid his brother, his right hand with the knife slowly beginning to come around, when a strong, authoritative voice from the doorway leading to the reception desk shouted,

"Stop! You had better look at this!"

Emilio walked into the room right up to the incredulous Petrucci. Glaring at the man, Emilio unfurled the black flag that had once adorned the headlight of the Isotta-Fraschini and handed it to the officer. Petrucci tore the flag from Emilio's hands, held it up, and looked at it. At once, his face turned white with fear and his hands began to tremble. He looked up at Emilio, whose face was filled with rage, and then back at the words that had been written on the flag years ago:

248

Bellaria di Rivergaro

"Bravo, Bellaria! Grazie a tutti.

Arturo Bocchini"

"Well done, Bellaria. Thanks to everyone," Bocchini had written.

Petrucci was terrified. He knew Bocchini was the head of the OVRA, Organization for Vigilance and Repression of Anti-Fascism, the dreaded Italian secret police. The flag that he was staring at could only mean that somehow these people at Bellaria had found favor with one of the most powerful and feared men in Italy. To show any disrespect to them was akin to committing suicide.

Petrucci snapped to attention, made the Roman salute that had been adopted by the fascists and said,

"There has been a terrible mistake. The people responsible for this error will be severely punished."

He turned and addressed Emilio and his family, who were now all huddled together.

"I beg your forgiveness," he said. Then he spun around on his heels, glared at the dumbfounded black shirts and shouted, "Out, out, you damn fools. Get out of here."

There was a mad rush for the door as the six black shirts dropped their weapons, ran outside, and jumped into the lorry that had brought them to Bellaria. Petrucci quickly joined them and the lorry sped off into the darkness.

Inside Bellaria, women and children were crying as the realization of the terrible danger that they all had been in fully hit them. Nino began picking up the fallen tray of plates. Antonio returned the cleaver to the kitchen and came back out to help. Evangelina and Maria hugged Carmela and told her how sorry they were that this horrible incident had happened on her birthday. However, Carmela said that she had just received one of the best birthday presents ever – seeing the black shirts, who reveled in terrorizing other people, themselves frightened out of their wits. Then one of the guests, a priest from Niviano, suggested that they should thank God that they had been saved from harm. In harmony, everyone knelt down on the stone floor of the *trattoria* as the priest led them in prayer.

Chapter 21

LUIGI DROVE HIS DARK GREEN, 1938 LASALLE up the driveway of his house and stopped in front of the garage. He left the engine running, got out of the car, and opened the garage door. When he returned to the car, a walnut from his least favorite tree fell on top of the car and clattered along the metal roof until it fell to the grass alongside of the paved driveway strip, laying among a couple of dozen others that had accumulated during the day. He hated that damn tree and once again vowed to cut it down. The problem was that Ines liked to gather the fallen walnuts; she ground them up and added them to a mascarpone torta or cookies and she used them to make delicious walnut liquor. Perhaps he would defer its execution a while longer.

When Luigi got in the house, Ines practically pushed a copy of the evening Cleveland Press in his face. She was obviously distraught.

"My God, Luigi, there's going to be another war!"

"What are you talking about," he said. He was annoyed at the greeting he received after another hard day at work.

"Look at this," Ines said. She opened the newspaper that she had curled in her hand and showed him the headlines:

HITLER INVADES POLAND

Luigi snatched the paper from Ines and began to read. According to the paper, at 4:45 AM that morning, Friday, September 1, 1939, without provocation, Hitler sent 1.5

251

million troops into Poland along its 1,750-mile border with German territories and sent hundreds of his Stuka dive bombers in a "blitzkrieg" attack on all major Polish cities.

Lina was at the kitchen sink peeling potatoes for the evening dinner.

"It's going to be a bad one, dad. I just hope that Mussolini does not get Italy involved. I always worry about Grandma, Grandpa, Aunt Maria, and the rest of the family over there."

"Mussolini is not as crazy as Hitler," Luigi asserted. "I can't imagine him doing something that stupid. According to the letters that we receive from Maria, things are bad enough over there – almost as bad as they were in the twenties."

"Well, they certainly seem to appreciate the occasional ten to twenty dollars that we send them. Ten dollars is almost 200 lire and that goes a lot farther at the grocery market over there than it does here," Ines added.

The sound of a car door slamming could be heard; a couple of minutes later the back door opened and Emil and Kay came in with little "Butchie." Emil, Luigi and Ines' son, was born "Emilio Luigi." However, as time passed Luigi and Ines decided to "Americanize" his name to "Emil Louis," the name that appeared on all of his school and work records. In fact, years ago, when Luigi thought about applying for U.S. citizenship, he used the name "Louis Emil" instead of the Italian form, "Luigi Emilio." However, to his close Italian amici and to Ines (and, of course to the family at Bellaria) he would always be "Luigi."

Lina wiped her hands in her apron and bent over to pick up her twenty-month old nephew who toddled over to her unsteadily. She picked him up and held him high in the air, much to his delight. Then she gave the smiling child to her mother saying, "Go say hi to grandma." Ines beamed as Lina passed Butchie to her. Butchie was the nickname that the boy had acquired from his immigrant grandmother Rose Petras, Kay's mother, who called him "Boochee" in a thick Slovak accent. In fact, the child was christened Louis Emil Tagliaferri, continuing a family tradition in which the first-born son was named after his grandfather, whether in English or in Italian.

"Did you hear the news about Hitler invading Poland?" Emil asked his father.

"How could I miss it," Luigi replied. "Your mother shoved the paper at me as soon as I got home from work."

Emil was also a carpenter and worked with his father in the Flats, but at a different job site. Emil's foreman, however, reported to Luigi.

"Italy is part of the Axis," Emil said. "Mussolini might have to join in the war. That would be bad news for the family at Bellaria. Then, if England and France get involved, it's the Great War all over again and eventually Roosevelt will have to send American troops over there."

Luigi sighed. At the moment, the conflict was far away from Italy, but who could know what might happen next. In the last war, Italy left the Axis and sided with the Allies. Perhaps, Mussolini would do the same this time.

"We'll have to wait and see," he said guardedly.

***

Luigi and the rest of the world would not have to wait for long. After occupying Poland, Germany relentlessly drove its army toward Paris, forcing the French Government to flee to Bordeaux. Although its military and economic infrastructure was totally unprepared for war, Mussolini claimed that he had no choice except to go the aid of his Axis partner. In June 1940, Italy joined the war and once again mobilized its population to fight and die for a cause they hardly understood. In Rivergaro and at Bellaria, fear and uncertainty prevailed as the people of the comune prepared for more hardship. Almost 5,000 miles away, Luigi and Ines had to confront their own challenges.

Once again, Ines greeted Luigi with a copy of the Cleveland Press when he got home from work. This time she was tearful and afraid. It was Friday, June 28. It seemed that bad news always happened on a Friday.

"What are we going to do, Luigi? They say that if we are not American citizens we have to register at the post office as resident aliens."

Luigi carefully read the evening newspaper. According to the headline story, Congress had passed something called the Alien Registration Act. That meant that all resident non-citizens had to register as Aliens at their local post office. They would be fingerprinted and given a registration card that they would be required to carry wherever they went. The article said that it was the patriotic duty of a resident non-citizen to register and that this was done for their protection and not persecution.

"I don't understand," he said. "It is true that we are not citizens of the United States, Ines, but we have lived here for almost forty years. Our children and grandchildren were born here. Our home is here – not in Italy. We have never gone back to Italy – not even for a visit. We have done everything possible to become 'Americanized' except for becoming citizens."

Lina was reading the newspaper article over his shoulders. "Dad, read further. Look what it says about restrictions on aliens."

"What? Where?" Luigi asked as he scanned down the column of the article. "It says that registered aliens must report any change in their address or employment to the post office," he said. Then he read further.

"It talks about aliens of German or Italian descent!" he exclaimed. "If the person is a fascist, anti-fascist, journalist, an Italian language instructor or a few other things, they can be restricted from traveling more than five miles from their homes. It also says they might have a curfew placed on them from 8:00 PM until 6:00 AM."

Ines was weeping softly, now.

"Mom, don't worry," Lina said. "Emil and I are both American citizens. We will protect you and dad. And, everyone here in the neighborhood will vouch that neither you nor dad have ever been a fascist or a supporter of Mussolini."

"I wonder if this affects Giovanni and Andrea," Ines said.

"I don't think so," Lina replied. "Andrea was born here in the United States and Giovanni became a naturalized citizen several years ago. However, it must affect Andrea's wife Paola. She is a resident alien like you and dad."

Three years earlier Andrea returned to Castel San Giovanni. He spent almost a year in Italy, visiting his relatives at Bellaria often. While in Castel San Giovanni, Andrea met and fell in love with Paola Maini. They married and after a few months, Paola accompanied Andrea back to New York. However, she had not yet become a naturalized American citizen.

Luigi was furious with the newspaper report. How could the government do this? Millions of Italian immigrants came over to this country to build a new life. In doing so, they had helped build a growing America. Italian immigrants were among the most loyal and dedicated supporters of American ideals and the American way of life. They were no threat to this country. However, he was also angry with himself for never following through on becoming a naturalized American citizen. It was just that, like several hundred thousand other Italian immigrants, he had never seen the need or benefit of doing so. Now he wondered if his failure to become an American citizen would result in a restriction on the freedoms that he and Ines enjoyed – or even their residency in America.

This past summer, for example, Luigi, Ines, and Lina had taken a month-long vacation. They drove in his new LaSalle all the way across the United States to California, following

256

Route 40, the Lincoln Highway. They stopped where they wanted, took photographs of whatever scenes they wanted and had a wonderful time. Was all of this now about to end – because of his Italian heritage?

Luigi handed the newspaper back to Ines. He was in no mood for dinner right now. He poured himself a double Haig & Haig, went into the living room, and sat down in his chair by the gas fireplace. He took a fresh Tampa cigar from the wood box on the table next to his chair, bit off one end, lit the cigar, and drew on it slowly. Then he sat back in the chair to be alone with his thoughts. This was bad news for him and his family in the United States. However, what about the family back in the old country? The United States was not even at war - but Italy was. What new hardships did this mean for his family at Bellaria?

Luigi rose to turn on the radio that was in a mahogany cabinet across the room from his chair. A framed photograph on the fireplace mantel caught his eye. Maria had sent the photograph to Luigi and Ines a few years ago. The photograph showed members of Emilio and Evangelina's immediate family, almost forty people, posing in front of Bellaria with Luigi's father and mother on the day that they celebrated their fiftieth wedding anniversary. Wistfully, he realized that two of the people missing from the photograph were he and Elisa.

***

It had been months since a letter from Luigi and Ines reached Bellaria. Even though Italy and the United States were not at war, both countries considered each other belligerent. Consequently, normal trade and communication was greatly reduced and restricted. However, it was still possible for an occasional letter to get through all of the political roadblocks and economic sanctions. Because of this, it was with excitement and anticipation that Maria opened the packet of three letters that had just arrived from Ines, the most recent postmarked five months ago. However, the others were over a year old. She opened the most recent letter first, scanned it quickly and then went back to the beginning and read it to her mother, who was sitting at the kitchen table cutting strips of coniglio that would be the main ingredient of tonight's rabbit stew.

"Ines said that they had a cold spring and that they were still having snow flurries in May, mamma."

"Well, it was colder than usual here, too," said Evangelina. "Now with winter setting in, it's cold again. What does she say about the family?"

"It seems that everyone is alright. Emil and Catherine moved from their apartment in Lakewood to the cottage near Lake Erie that Luigi and Ines own. They are so close to the lake that they can walk to the beach."

"Does she say anything about the baby?"

"Yes, your great grandson is fine. He will be three years old in January." Maria handed Evangelina one of the photographs enclosed with the letter. "Look, he's playing in the sandbox that Luigi made for him. He's so cute!"

The photograph showed a tussled hair little boy in a sun suit sitting in a sandbox. A child-size shovel was in his hand and he was filling a toy truck with sand.

"Who do you think he looks like?" Evangelina asked.

"Oh, he looks like Emil, for sure," Maria replied. "Not so much like his mother's side. Ines did say that he has some kind of bronchial problem. Last winter Catherine had to use a steam inhaler several times to help him breathe."

"Well, that's not good," Evangelina said. "We better make sure that he visits us when it's summer, not..." She paused, suddenly realizing that her great grandson lived many thousands of kilometers away. She wondered if this boy would ever see Bellaria and his extended family in Rivergaro.

"Did Ines say anything about Nino and Erminia or the baby?" Evangelina asked.

"No, nothing. That must mean that they never got our letters about Nino's marriage to Erminia."

"It's probably true, then, that since Italy sided with Germany and declared war against Britain and France few, if any, letters from here are getting through to America.

"Anything else?" Evangelina asked.

Maria opened and scanned the other two letters. She filled her mother in on the rest of the news from Ines. Everyone there was sad to learn that Emilio's older brother Giuseppe had died. They were glad that Emilio was still able to ride his bicycle into Rivergaro to meet with his old friends; but he should be very careful because a fall at his age would be dangerous. Ines wrote that under a new law, she and Luigi had to register with the government as resident aliens. However, that turned out not to be too much of an issue because Luigi has an important job building steel plants for the defense industry and he was exempt from all other restrictions on aliens. Of course, Ines asked how everyone at Bellaria was doing and whether anyone needed anything. Lastly, along with a couple more photographs of Ines, Luigi, Emil, Catherine and baby Louis there was an American twenty-dollar bill.

"God bless them," Evangelina said. Italy's war effort continued to drain the country's resources severely. There was always enough food for people like Evangelina and her family, who lived in the country and worked the land. However, other necessities, like medicine, fuel, clothes, tobacco, and blankets were in short supply or were very costly. Some of these supplies were available on the black market, but at a premium cost. American dollars were now worth much more on the black market than their official exchange value. This made it easier to obtain necessities that were scarce or rationed.

***

When Emilio was a child, most Italian children received no more than a third grade education – just the basics of reading, writing, and arithmetic. However, that was enough for people who grew up and lived their lives in Italy's nineteenth century agrarian society. What he might have lacked in formal education, Emilio's innate ability and skills, including his conceptual skills, more than sufficed. He was always able to anticipate future events and develop plans to meet those eventualities. Over the past several years, in the twilight of his life, his planning skills served him well.

In February 1938, when he was eighty-four years old, Emilio asked Pietro Faustini, a trusted friend and notary from Rivergaro, to help him draft a Last Will and Testament. He carefully divided his estate among his children, bequeathing parcels of Bellaria's property and buildings to some and cash sums to those for whom he believed real property would not be appropriate. Luigi, and Emilio's nephew Andrea, who both lived far away from Bellaria, were each bequeathed 1,000 lire. Of course, he bequeathed a life interest in Bellaria to his wife, Evangelina.

Several months later, Emilio rode his bicycle into Rivergaro, this time to meet with Padre Don Veneziani, the pastor of Sant'Agata. He told Don Veneziani that he had already lived too long and that it was time to make arrangements for his funeral. The priest chided Emilio and told him not to be foolish, that God would take him when He was ready – not a moment earlier. However, Emilio persisted, telling Don Veneziani that he wanted to spare his family the pain of having to make those arrangements whenever the time of his death might be. So, he discussed with the priest every detail he wanted for his funeral. He told Don Veneziani who he wanted for pall bearers, what music and hymns should be sung, and even that he wanted his body to be transported to the church, and later to the cemetery, in a horse-drawn funeral carriage. He even picked out his own casket.

Emilio planned not only for his own death, but also for the death of his immediate family. In late 1942, he purchased space in the Rivergaro cemetery and built a mausoleum large enough to inter his own remains and eventually those of his children and their spouses. He put a sign above the entrance to the open mausoleum that read:

"Famiglia Tagliaferri Emilio - Bellaria.."

Emilio knew that at age eighty-nine his time in this world was very limited. He could feel it in his bones. There were fifteen vaults in the mausoleum. His remains would occupy the first of them.

***

Emilio stepped outside of Bellaria to check the weather. The air was chilly but the sun shined brightly, so he decided to ride his bicycle as usual to Rivergaro to meet with his friends. Only one of his old friends, Edini Massimo who was now eighty-two years old, was still alive. However, over time two or three other elderly men from the surrounding towns, such as Francesco Molinari from Quarto and Giuseppe Frontari from Gragnano Trebbiense, replaced those who had passed away.

It was difficult for Emilio to move around most anywhere these days. He could no longer walk down to the Trebbia where the *mulino* was. It was painful for him to climb the stairs to the family quarters at Bellaria each night. He did not even try to walk the steep Via Castello to the Santuario anymore and in so many other ways, his mobility was restricted. However, amazingly, the one thing that he could still do with minimum discomfort was to ride his bicycle into town to meet with his friends, smoke a stogie, play cards and have a caffè, if it was the morning, or a glass of wine, if it was the afternoon.

Emilio pedaled his ten-year old Bianchi bicycle (a gift from his son Antonio) into Piazza Grande and spotted his amici waiting at a table outside of a small pasticerria. He propped the bicycle against the wall of the pasticerria and sat down at the table. The proprietor, an old acquaintance of Emilio's group came out and took their orders. Ten minutes later, Emilio, Francesco, Giuseppe, and Edini were laughing, smoking, and enjoying the fresh brewed espresso and an enticing variety of cream and fruit-filled mini-pastries. Then, Edini glanced up at Emilio and said,

"*Emilio, stai bene?*" He expressed concern, wondering if Emilio was OK.

"*Si, sto bene,*" Emilio replied. "*È solo un pò di agita,*" Emilio said, pounding his chest. "Yes, I'm OK. It's only a little agita."

However, the agita did not subside; so the proprietor told his son Marco to bring the family Renault around to the front of the pasticceria. They loaded Emilio into the back seat of the car and tied his bicycle on the top. Then they drove off toward Bellaria as fast as prudence would permit. When they arrived at Bellaria, Marco ran into the building and a moment later came out followed by Antonio, Nino, Evangelina, and Maria – all very worried.

By this time, Emilio was breathing a little easier and was strongly protesting all of the attention. His sons, however, practically carried him up the stairs and placed him on his bed. Evangelina followed as best as she could – she was

263

seventy-five years old, herself, and had her own problems
climbing stairs. Maria came up a few minutes later with a
cup of hot tea. Nino took off Emilio's shoes and Evangelina,
with the help of Antonio, took off Emilio's vest and loosened
his shirt. Then, his two sons helped him up enough so that he
could sip the hot tea. His breathing improved and soon
Emilio seemed to be resting comfortably, to the relief of
everyone present.

The next day, Emilio felt a little better; however, he was
too weak to get out of bed and go downstairs. Two days
later, he surprised Evangelina and Maria as they were baking
fruit pies when he walked into the kitchen.

"Papà, you look much better," Maria said.

Evangelina went over to Emilio and put her hand on his
arm. "Sit here, Emilio," she said pulling out a chair at the
table for him. "Can I get you something?"

"No," Emilio said. "But, I want you to ask Antonio to
come here for a moment."

Maria walked to the bicycle shop attached to Bellaria and
told Antonio that his father wanted to see him. Antonio
wiped his grease-streaked hands on a rag, told his assistant,
Gino Ghilardelli that he would be right back and
accompanied Maria into Bellaria's kitchen.

"You wanted to see me, papà," he said.

"*Sì*, Antonio. I want to talk to you alone for a moment."

The women and Nino looked at each other and then left
the room. When Emilio and Antonio were alone, Emilio said,

"Son, it's time. Please get everyone together. I want to talk to them."

"It's time? What do you mean papà?

"You know what I mean, son. I want to talk with everyone for one last time."

When Antonio told his mother what Emilio had requested, she became alarmed and told Maria to call the doctor. Later that afternoon, Dottore Fabbriani visited Bellaria and examined Emilio. He checked Emilio's pulse, took his blood pressure, and listened very carefully to his heart and lungs. When his examination was finished, he went downstairs and met with Evangelina, Maria, and Antonio.

"Emilio is a strong man," he said. "However, he is very old and his body is simply wearing out. His vital signs are weak. I believe that he might be suffering from congestive heart failure. There is nothing that can be done except to make sure that he has plenty of rest and that he is kept as comfortable as possible. I will check back with you next week. However, call me if anything happens in the meanwhile."

Antonio escorted the doctor to his car.

"How bad is it, Dottore?" Antonio asked.

"I think that you should call the family and also Don Veneziani," Fabbriani replied.

By early evening, all of the immediate family had gathered at Bellaria: Evangelina, Maria and Antonio, Pietro and Paola, Giuseppe and Natalina, Nino and Erminia, Elvira and Severino and Silvio and his wife Maria. They kept a watchful vigil, as Emilio visibly grew weaker. Don Veneziani came and administered the last rites of the Catholic Church to Emilio. He led the family in the Holy Rosary and told them that he would stay with them until the end.

Emilio was aware that the family was in the room with him, but he was very weak and he could not see them clearly. He was aware that some of them were crying. He could not understand why. He had no pain – just some discomfort breathing. But, he did feel tired – so very tired. His mind was filled with thoughts and memories, some of them so real that he was sure they were happening right then. He was a child running through the wheat fields on the slope of the hill behind his mother's house. He was looking at Evangelina, so beautiful in her red wedding dress, walking up the aisle of the church in Montechiaro.

Emilio's breath became more labored. He felt a weight on his body. Perhaps, he thought, it was simply the weight of the rough stones from the Trebbia in his hands as he passed them to his brothers Giuseppe and Silvio so they could add another layer to the walls of Bellaria. He again felt sadness as he watched his son Luigi board the train that began his journey to America, knowing in his heart that, despite his promise, Luigi would never return home. The sound of people crying faded as he saw figures approaching – one of them a beautiful, young woman, who was smiling and holding out her hand to him. Elisa! He reached out joyously to take her hand and then sighed as the last breath of life left his still body.

A shudder seemed to go through the room. It was as though Bellaria, itself, knew that it had just suffered a terrible loss. Everyone was crying and hugging each other for comfort. Don Veneziani approached Emilio's lifeless body, closed Emilio's eyes, and made the sign of the cross over him. Natalina walked over to the dresser that Emilio had shared with Evangelina and stopped the clock. It was nine o'clock at night on Wednesday, March 25. Evangelina knelt at the side of Emilio's bed, took his hand, placed it against her cheek, and wept.

Four days later, following the Funeral Mass that Emilio had planned with Don Veneziani earlier, Emilio Luigi Tagliaferri was laid to rest in the Mausoleum that bore his name. He had chosen the vault that was second from the top in the center column to be his. In the years to follow, one-by-one, each of the other vaults would bear a name of a member of the family at Bellaria.

Bellaria di Rivergaro

Chapter 22

SERGEANT PILOT KEITH HENDERSON of the British Royal
Air Force stood on the open parapet of the ancient monastery.
The view of the Pietra Parcellara, a dark serpentine mountain
of stone thrust up from the surrounding hills north of Travo,
was spectacular – most enjoyable. That is, as enjoyable as
possible for someone who for the past two years had been a
prisoner of war. Henderson was flying a British Hurricane
single-engine fighter over Tobruk when he was spotted by a
camouflaged Italian anti-aircraft battery. His aircraft was
struck by ground fire when he tried to go around and strafe
the gun emplacement.

He bailed out of the plane but was taken prisoner by the
Italians. Later, when Montgomery's Eighth Army pushed
back the Italian army, his captors transferred him and several
other POWs first to Sicily and then to the Italian mainland.
Eventually, he was interned at a former 15th century
monastery, now home to about fifty British POWs, that was
known as the *Torre dei Farisi*, Tower of the Farisi. The facility
was named after the Italian noble family from Parma that
built the medieval tower to guard their trade interests in the
Val Trebbia.

"If the cuisine and service was better, I could get to like
this place," fellow POW Evan Ramshaw joked.

Henderson chuckled and offered Ramshaw a cigarette
from a pack recently distributed to the POWs at the "Tower"
by the International Red Cross. The two men lit up and

looked down at the field of burnt-orange colored poppies stretching across their view about 300 meters downslope from the "Tower."

"Now, there's a paradox for you," said Ramshaw. "Over to the left we have a view of the rolling countryside extending across the Trebbia to the Pietra Parcellara. Behind us and slightly uphill is the town of Montechiaro with its medieval church and even older campanile, bell tower. Then, in front of us, below the beautiful field of poppies are those ugly oil derricks. Isn't that one for the books?"

He was right. The last thing that one would expect to see in this beautiful panorama was Texas-like oil derricks fouling the otherwise pristine scene. There were only three working derricks in the small Montechiaro oil field. But, in nearby Montechino there were more than a dozen. In the late 1800s, geologists speculated that the unique subterranean formations along the base of the Ligurian Apennines and Pianura Padana could be a source of petroleum. In the early 1900s, serious exploration began and small, but high quality, pockets of oil were found about 500 to 1,000 meters below the surface. Ground seep fouled one of the streams flowing below the town and sickened grazing sheep, helping to pinpoint the location of the Montechiaro field that produced light, sweet crude oil and natural gas. Already, however, each year fewer barrels of oil came from the wells. It was unlikely that the Montechiaro field would still be economically viable ten years in the future.

"Here comes our minder," Henderson said, nodding toward the guard who they knew only as Peppe.

Bellaria di Rivergaro

After almost two years in Italian POW camps, both
Henderson and Ramshaw could speak a little Italian. That
was fortunate for them because their Italian guards seemed to
have little interest in learning to speak English. Only the
camp commandant, Primo Capitano Maurizio Rebolini and
interrogators from Piacenza spoke even passable English.
Despite the language issue, a relaxed atmosphere and
relatively cordial relationship existed at the "Tower" between
captors and prisoners.

"*Ciao, Peppe*," Henderson said. Despite his age – he must
have been almost forty – Peppe was only a Corporale,
equivalent to a Private.

"*Come va*?" Henderson asked. How goes it?

"*Problemi, miei amici*," Peppe answered. "Problems, my
friends."

Ramshaw asked what was going on and he and
Henderson strained their Italian to the maximum trying to
understand what Peppe told them. There was both good and
bad news. Mussolini had lost his support among most of the
population in Italy. However, the heavy presence of German
troops in Italy resulted in the Italian government and its
people virtually being held hostage by the Nazis. Then,
according to Peppe, some political event happened in
southern Italy and Mussolini was overthrown. Soon
thereafter, the Allies invaded mainland Italy and were
driving northward. The Italian government had switched
sides and declared war on Germany, which immediately sent
twenty divisions over the Alps to control the Northern
Apennines and the entire area north of the Po River Valley.

271

Bellaria di Rivergaro

"Molto interesante," Henderson told Peppe. *"Ma, che dire di noi?* That was all very interesting, but what about us?

That was the problem, Peppe told him. The Germans were coming to take over the Tower. The word was that they planned to take the prisoners to POW camps in Germany.

Henderson and Ramshaw were stunned. That was terrible news. According to the camp grapevine, as the Germans suffered defeat after defeat, their treatment of Allied POWs became more brutal.

Henderson asked Peppe when this would happen, but he did not know. He simply said that they should be prepared for anything and then he walked away.

The Tower was only part of the ancient monastery that now served as a POW camp. Below, to the south of the Tower, were two, two-story buildings separated by a courtyard that was now a vegetable and flower garden maintained by the prisoners. The buildings were constructed of rocks and fieldstones, like most of the *cascini* and *stalle* that dotted the countryside. The building to the east housed the British prisoners, who slept on three-inch mattresses over steel spring bunks. Across the courtyard were the quarters for the dozen camp guards and administrative personnel with private facilities for Primo Capitano Rebolini. The guards worked in shifts with two men always patrolling the monastery grounds, which were encircled by a barbed wire fence.

At 2:30 AM, Henderson got up to use the latrine that was located in the base of the Tower. He passed Peppe, who was standing guard duty, and had just entered the lower level of the Tower when he heard the rumble of a lorry coming up the hill from the Bobbio-Rivergaro Road down by the river. Peppe burst into the latrine, put his finger to his mouth in the international symbol meaning silence, and whispered:

"Loro stanno arrivando. Vieni con me. Ora! Presto," he said. "They are coming. Come with me now. Hurry!

Henderson could hear someone at the gate of the compound shouting in German and realized that the Nazi takeover of the camp was happening now. He wanted to go back into the barracks to rouse Ramshaw and the other prisoners, but there was no time for that.

Peppe beckoned to Henderson to follow him down the slope in front of the Tower toward the poppy field. At the bottom of the slope, they reached a section of the barbwire fence that Henderson could see was pulled away from the wooden pole to which it was attached. Someone had previously used this spot to exit the compound. Henderson suspected the guards themselves occasionally used it when they wanted to sneak out of the camp for a little local entertainment. Peppe motioned to Henderson to crawl under the fence. Henderson needed no prompting. A moment later, Henderson was standing outside of the camp compound running for his life and freedom. He glanced back, but Peppe was nowhere to be seen.

Henderson now had another problem. With the help of Peppe, he had broken out of the POW camp. However, he had to avoid recapture and somehow make his way to safety and he was completely on his own. Henderson knew exactly where the camp was located. He was about ninety kilometers southeast of Milan. From there it was another seventy kilometers to Switzerland. If he could reach neutral Switzerland, he faced internment there for the rest of the war. However, that was a much better alternative than winding up in a Nazi POW camp somewhere deep in German territory. He decided to try to make it to Switzerland.

Henderson quickly took in the surrounding countryside as best he could in the near total darkness. Several hundred meters to the north, the oil field was heavily guarded. He could see lights in the guard shacks around the perimeter of the field and he could hear the faint barking of dogs the guards used to patrol the facility. That direction was blocked. The "Tower" was behind him and he could hardly return anywhere near there. Apparently, no one had yet noticed that he was missing, however that could change at any minute. He did not know what obstacles lay between his current position and the river a half kilometer or so downhill from the camp. Too risky! That left only one alternative; Henderson ran as fast as he could eastward toward the small, sleeping hamlet of Montechiaro that he knew was less than a kilometer away.

The night air was cold and soon chilled Henderson, who was dressed only in the light flight suit like the one that he had worn when he was shot down over North Africa. In Sicily, he had "inherited" a RAF flight jacket from a pilot who had died of his injuries, but that was left back in the camp barracks. Not to worry, he told himself, comfort later. His first priority was to find some safe shelter. He pushed through some tall brush and suddenly stumbled into a dry ditch alongside a narrow dirt road that seemed to head uphill. Rubbing a knee that smashed into a rock as he fell, Henderson climbed out of the ditch and followed the road uphill, hoping that it would lead to the hamlet. He had no idea what he would do when he got there.

Henderson had to be careful where he was walking. The right side of the road fell off sharply toward the farmland below. He did not want another tumble. On the left side of the road, the earth banked steeply, preventing him from seeing what was above. About 300 meters later, the road split. One fork seemed to go downhill toward a farmhouse with some outbuildings, the other continued upward. He chose the fork going uphill. A quarter of an hour later, he could make out the silhouette of several buildings clustered around a church with a tall bell tower – Montechiaro.

Henderson moved silently through the sleeping hamlet. The last thing that he wanted to do was to awaken and startle anyone. He moved from one dark recess of a building to another, always on the alert for any movement or sign that he had been detected. He could barely make out the name on the church, Sant'Ilario Vescovo. In front of the church was a small piazza. Across the piazza, in front of the church, was a small two-story stone house. He was careful to make no noise that might be heard by anyone in the house. Henderson spotted a side entrance to the church that was to the left of the five stone steps leading up to the main entrance. He hugged the perimeter of the church until he reached the wooden side door. As expected, the door was locked. Henderson saw that the lock was as ancient as the church itself, easily picked with the help of a long, rusty nail that he was able to pry out of a rotting fence nearby.

Henderson closed the heavy wooden door behind him.
He could see nothing. The darkness was absolute. He
tentatively took a few steps forward, stumbled, and fell
against what must have been two or three stacked wooden
chairs. He remembered the cigarette lighter in his pocket and
lit it just for a moment. He could see a tall cabinet to his right
with the words "*Archivio Parrochiale*" at the top. He opened
the cabinet and saw that it was filled with ledgers, some of
them obviously very old. Nothing useful there, he thought.
He also noticed that the passageway was not straight – it
jogged to the right in the darkness ahead. He extinguished
the lighter and out of prudence decided that crawling would
be safer than walking. The passageway led to a single stone
step above which was another door, this one not locked.
Henderson pushed the door open and was relieved to find
that the faint starlight coming in through the room's stained
glass windows enabled him to see well enough to stand and
move about.

The room must be the church's sacristy, he thought.
Luckily, the Anglican Church that his family attended back in
Oldham, outside of Manchester, shared many design
similarities with Catholic churches; among them, both had
sacristies. He looked around the room, recognized an
armoire, opened it and saw that it contained black cassocks,
white surplices, and other vestments for the priest and altar
boys. Now, that might be useful. A heavy wooden table
stood in the middle of the sacristy. A pair of candelabras
rested on the table together with a large, ornate book that
Henderson assumed contained the rite of the Catholic Mass.

To the right of the table was another door that he correctly assumed gave access to the inside of the church and to the main altar. Glancing back at the armoire, he saw more cabinets to its left hung over a long counter. An open bottle of holy wine was on the counter, next to a sink with a single faucet. A chalice and two candelabras stood next to the bottle of wine. He rummaged through the cabinets, finding nothing particularly useful except a couple of candles and several sulfur matches. Then he saw a ladder leading up to a dark square hole in the ceiling.

Henderson quenched his thirst from the faucet in the sink, hoping that the water was potable. If not – oh, well. Then he took the candles and matches and climbed the creaky ladder up through the hole in the ceiling. He pulled himself up onto a dusty platform and lit one of the candles. He was in the campanile, the church bell tower. In front of him were two ropes that led up into the darkness, where he assumed the church bells were located. He estimated that the platform measured about nine meters square with the access hole being in the center. Apparently, it was also used for storage because in one corner was a canvas covering old picture frames and a small wooden chair – all heavily coated in dust.

Henderson was exhausted. He needed to sleep. Daybreak would bring whatever it would bring. He pulled the canvas off the picture frames and shook the accumulated dust and bat guano off it. Then, he wrapped it around himself, stretched out on the wooden platform and immediately fell asleep, unmindful of the occasional rat scurrying across the platform.

***

Bellaria di Rivergaro

Tonino Piergiorgi lived in the little stone house across the piazza from the church of Sant'Ilario Vescovo in Montechiaro. The house had once been the home of his great aunt Evangelina, who was now a widow and lived with her children at Bellaria in Rivergaro. Tonino worked at the oil field between Montechiaro and Rivergaro that was owned and operated by Azienda Generale Italiana Petroli (AGIP). He was a mechanic and maintained the Deutz diesel engines that powered the pumps that extracted crude oil from the Montechiaro field. He had another job, as well – ringing the bell in the campanile of his church three times each day, at 6:00 AM, 12:00 Noon, and at 6:00 PM, to signal that it was time for the faithful to pray the Angelus, a Christian prayer proclaiming the incarnation of Jesus Christ.

However, Tonino hated to be the church bell ringer. He hated having to climb up through that dark hole in the ceiling of the sacristy. It was musty and claustrophobic up there. There were rats, which he hated, spider webs, and several times bats had swooped so close to him that he could feel the beat of their wings in his hair. Most of all, Tonino was convinced that the campanile was haunted. He had heard rumors that centuries ago, a monk was ringing the bell before Holy Mass when he slipped and fell to his death through the hole in the sacristy ceiling. Supposedly, the monk had been unfaithful to his vows of chastity and died before he could confess his sins; his tortured soul roamed the bell tower seeking forgiveness.

At ten minutes before six in the morning, Tonino trudged across the piazza. He walked to the entrance on the left side of the church, took out the over-sized key for the lock, slipped it in, and opened the door. He did not notice that the door was already unlocked. When the sun rose higher in the day, the light finding its way through the slits of windows near the passageway ceiling would enable a person to see where he or she was going. However, it was still dark outside, so Tonino pulled out an electric torch from his pocket and made his way to the sacristy.

Henderson woke with a start. He heard someone come into the sacristy below. Oh no, he thought. The Angelus! They are going to ring the Angelus. Henderson was Anglican – not Catholic. However, he was familiar with the Angelus because many Anglicans also followed that practice. He remembered that back in Oldham, Anglican churches customarily rang their bells at 6:00 AM, Noon and again at 6:00 PM, following the same tradition as their Catholic brethren. He cursed himself for forgetting about this and huddled deeper under the canvas.

The larger windows in the sacristy provided more than ample light for Tonino to see that everything seemed to be in its proper place. He opened a cabinet drawer and took out a candle, candleholder, and some matches. He fitted the candle into the holder, lit it, and began to climb the ladder up to the bell tower platform, carefully holding the lit candle in front of him. As he reached the platform, a rat scurried past startling and disgusting him. He set the candleholder down on the platform and stood up, grateful that there were no bats flying around this morning. Paying little attention to the material stored in the corner of the platform, he reached over and grabbed the closest of the two bell ropes. Only one of the church's bells would be rung for the Angelus; it would be rung nine times: three rings, a pause, three more rings, a pause, and three final rings. It was 6:00 AM, time to ring the Angelus. At that moment, Tonino saw the canvas in the corner move.

Tonino froze in complete terror. He watched in horror as the canvas slowly lowered and a face emerged, made ghastly by the dim light of the candle. His knees became so weak he could not stand and he slumped to the floor of the platform. His heart raced as adrenaline pumped through his veins. He was certain that the ghost of the dead monk had come to kill him and carry his soul to hell. Then the ghost spoke,

"Sono inglese. Ho bisogno di aiuto." Henderson said that he was English and that he needed help.

However, Tonino did not hear him. He was now on his knees repeatedly making the sign of the cross and begging for God's mercy and deliverance. Henderson realized that if the Angelus bells did not ring, it would cause concern and alarm in the hamlet. However, it was obvious that the man who was kneeling on the platform and praying was incapable of ringing the church bell. Henderson threw off the canvas reached for the rope and began to ring the Angelus, himself, hoping that he remembered the proper series of rings.

Throughout Montechiaro, the faithful heard the familiar ringing of the Angelus and began to pray.

"The Angel of the Lord declared unto Mary…"

Rico Costello was one of the faithful who responded to the ringing of the Angelus. When he heard the sound of the bell in the campanile of Sant'Ilario Vescovo, he knelt on the bedroom floor of his home that was just a few doors away from his friend Tonino's house. He also glanced at the clock on his bedroom dresser and saw that it was 6:04 AM. He wondered why Tonino was late that morning. He was usually very punctual. Perhaps he overslept. He would be sure to chide Tonino when he saw him later in the day.

***

Henderson grabbed the trembling man by the arm and hauled him to his feet. He prayed that his limited Italian would be sufficient to explain his plight.

Tonino began to realize that the man in what appeared to be a flight suit was human – not a ghost.

"Who are you?" he stammered. "What are you doing here?"

Henderson responded in broken Italian. "I am English. My name is Henderson. I was in the Torre dei Farisi," What is your name?"

Tonino studied Henderson carefully. Everyone in Montechiaro knew that the Torre dei Farisi was a POW camp.

"You are a prisoner of war?" he demanded.

Henderson had no choice. He tried to explain that he had escaped from the "Tower" and that he had to get to Switzerland. He was frustrated when he finished; it was obvious that his command of Italian was inadequate. But then Tonino pointed at him and slowly said,

"Prigioniero…sfuggito…torre…vai in svizzera."

With deep relief Henderson nodded his head and repeated what Tonino said, "Prisoner, escaped, tower, go to Switzerland." He knew that Tonino understood he had escaped from the "Tower" and that he had to get to Switzerland.

Tonino relaxed, smiled, and patted Henderson on the back. In as simple Italian as he could muster, he told Henderson that he should remain in the campanile platform while he made some arrangements. No one except Tonino would be in the sacristy until Sunday because there was no priest in the hamlet to say daily Mass. Tonino said that he would return as soon as possible. Then he climbed down the ladder and disappeared from Henderson's view.

Henderson was unaware that a network of partisans ran from Bobbio through the lower Val Trebbia and that Tonino Piergiorgi was one of them. Later in the day, Tonino and a fellow partisan received instructions from their command to take Henderson to a different location several kilometers north of Montechiaro. Only the most senior partisan commanders knew that his new destination was a safe house. The locals knew it as Bellaria, Bellaria di Rivergaro.

Chapter 23

IN THE MIDDLE OF THE NEXT DAY, a young man was riding his bicycle on the way from Montechiaro to Rivergaro when the chain broke. He forgot to carry any extra links with him, so he "walked" the bicycle until he came to Antonio's bicycle shop at Bellaria. Antonio and the young man chatted a few minutes while Antonio fixed the bicycle chain. The young man paid Antonio for his services and Antonio gave him a couple of extra links in case the chain broke again on the fellow's way home. As soon as the young man left the shop, Antonio wiped his hands with an oil rag and quickly went into Bellaria to find Maria and Nino.

It was chilly that evening so Nino made sure there was plenty of wood available for Bellaria's fireplaces. Earlier he had strolled around the back of building and unlocked the door of the old workshop. He entered the cluttered space and walked over to a stone-sided pit in the corner of the workshop that once served as a "cold cellar" for the storage of milk, butter and other perishables. He lifted one of the wooden planks covering the pit, saw that it was dry, replaced the plank, and went back inside Bellaria.

At 8:15 PM that night, an older man and a young priest walked through the front entrance of Bellaria. The older man said that they were on their way to Piacenza and decided to stop for supper. The priest was wearing a black traveling cassock with a black beretta on his head. Nino's wife Erminia was helping Evangelina in the kitchen, so Maria greeted the two travelers and showed them to a table in the smaller of the two dining rooms. Maria did not acknowledge that she recognized the older man as being Rico Costello from Montechiaro, nor did she ask the priest his name or even speak directly to him. Nino came to the table a minute or two later and took the pair's supper order.

A little later, Maria brought the guests a bottle of mineral water, a bottle of white wine, two orders of broccoli risotto, and a plate of crusty bread. The priest made the sign of the cross. He mumbled something that presumably was the prayer before dinner and then dove into the risotto as though he had not eaten in a week. When the only other supper guests that night finished their meal, they rose from their table, paid the bill and left, paying no attention to the priest or the older man.

As the two travelers were completing their meal, Nino came over and asked if they would like dessert; perhaps a fruit torta, and caffè. They both declined. However, the priest asked Nino, in carefully practiced Italian, where the toilet was. Nino said that it was in the back of the building and that he would show him how to get there. Meanwhile, the older man stood up, walked into the lobby, and paid the bill for both of them. He said that he would wait for the priest outside. Then, he walked out of the building and melted into the darkness. Maria quickly cleared the table and in a few moments, it was as though no one had dined at Bellaria that night.

Nino put on a sweater and went outside Bellaria to smoke a cigarette. He leaned against the building, occasionally glancing down the road toward Bobbio. At exactly 9:35 PM, he saw a single flash of light far down the road. Three rapid flashes, a pause, and then a single flash followed. Nino took one more puff of his cigarette, threw it to the ground, and crushed it with his left foot. Then he went back into the building, through the now- darkened kitchen, and slipped out the back door.

A partisan who he knew only as *"Meme"* met Nino at the entrance to the old workshop. They quickly went inside, removed the planks covering the cold cellar, and helped Henderson climb out of the cramped space. Henderson shed the black cassock and replaced it with a heavy, dark wool sweater over a pair of black trousers. He threw a black wool knit cap over his head and shook Nino's hand vigorously. As Henderson turned to leave with *Meme,* Nino gave him a letter and asked that he mail it if he safely reached Switzerland. Then Henderson and Meme disappeared into the night. Nino took the cassock and beretta and put them in an oil drum outside of the building that he used to burn trash. He poured kerosene on top of the clothes, threw in a lit match, and warmed himself by the fire as the priestly garb turned to ashes.

***

At the *Torre dei Farisi* POW facility, Wehrmacht Hauptman Kurt Bauer, the new camp commander, was furious. One of the English prisoners at the camp was missing. Bauer assumed the prisoner had escaped with the help of local partisans. Bauer had previously been stationed in Piacenza, where his job was to ferret out partisan sympathizers, who were either executed or imprisoned. He took it as a personal insult that partisans likely helped one of the "Tower's" prisoners escape. The Germans had just taken

285

over control of the POW camp from the Italians in order to facilitate the transfer of its prisoners to other, more secure POW camps deeper in German territory. It was Bauer's job to make sure that happened smoothly.

It was also Bauer's job to suppress partisan activity in the lower Val Trebbia. He knew there were two partisan groups operating in the Val Trebbia and he even knew the code names of their commanders; one was code named *"Bisagno"* and the other *"Scrivia."* However, it was Bauer's understanding that both of those groups usually confined their activities to the Alta Val Trebbia, the higher part of the valley mainly in the region past Bobbio. In recent weeks, though, partisans had successfully ambushed several German patrols on *Strada Statale* 45, the only road between Bobbio and Rivergaro in the lower valley. Several lorries of German troops had been blown up as they traversed the road resulting in the loss of dozens of German troops. It was impossible to catch the partisans after those attacks because they used barely discernable mule trails to disperse into the surrounding mountains. Now this! Bauer decided to take action. He intended to check out a few places in the area suspected of being sympathetic toward the partisans. If he found anything conclusive, he would execute the partisans on the spot.

An open German staff car with a driver and an armed soldier in the front seat and Hauptman Kurt Bauer in the rear seat screeched to a stop in front of Bellaria. Behind the staff car, an Opel-Blitz troop carrier stopped, blocking the road. Eight German troopers carrying assault rifles and submachine guns leaped out of the carrier and stood at attention waiting for Bauer's orders. Bauer nodded toward the entrance of Bellaria and the soldiers stormed inside terrifying everyone.

"*Heraus! Heraus!*" Shouted the troopers, as they dragged everyone out of the building, forcing them to raise their hands over their heads. Most of the family was there: Evangelina, Antonio, Maria, Giuseppe and Natalina and their two sons, Nino and Erminia and their baby, and two male friends of the family. In heavily accented Italian, Bauer demanded to know who the proprietor of Bellaria was. Nino stepped forward.

Bauer gestured to the front wall of Bellaria and pointed to Nino and his two friends. Immediately, the German soldiers roughly pushed the men up against the wall. Baurer ordered the soldiers to prepare to shoot the trio and then said,

"Now listen to me carefully. An English aviator escaped from my camp two days ago. I want him back. Where is he?"

There was silence. No one said a word.

"You," Bauer said to Nino. "Where is he?"

Nino looked directly at Bauer and said that there were no English aviators at Bellaria, nor had any been there. Bauer turned to his sergeant, Feldwebel Hans Koch and ordered,

"*Koch, suchen Sie den Platz,*" he said, telling Koch to search Bellaria. Then he turned back to Nino and the other two men and said, "If you are lying I will have you executed."

Koch took half of the soldiers and ran into Bellaria. The remainder of the soldiers kept their weapons trained on Nino and his friends and the family. The noise of glass being smashed could be heard as Koch and the soldiers searched

Bellaria room by room. Koch and the soldiers returned outside and Bauer motioned for them to search the bicycle shop. Koch, however, walked over to Bauer saluted and handed him a small object.

Bauer took the object and unfolded it. What the hell is this, he thought? He studied the fascist flag with Arturo Bocchini's signature and the inscription above it. Bauer knew who Bocchini was, but the man died almost five years ago. Further, Mussolini was no longer an important factor in either the politics or war in Italy. Hitler recently set him up in a resort castle on the shore of Lake Garda to keep him out of the way. Yet, the fascists were still allies of Germany, so was it possible that things were not as they might seem?

Bauer ordered his men to stand down and return to their vehicles. He folded the flag, sauntered over to Nino, and handed it to him with a glare. Without a word, he spun on his heels, returned to the staff car, and drove away in the direction of Bobbio. Erminia passed her young son to Maria and ran over to Nino, hugging him tightly and sobbing with relief. Everyone slowly went back into Bellaria to clean up the damage that the Germans had caused, unsure that the danger had truly passed.

An hour later, there was a loud explosion somewhere down the road toward Bobbio. Antonio hopped on a bicycle to see what happened. He came back a half-hour later, swearing bitterly.

"The *bastardi* blew up the old Sconti house," he told Nino. "No one was injured but the house was destroyed. The Germans said that it was a partisan safe house."

The two men looked at each other knowingly and then turned to help the others straighten up after the near fatal intrusion by the Germans. Nino returned the fascist flag to the cupboard where it had laid forgotten. He found it incredible that this hated symbol had saved his family from tragedy not once, but twice.

***

The mood at Bellaria was definitely brighter. Not only was it a beautiful April, but more important the Germans were being routed from Northern Italy. Allied forces had recently launched a Spring Offensive against the Gothic Line, a formidable series of German defensive positions that extended across much of the Po River Valley. Then on April 19, 1945, British forces launched an attack toward Bologna while the United States Fifth Army pushed out of the Northern Apennines and entered the Po River Valley. The Americans attacked the Germans and pushed them back from Bologna through Modena, Parma, and Piacenza toward Milan, Turin, and Como. In the northeast, the Germans were being attacked north of Brescia, west of Lake Garda, and north of Belluno in the Trentino region.

It was now common to see Allied troops, mostly Americans, pass by Bellaria on their way to the front in northwest Italy. One day, in late April, a U.S. Army jeep with four American soldiers pulled up in front of Bellaria and blasted its horn. Maria and Erminia rushed to see what was causing the commotion. Just then, a tall, thin American GI walked through the front entrance of Bellaria and in perfect Italian said,

Bellaria di Rivergaro

"Hey, can a guy get a decent meal in this place?"

Maria and Erminia stared in disbelief. Then Maria ran over and threw her arms around her nephew. Andrea had come back to Bellaria! It had been almost seven years since they had last seen Andrea. That was when he met and married Paola Maini in Castel San Giovanni.

Everyone who was in Bellaria dropped whatever they were doing and crowded into the small reception area. There were shouts of joy, crying and the clapping of hands as everyone tried to get closer to Andrea and his fellow GI's. Finally, Nino led Andrea and the other three American soldiers into the main dining room and seated them at a table. He hurried to bring out several bottles of Bellaria's best Gutturnio red wine.

Andrea explained that he was part of a headquarters unit serving as an interpreter. In addition to being fluent in Italian, Andrea also spoke German and French. He was on his way to Milan where he would likely be involved in translating material relevant to the capture and surrender of German forces in Italy. In the meanwhile, however, was there any possibility that his family at Bellaria would show his three pals what good Italian food was really like?

Evangelina, Antonio, and Giuseppe stayed with Andrea and the other GI's while the younger women rushed into the kitchen to prepare a special *pranzo*. Nino set the tables and made sure that the wine glasses remained full. Meanwhile, Andrea's friends went back out to the jeep and returned with box after box of the kind of foodstuff that had been a scarcity since the war began. Andrea and his friends enjoyed a wonderful *pranzo* that passed much too quickly. When they were finished with the meal, Andrea said that the four of them had to move along because they needed to be in Milan by evening. He promised to return as soon as he could get leave. There was a brief, tearful goodbye and the jeep headed off in the direction of Rivergaro.

After Andrea left, Nino went to the cupboard behind the reception counter where he had placed the flag that Arturo Bocchini had given them. He took the flag in to the main dining room and threw it into the fireplace. Then, he lit a match, set the flag on fire, and watched as the flames consumed it completely.

***

On April 28, 1945, Mussolini and his mistress, Carla Petacci, were captured and shot by Italian partisans. Their bodies and the bodies of several other high-ranking fascists were hung from the roof of an Esso gas station in Milan. That same day, German forces in Italy surrendered to the Allies. Two days later, April 30, 1945, Hitler committed suicide in a Berlin bunker. In two more days, Germany formally surrendered to the Allies and the war in Europe was over.

When the people of Rivergaro heard that the Germans had unconditionally surrendered to the Allies and that the war in Europe was over, they joined Italians throughout the country in a massive celebration that lasted for days; their personal and national nightmare was finally over. During the war years, the Italian people suffered terribly. Over 300,000 Italian military personnel were killed and there were over 153,000 civilian casualties, including those killed as a result of crimes against humanity committed by the Nazis and Italian fascists. In addition, many thousands of Italians suffered severe deprivation from war-related shortages of food and essential supplies. Hundreds of thousands were left homeless when their cities and villages were destroyed by bombs and artillery fire.

The family at Bellaria experienced its share of suffering; but, thankfully, not as severely as many other Italian families as close as Parma, Modena and Bologna. Still, food shortages, especially meat, were common and danger was always present. The Statto Bridge, just a few hundred meters downhill from Bellaria, was bombed on more than one occasion and bomb craters speckled the fields near La Casella on the Statto side of the Trebbia.

Chapter 24

THE LETTER WAS UNEXPECTED. It had been at least three years since Luigi and Ines had received a letter from the family in Italy; the war prevented communication of any kind between them. Then, earlier in the past week, they received a letter postmarked Switzerland. When they opened the letter, they saw that it was from Maria. She said that Emilio died two years earlier but they had no way of informing Luigi about his death. They even tried to contact the International Red Cross, but were denied access to that organization. Then, unexpectedly, they made contact with someone who was trying to go to Switzerland. Without providing details, Maria said that the person agreed to mail her letter from Switzerland if he was able to get there. If Luigi and Ines received the letter, the person obviously succeeded. Maria gave them the family's love and asked them to pray that the terrible war would end soon. She had no way of knowing that by the time they received her letter the war would indeed be over.

It had been forty years since Luigi had last seen his father, mother, and siblings. He had tried to keep in touch with them, but forty years is a long time. Luigi felt very sad to learn his father died. However, his greatest regret was that he never returned to Italy, even for a visit. Yes, at first there was concern that young men like Luigi, who emigrated from Italy without completing their military service, could be arrested and forced to complete their military obligation upon their return. However, the Italian government did not consistently enforce this practice. Many other young, male Italian immigrants to America returned to Italy under the same circumstances without a problem. Luigi could offer many other reasons why he never returned to Rivergaro, but they all seemed hollow. The fact was that he never again saw his father alive, nor would it be likely that he would see his mother and siblings again, either. Luigi was painfully aware of this and grieved deeply for what might have been, but what never was or would be.

Luigi and Ines' grandson Louis, "Piccolo Luigi," was staying with them for the weekend as he did often. He always had fun at Gramp's house. Aunt Lina would usually take him to the park on Hilliard Road at the top of Orchard Grove or maybe even to the Hilliard Movie Theater, where he would see the latest Lone Ranger film. He also loved going with his grandparents and aunt to the Rocky River Valley. In nice weather, Gram and Aunt Lina packed a basket filled with sandwiches, potato salad, Charlie Chips potato chips, and homemade lemonade. They had a favorite picnic spot near the creek that ran through the valley where he could throw stones in the water and skip flat stones across to the other side. There was also a stable in the valley and every once in a while Gramps would surprise him with a pony ride.

Emil and Kay dropped Louis off with Luigi and Ines the previous night. Then they left with their youngest son, Norman, who was only two years old – too young to stay overnight with his grandparents. Saturday morning Louis got up and went downstairs, sliding intentionally on his rump as he bounced from stair to stair. He went into the kitchen, gave Gram, Gramps, and Aunt Lina a hug, and sat at the chair to the right of Gramps – his usual spot. Gramps was having a cup of coffee and reading a copy of the Saturday morning paper, the Cleveland Plain Dealer. Aunt Lina asked Louis if he wanted pancakes or a soft-boiled egg. He liked both. Soft-boiled eggs were certainly a favorite. Aunt Lina would boil an egg and put it in an egg cup. Then, she would crack and peel the top and slice it so that the yolk showed. Next, she gave him several strips cut from a piece of toast that he dipped into the egg and ate, savoring each tasty bite. The thought was tempting. This morning, however, when Gramps said that he would have pancakes, Louis asked for the same.

Louis noticed that his grandfather was not very talkative. In fact, he was very quiet and frequently dabbed his eyes with his handkerchief. Louis tugged at his grandfather's shirt and asked,

"Are you OK, Gramps?"

Luigi sniffled a little and then patted Louis on the head.

"I'm OK, boy. Everything will be alright."

Lina looked at her mother, who was standing next to the stove, and raised her eyes. Then, she decided that Louis was old enough to be told what happened. She sat down next to Louis and said,

"Yesterday, your grandfather got some very sad news. God took his daddy to heaven."

Louis said, "You mean his daddy died?" He knew a little about death. The Lone Ranger and Tonto were always shooting somebody, mostly train robbers and bank robbers.

Bellaria di Rivergaro

In addition, he was in the second grade at St. Theresa Catholic School, a two-room school in rural Sheffield Lake. The nuns taught him and the other children that people die and go to heaven. It did not seem that awful to Louis because heaven was supposed to be a nice place, but Gramps was sure unhappy about it. He looked quizzically at his aunt.

"Yes, honey. Grandpa's daddy, Emilio, was very old and he died."

"Oh," Louis replied. He wrinkled his brow and thought about it for a minute. Then he said, "Can I have another pancake?"

Later that morning, Louis came up to Luigi and asked if he would take him to ride the ponies. Luigi looked at his grandson and recognized that at such a young age, it was not possible for Louis to understand the loss and sadness that he was now feeling. He gave the boy a hug and went into the kitchen and told Ines and Lina to pack up a lunch because they were going to Rocky River Valley for a picnic. Then, he gathered the four of them into his LaSalle and drove the five miles to the park. They found a picnic table alongside the creek, set up a couple of folding chairs and laid out their lunch. Luigi took Louis down to the water and showed him how to select the flattest stones for skipping across the water. He watched Louis clumsily throw the stones into the river and finally said,

"Louis. Here, let me show you how to do it. Hold the stone this way and flick your wrist..."

He did not finish what he was saying. In that moment, Luigi remembered the day that he left Bellaria for the last

296

time. Before leaving for the train station, he had taken his younger brother Pietro down to the Trebbia for a talk. While he was there, he watched Pietro try to skip stones across the river and he showed him how to get the most skips, just as he was now showing Louis. He remembered little Giuseppe crying as the *calesse* his father and he were riding in pulled away from Bellaria, and he remembered the promise he made to his family that he would come back – the promise that he never kept. He walked back to the table where Ines and Lina were waiting, sat down in one of the folded chairs, and felt tears well up in his eyes. Ines intuitively knew what he was suffering. She put her arm around his shoulder, kissed him gently, and asked Lina to get Louis. It was time for lunch and then the pony ride.

On the way back home from the park, Luigi stopped at Fazzio's, the Italian market on Hilliard Road. It reminded him of the *salumeria* in Rivalta on the grounds of the Castello Rivalta just past Statto, where his mother would send him to buy salami, cheese and olive oil. Fazzio's was just like that and Luigi could not go by the place without stopping and buying something.

Louis loved Fazzio's just as much as his grandfather did. There was something special about seeing the different kinds of olives in the wooden barrels, glistening in brine and olive oil, or the smell of salami and capicola hanging from the ceiling with their hint of garlic. There were rounds of cheese of every type and Mr. Fazzio would always ask Louis if he would like to taste them, which he always did. There was also Torrone, that chewy almond treat from Cremona, Italy

that came in cream-colored, log-shaped triangular boxes.
They were hard to chew, but ever so delicious.

In less than a half-hour, the four of them walked out of
Fazzio's carrying several paper bags of Italian groceries.
Inside the bags were sliced Genoa salami, hot capicola, and
sopressata; sharp provolone, gorgonzola dolce and
parmigiano reggiano; seminola flour from Sardinia to make
Ines' raviolis; and cans of Cento Pomodoro Pelato, peeled
tomatoes direct from the vast tomato fields of the Po River
Valley. Of course, at Louis' pleading, there were also a
couple of boxes of Torrone and some Perugina Chocolates.
During the summer, Louis might also walk out of the store
with a cone of delicious homemade gelato. However, Mr.
Fazzio had not made any yet; the weather was still too cool.

When they returned home, Lina helped Ines put the
groceries away. It seemed as though they had everything
they needed to have a terrific Italian *pranzo* later that
afternoon. Meanwhile, Luigi decided to sit on the front porch
and listen to the baseball game between the Cleveland
Indians and the New York Yankees. Louis joined his
grandfather; however, instead of paying attention to the
baseball game, he turned the pages of a photo album that his
aunt had let him see.

There were many photographs of old people in the album,
but also some of children. The children, however, were
dressed in funny clothes and the photographs seemed to be
very old. One of the photographs showed a building that
looked like a large house. Several people were sitting at
tables in front of the house. Behind it was a river and across
the river, there were hills.

"Gramps, what is this?" Louis asked, showing him the photograph.

"That is the house I lived in when I was a boy," Luigi said.

"Look, Gramps," Louis said. He pointed to a sign on the front of the building. "What does that say?"

"It says Bellaria, *Trattoria* con *Locanda*," Luigi replied. "It means, Bellaria Restaurant with Inn," he explained. "It is a wonderful place that has been part of our family for many years and it has a very interesting history.

"Where is Bellaria?" Louis asked. "Can we go there?"

"Oh, it's very far from here," Luigi said. "It's in Italy. Do you know where Italy is?"

"No," Louis said slowly. "But is that where all of the food in Mr. Fazzio's store comes from?"

"Yes, it is," Luigi replied. Then, out of curiosity he asked, "Would you like to learn how to speak Italian?"

"I heard you and Mr. Fazzio talking," Louis said. "And sometimes you talk to Gram the same way. It sounds funny."

"Well, someday I will tell you about Bellaria and I will teach you how to speak Italian. OK?"

"Ok, Gramps," Louis answered. Then he closed the photo album and went into the kitchen to see what his grandmother and aunt were making for dinner.

Luigi smiled and wondered if his grandson would ever see Bellaria. It was possible. Perhaps someday Louis would help him fulfill the promise that he made but was never able to keep. He took some comfort at the thought, then lit up a stogie and listened as Dutch Meyer hit a home run for the Indians. The radio erupted with the sound of cheering as the crowd at Cleveland Stadium went wild.

***

At Bellaria, the family was trying to recover from the disaster of over ten years of war. From the time of the second Ethiopian War through the end World War II, the economy of Italy descended in a downward spiral, culminating in near collapse. Bellaria as a business had suffered, also. Wartime shortages of materials, supplies and commodities coupled with a significant reduction in *locanda* and *trattoria* guests and patrons had caused economic hardship on the family. Nino and Maria operated the facilities at Bellaria. Giuseppe took a job as a telegraph lineman responsible for maintaining the line between Piacenza and Bobbio. In weather of any kind, he rode his bicycle as far as 30 kilometers from Bellaria to make repairs and check lines when he was notified of a problem.

Antonio operated the bicycle shop attached to Bellaria, selling and repairing both bicycles and motorcycles. He also used the *calesse* as a form of taxi, transporting people or goods around town by horse. Antonio even made a sign that read "*Trasporti Celeri*" meaning "Quick Transport" that he put on the side of the *calesse* to drum up business. Pietro worked as a carpenter, both at Bellaria and doing repair work and new construction for families in Rivergaro. When there was little carpenter business, he would work in the various *mulini* in the area making and replacing the hardwood that served as "teeth" in the gears of the machines. In order to continue to

300

cut slats and gear teeth for his customers, he still maintained the old sawmill down by the Trebbia, which was being used right now.

Pietro recently purchased hardwood logs from a logging company in the Alta Val Trebbia. He planned to use some of the lumber from the logs he would cut to make tables for a customer in Rivergaro. Three men from the area past Bobbio delivered the load of logs to the *mulino* in an old horse-drawn cart. In the years immediately following World War II, Italy's economy was still primarily agrarian. Horse and ox drawn carts and plows would remain a common sight for several more years.

Giuseppe and Nino were already at the *mulino* to help unload the heavy cart. Pietro followed a few minutes later. As Pietro approached the *mulino*, he immediately noticed that something was wrong. Giuseppe and Nino seemed to be struggling with one of the logs on the heavily loaded wagon, while the workers who had been helping started shouting and backed away. Pietro ran to the wagon. The problem was obvious; a large log had slipped and was threatening to tip the load over. Giuseppe and Nino were caught halfway along the side of the wagon, where they tried to push the log back in place. They could not back away because the minute they stopped pushing against the side of the wagon, the entire load of logs would fall on them.

Pietro ran to join his brothers shouting and swearing at the workers, who were standing at a safe distance from the tilting wagon. They did not want to risk being caught under a pile of falling logs.

"Get your ass over here and help push back the logs, you stupid sons of bitches!" he yelled, as he joined his brothers trying to right the leaning pile of timber.

Guiseppe and Nino were struggling too much to say anything. They just grunted as they used every ounce of their strength to hold back the logs. However, it became clear that the load was too heavy and that their strength would soon give out.

"Grab a couple of those 'god damn' studs – the big ones," Nino shouted at the workers, referring to the sturdy framing studs that the workers had been cutting earlier. "Bring them over here and prop up the 'fuck'n' wagon."

The workers stood frozen in horror waiting for the logs to tumble on top of the three brothers. However, when they saw that none of the brothers intended to leave the others, they jumped into action and helped them try to prop up the leaning side of the wagon. They got the studs in place and all of them leapt back, just as one of the studs slipped and wagon with its entire load tipped over, crashing into the spot where Giuseppe, Nino, and Pietro had been struggling just a moment earlier.

Giuseppe, who was the heaviest among them collapsed to the ground gasping for breath. Pietro called the workers from the logging company every name under the sun. He picked up a stout piece of scrap lumber and set out to do damage to the workers, who escaped only because he was too exhausted to chase them. Then Pietro, too, sat on the ground and shivered at the realization that all three of them narrowly escaped serious injury, if not death.

Bellaria di Rivergaro

***

Evangelina was eighty years old. Her health was failing and the cold, damp winter took an even greater toll on her. The family was not sure she would make it through the holidays, but she surprised them and brightened Christmas *pranzo* at Bellaria with her gentle presence. However, now she was suffering from some type of respiratory ailment and was confined to bed, coughing heavily despite the medicated syrup that the doctor insisted she take at least three times a day. Her breathing was raspy and seemed to be labored.

There was always someone at her side. Maria, Elvira, Natalina, and Erminia all took turns checking on her, sitting with her and responding to her needs. Erminia was expecting her and Nino's second child in the spring. She kept reminding Evangelina that soon she would have another grandchild to hold and cuddle. That always brought a smile to Evangelina's face.

That night, Maria kissed her mother goodnight and went to bed, leaving the door to her room open as usual so that she could hear if Evangelina needed help. An hour before dawn Maria woke with a start. For a moment she was puzzled, something was not right. Then she realized what it was. She had become accustomed to the sound of Evangelina's raspy breathing. Now there was silence. Maria quickly got up and went into her mother's room. She turned on the lamp on the table next to the bed and gazed at her mother's face. It had such a beautiful, calm appearance. Maria knew that her mother was now at peace with her beloved husband. Bellaria had lost its mistress.

A funeral High Mass was said at Sant'Agata. Then, with great sadness and mourning, Evangelina was laid to rest in the crypt to the right of Emilio's at the family mausoleum in Rivergaro. In addition to her name, the dates of her birth and death and a porcelain cameo photo of her, the family added another inscription to the crypt marker. When a child who lived far away from the parent died, it was traditional to put an inscription with the child's name, dates of birth and death and a porcelain cameo photo on the parent's crypt marker. Therefore, a second inscription also appeared on Evangelina's crypt marker - that of her daughter, Elisa Tagliaferri Guasconi.

Chapter 25

BELLARIA WAS STILL STRUGGLING FINANCIALLY, so Nino decided to call a family conference. They had always been a close family, therefore whenever any member of the family felt a need, all he or she had to do was to contact the rest of the family and ask that they meet together to discuss the problem. Spouses were invited, too, but rarely attended any of the meetings unless it pertained to them personally.

As customary, the family conferences were held at Bellaria. Maria, Giuseppe and his family, and Nino and his family lived there. Antonio, Pietro and his wife Paola and Elvira and Severino all lived in Rivergaro. Bellaria was the logical place to meet. Besides, this time, it was the subject of the meeting. The six brothers and sisters sat at a large table in Bellaria's small dining room. Natalina, Erminia, and Severino volunteered to take care of the *trattoria* diners. As was becoming more common, there were no *locanda* guests. Everyone knew the reason for the meeting. It was increasingly difficult to make Bellaria a profitable venture. Nino began the meeting.

"The war and the events leading to it have been very damaging to Bellaria's business. We hoped by now, three years after the war, things would be a lot better. They have improved somewhat, but we are still struggling. Maria and I need your help to think of what we can do to improve our very tight family budget. First, however, we received a letter from Luigi about Mamma's death. Maria will read it to you."

Bellaria di Rivergaro

"Mamma died on January 19; however our letter informing Luigi of her death did not reach him and Ines until six weeks later," Maria said. "Ines wrote a short note to us immediately with their condolences. She said that Luigi was too upset to write then, but that he would write to us soon. This is his letter."

My Dear Sisters and Brothers,

It was with great pain that we received your loving letter telling us that Mamma had departed this Earth. Forgive me, but I could not think of what to say, my pain was so great. But, it has now been a week and I want to send all of you my love and condolences in your pain.

At least I take comfort knowing that all of you were with Mamma in her final moments. But, now both of our parents are gone and I must live with the knowledge that I never fulfilled my promise to return to Bellaria to visit them and to visit you. I was not even able to see our beloved sister Elisa before she died, although she lived much closer to us than all of you do.

You have a right to ask why I never returned to Bellaria. I have asked myself that question almost every day. The answer is that I was afraid. At first, I was afraid that if I returned I would be imprisoned and then forced into military service because I violated the Italian law that prohibits men under the age of 20 from immigrating to other countries. Then I was afraid to leave my good paying job for fear of not finding one like it when I came back to America. I was afraid to leave my growing family. I was afraid of fascism and then the war. And then, after Ines fell and suffered a serious injury to her hip and leg, I have been afraid to leave her alone. Now, I am afraid that it is too late.

I have wonderful memories of Papà, Mamma and all of you. I remember how much Papà liked to play cards with his friends and play bocce. I remember how gentle and loving Mamma was. And, I remember each of you, even Nino who was still in diapers when I left Bellaria to come to America. Please tell Giuseppe and Antonio that I will answer their letters very soon. But, most of all, I send each of you my love and affection and ask you to forgive me for not keeping my promise to return to Bellaria.

Your brother Luigi

There was silence when Maria finished reading the letter. Even though he had never returned to Bellaria, Luigi had always been very close to his mother, father, and siblings. It was obvious that he was filled with remorse that Emilio and Evangelina died without him seeing them again.

"Our poor brother is suffering, too," she said.

"Perhaps he will come back someday," Pietro said.

"I doubt it," opined Giuseppe. "But, maybe someone will come to Bellaria in his stead – perhaps his son or his grandson."

Maria nodded in agreement. "Yes, someone needs to fulfill the promise that he made so that he can be at peace with himself – or rest in peace."

Nino sighed. "Well, let's talk about Bellaria."

When Emilio died, his will specified how he envisioned the distribution of his assets should be made. In the event that he predeceased Evangelina, everything was to be left to her. In turn, Evangelina provided for the distribution of the estate among her surviving children. Bellaria and its operation were given to Nino and Maria. Giuseppe inherited the parcel of land across the *Strada Statale*, the road to Bobbio. Cash was given to Elvira, Luigi, Antonio, and Pietro and even to Andrea in lieu of the share that would have been given to his mother Elisa. However, now after the passing of both Emilio and Evangelina, the issue was clear. Something had to be done to improve Bellaria's revenue or the family would be faced with the possibility that it would have to be sold.

The family grappled with the issue until they were exhausted. In the end, they concluded that the *locanda* was the least profitable part of the business. They decided to reduce the *locanda* rooms to only two and instead, focus on expanding the business of the *trattoria* by soliciting more banquets and parties. The other two rooms would be used for family purposes. Pietro was charged with building a two-story *stalle* on Giuseppe's property that would have six stalls on the ground floor and a portico above. The facility would be used to breed wild pigs, boars, and brooding hens. The boars would be sold on the open market and the chicks from the brooding hens would be sold to traveling commercial traders.

Pietro agreed to rent a farm plot in nearby Roveletto and use it to raise sheep for their wool, from which Natalina would use her skills to make wool quilts, also for sale to traveling commercial traders. Antonio was asked to continue the bicycle shop and to help run the private store that sold Bellaria's wine, jams and preserves, honey and summer vegetables. The postal substation, of course, would continue as long as Bellaria held the franchise. Lastly, the *mulino* would continue to produce the wood slats and hardwood teeth needed for the flourmill machines. The plan made sense and the entire family was committed to it. Only time would determine if it would be successful.

***

The years passed and Bellaria's business improved, not as much as the family hoped, but enough to sustain them. The new generation of the family attended school at Sant'Agata, as had their parents. On Sundays and Holy Days, the family continued to attend Holy Mass together, alternating between Sant'Agata and the Santuario up on the hill over Rivergaro. The face of Rivergaro began to change. Buildings were renovated, streets were paved, and shops and cafes were given upgrades. The train station disappeared, but a park with a long walkway along the banks of the Trebbia was built across from where it stood. The local delicatessen, pastry shop, and butcher shop continued to thrive; however, a new grocery store on Via Roma across the street from the Flower shop and Gelateria, gave them serious competition.

The face of Bellaria changed, too. The stone exterior wall at the rear of the building was sheathed in concrete and painted white, as was the old workshop and bicycle shop. Only the front of Bellaria and the side facing Rivergaro remained in the original stone facing. The tables in front of the building yielded to parking spaces and were relocated to a newly constructed terrace in the rear of the building that overlooked the hills across the Trebbia.

At Bellaria, life continued much the same as it had for decades, albeit more stable and with fewer notable events. However, only two years after Evangelina passed away,

Bellaria di Rivergaro

Bellaria lost a son when Giuseppe died following a long illness. His wife, Natalina, and the two boys continued to make Bellaria their home. Not many years later, the family was saddened to receive news that Luigi's wife Ines, herself invalided for several years, passed away.

Maria continued to serve as the family letter writer and kept in close contact with Luigi and his daughter Angelina. There was not much news about Luigi's son Emil, who had gone his separate way from his father, or about his two youngest sons. However, Luigi's oldest grandson *"Piccolo Luigi"* was now an adult. He was married, served in the military and had his own family. Luigi was delighted that Lou (the nickname that he was now called by his adult friends) married a good Italian girl from Hamden, Connecticut, Judy Pavoratti Biondi, who was from the very same town that Ines and her parents lived in after they emigrated from Italy. Luigi and Ines met Judy and her parents, Jim and Nelda Biondi, several years earlier when they were in Hamden visiting Ines' cousins, Rico, Aldo and Fred Veneris, long before Lou knew Judy.

***

At Easter in 1965, Lou and Judy flew to Cleveland with their four small children to spend the holiday with Luigi and Angelina. "Gramps" and "Aunt Lina" enjoyed having the house on Orchard Grove filled with the sound of children's laughter once again and everyone had a great weekend. Of course, there was the almost obligatory trip to Fazzio's Italian Market to stock up on imported delicacies. This was followed by a drive through Rocky River Valley with a stop at the stables so that Luigi could give his great grandchildren Lou

310

Ann, Stephen, and Susan a pony ride, while Aunt Lina held baby David. Then, after Mass on Easter Sunday, they drove to the cemetery to place flowers on the grave of great grandmother Ines.

After Easter dinner, Judy and Aunt Lina were in the kitchen cleaning up and washing the dishes. Lou and his grandfather were in the parlor, Luigi now sitting in the recliner that had been Ines' favorite, smoking another Tampa cigar.

"You know, I have been thinking," he said to Lou. "After your grandmother died, your aunt and I took that long trip to Hawaii."

"I know, Gramps. You always wanted to go there. I'm glad that you had a good time."

"Well," Luigi said, "That was the first time that I had ever been on a jet airliner and it wasn't bad at all."

"No, they're great. I have taken several business trips on jets."

"Anyway," Luigi continued, "I've been thinking a lot about the family in the old country lately. They say that it takes about twelve hours to get to Milan from here with a stop in London. Perhaps this summer I will get a passport for Lina and me and maybe we'll go over in the fall. As I remember, late September or early October is a beautiful time of year at Bellaria."

"That would be terrific, Gramps, and that reminds me; you never did tell me the story about Bellaria."

"When are you, Judy, and the kids coming back?"

311

Bellaria di Rivergaro

"Oh, Christmas, for sure," Lou answered.

"In that case, I'll tell you the story of Bellaria then and I'll teach you a little Italian, too. I promise."

***

It was an unusually warm day in late September. Luigi was outside picking the last of the summer vegetables from his garden. Lina came to the back door and hollered that it was time for lunch. Luigi gathered up the eggplant, peppers, and tomatoes he picked and put them in a wicker basket. He walked across the driveway past the stump of the walnut tree and stopped for a moment to talk to his neighbor Bill Fedor, who was repairing his car. Luigi gave Bill a few tomatoes and then went into the house. Lina made tortellini in chicken broth for him to which added a little red wine. In addition, he slathered butter on a fresh cut slice of Italian bread, added soft gorgonzola cheese and topped it all with a couple of thick slices of Genoa salami.

When Luigi finished lunch, he went into the parlor and sat in Ines' recliner. This time he did not light up a stogie. A little later, Lina came into the parlor and looked at her father with concern.

"Dad, are you OK? You look like you are sweating."

"It's just a little 'agita'," he said, rubbing his chest.

"Are you sure? Maybe I should call the doctor."

"No, the pain will go away in a few minutes."

***

312

Bellaria di Rivergaro

It was October 3, 1965, Luigi's birthday. Lina walked over to the mahogany secretary cabinet that Luigi bought for Ines many years earlier. She pulled down the lid of the secretary, converting it into a writing table, and sat on the chair that she placed in front of it. She opened one of the drawers inside the secretary, removed a sheet of stationery, a pen and a small jar filled with the green ink that was characteristic of the letters she wrote. For a few minutes, she looked at the framed family photos in front of her, including one of her mother and father. Then, she began writing:

Dear Aunt Maria:

It is with much pain and a heavy heart that I write to inform you and the family that three days ago…

***

Luigi died three days before his seventy-seventh birthday. Lina passed away less than three years later. Her brother Emil was the sole heir of Luigi's estate. Among Luigi's possessions were important family mementos such as copies of immigration documents, early passports, alien registration cards, letters from the family in Italy, and photo albums that contained a historical record of Bellaria and the family in Rivergaro. Emil packed all of this material in a shipping box, where they remained forgotten for the next quarter of a century. Luigi's house on Orchard Grove was sold and all of its contents, including the personal effects of Luigi, Ines and Lina, were auctioned – except for the old grandfather clock that Luigi gave to Ines for a Christmas present in 1943 and Lina' mahogany secretary. Many years later, both would find their way to the home of Luigi's grandson, *"Piccolo Luigi."*

313

Bellaria di Rivergaro

Meanwhile, Emil took his wife and youngest son on a tour of Europe that included a brief visit with the family at Bellaria. Maria, Pietro, Antonio, Nino, and Elvira received the three very warmly. They found it strange that Emil had anglicized his last name, but were too polite to ask why he did this. Still, they felt it awkward that their guest did not seem to want to share their family Italian heritage. In any event, they expressed a desire to maintain contact between the families, which both sides did for the next several years.

As time passed, other members of Bellaria's original family passed away and eventually, the surviving members of the family decided that it was no longer feasible to operate the inn and restaurant. In 1980, Bellaria passed to other owners, and the story of that special place in the Val Trebbia drew to a close – or so it seemed.

Epilogue

THE ELDERLY COUPLE TRIED TO RELAX on the uncomfortable solid plastic seats of the Ryan Air flight from Dublin to Milan-Bergamo. Earlier, they traveled from their home in northeast Florida to Dublin via Boston, resting a few days in Ireland before continuing to Italy. The Ryan Air flight was scheduled to arrive at Bergamo at 8:20 PM, too late to drive to Rivergaro that night. Besides, it was raining throughout northern Italy and Lou did not want the challenge of driving over sixty kilometers on unfamiliar roads in the rain at night. Therefore, he had booked a room for him and Judy at the Hotel Wintergarden right at the airport. By morning, the weather began to clear and the two set out for Rivergaro.

The trip was years in planning. It began after Lou's father, Emil, died in 1993. After his death, Lou acquired the cardboard box that contained the old family photo albums and documents once belonging to his grandfather. He also acquired the mahogany secretary and grandfather clock that his grandfather once gave to his grandmother, Ines – the only physical remembrances that he would have from the combined estates of his grandfather, father, and aunt. In the secretary was an address book with the names and addresses of people in Rivergaro and Piacenza who apparently were his cousins – cousins who he had never met and until now, of whose existence he was unaware.

Lou was the eldest of Luigi's three grandchildren. He was also his grandfather's namesake and the only one of the three still bearing the original family name. He decided to write to his cousins in Italy to inform them of his father's death. They quickly responded. They said that they were sad to learn Emilio died, but they were very happy to receive his letter. One of his cousins said the family thought they lost all contact with their extended family in America because none of the letters they sent to Emilio over the past several years had been answered.

During the years that followed, Lou exchanged many letters with his cousins in Italy. He studied Italian so he could communicate better with them and as technology advanced, email and Skype video calls replaced letters sent by post. Eventually, Lou and his wife Judy, both now in their mid-seventies, decided to travel to Italy to meet the family and to finally learn the story of Bellaria – the story that his grandfather had promised to tell him.

They stayed at a lovely country house near the Castello di Rivalta, not far from Rivergaro, that was generously offered to them by the wife of one of Lou's cousins. The house was reserved for the use of family and friends, so they had the entire place to themselves. They stayed a month, first meeting all of the members of the family, whose warmth and welcoming was overwhelming. Family *pranzo* followed family *pranzo* until neither of them thought they could handle another three-hour meal. However, in order to repay all of the courtesies showered upon the two of them, Judy invited everyone in the family to the country house where she prepared and served an Italian-American *pranzo*, "Biondi" style, for sixteen people.

Bellaria di Rivergaro

Lou and Judy spent most of their time touring throughout the beautiful Val Trebbia, learning about the area, the family's history and about Bellaria. Sometimes their cousins escorted them, taking the couple to remote places that no tourist was likely to see, like the decaying Castello di Monticello high atop a hill, not far from Pigazzano, that was the site of a major World War II battle between Italian partisans and German and Italian fascist forces. Sometimes they drove kilometer after kilometer by themselves through the countryside, frequently stopping to take photos or just to admire the scenery. They often got lost, but always found their way back with the help of a hotspot and a GPS.

They explored Rivergaro, Niviano, Ottavello, Settima, Grazzano Visconti, and more – all the places that were known to Lou's grandfather Luigi and his parents and siblings. The elderly couple drove the twisting road that ran past Bellaria to Bobbio, through the vistas that had so impressed Ernest Hemmingway, noting that they were seeing the Val Trebbia almost exactly as Emilio and Evangelina and their children knew it. They saw the original Statto house, drove over the Statto Bridge, and went to Travo, past the *fornace* where the limestone used to make the mortar at Bellaria was made.

They drove up the mountain to the church at Pigazzano where they stood on its terrace overlooking Rivergaro, Statto, and the Pianura Padana beyond, thinking how it looked to Emilio and Evangelina on the day he proposed to her. Then, they drove to Montechiaro and saw the childhood home of Evangelina and the church where Emilio and Evangelina first met. They entered the ancient church by the side door and walked carefully through the dark stone passage leading to the main church. There, in an old cabinet marked *"Archivio Parrochiale,"* among dusty ledgers dating back to the sixteenth century, they found the one in which Emilio and Evangelina's wedding was recorded. They passed an old wooden ladder leading up to the bell tower as they walked through the sacristy into the main church and were impressed with its simple beauty. Then, they stood on the spot in front of the altar where Emilio and Evangelina, exchanged their marriage vows.

There was much more. There were the tranquil fields on hillsides where sheep grazed under the watchful eyes of a shepherd guiding them with his crook. They walked along the Trebbia and even tried to skip stones across its rapidly flowing waters. They walked the ancient alleys on the grounds of Castello di Rivalta, visiting the *salumeria* where Evangelina often sent young Luigi to buy cold meats, cheese, flour, and olives for their supper. When finally they were exhausted, they returned to the country house to rest and reflect on how it all had once been.

Of course, they also went to Bellaria, easily recognizable from the photos that Lou had seen in his grandfather's photo albums. The building sported new whitewash on the sections sheathed in concrete. However, much of the original stonework remained, adding to the character of the structure. The bicycle shop was gone - Antonio moved it to Rivergaro in the late 1960s – and there were some changes to the terrace and rear of the building. The new owners did a great job renovating it. Lou was sure that Emilio would have approved. Still, it was undeniably Emilio's Bellaria.

Bellaria di Rivergaro

Lou walked around the building, touching the same stones that his grandfather handed to Emilio and his brothers when Bellaria was being built. He scanned the fields below Bellaria, visualizing the *mulino* by the river that was now long gone, as were the cows and sheep that once grazed in the open fields. He looked toward the Trebbia and imagined an adult Giuseppe, Uncle Pipòn, cutting bundles of willow and poplar and loading them on the horse-drawn *barra* until it was full; the children climbing on top and shouting in excitement as Uncle Pipòn drove the cart through the shallow water as fast as he could.

As the month passed, the story of Bellaria unfolded more and more. It was a fascinating story about an incredible place and an incredible family. It gave Lou great pride that he and his family were a part of that story. However, there was another reason that he and Judy traveled to Rivergaro. It was to help fulfill a promise made many years earlier.

The next morning, Lou and Judy drove their rented car to the Rivergaro cemetery to visit the family mausoleum built by his great grandfather Emilio. They parked the car and walked through the complex of mausoleums, tombstones, and crypts until they came to the mausoleum above which was inscribed:

"Famiglia Tagliaferri Emilio - Bellaria.."

Their eyes scanned the crypt markers, focusing on one in particular. It was the marker for Emilio's crypt and it had recently been altered. Two years earlier, when his cousin Luigi's son Lorenzo and his bride Anna spent Christmas with Lou and his family in Florida, Lou gave them a photo of his

319

Bellaria di Rivergaro

grandfather and asked them a special favor that they graciously granted. Now, just like the cameo photo and inscription of Elisa that had been placed on Evangelina's tomb when she died so far away from the family, Luigi's photo and inscription had been added to the marker for his father Emilio's tomb. Lou walked up to the marker and touched the porcelain cameo photo of his grandfather. He felt a sense of peace. A promise had now been kept and everything was as it should be. After so many years, Luigi had at last come home.

On their last day in Rivergaro, Lou and Judy had lunch at Bellaria. Several photos and paintings showing how the *trattoria* and *locanda* looked in past decades hung on the walls around their table. One was especially beautiful. It was a scene of Bellaria in the winter painted by Pietro Zangrandi, a well known local artist. The couple could only imagine how it must have been in times past when Bellaria bustled with guests and when Evangelina and Maria skillfully prepared meals for them in Bellaria's kitchen, right behind where Lou and Judy were now sitting. They looked at the counter outside of the dining room where a cashier now sat and imagined Emilio sitting there instead, smoking a stogie, his hand not far from a glass of his favorite Gutturnio wine.

They both ordered a salad, *agnoli* in butter sauce and a glass of white Trebbiano wine. In a few minutes a pleasant young lady brought out their plates. Ah, Lou thought, that would have been the job of Nino. He ate his meal mostly in silence, occasionally looking out the window at the view of the Trebbia below them. Across the river, he could clearly see the Statto Castle and the church of Sant'Antonio Abate.

These were places his grandfather often spoke about and where just yesterday, he and Judy walked their grounds. Judy could see emotion beginning to well up in her husband's eyes. She reached across the table and took his hand in hers.

"Bellaria will always be a part of your heritage, Lou. It is now my heritage, too. You have a wonderful story to tell to our children and grandchildren when we get home. It's a story that your grandfather intended to tell, but never did. Now, you can tell it for him."

She gave his hand a squeeze and raised her wine glass in a toast saying, "To Bellaria."

Lou nodded and then a thought began to form in his mind. He smiled as the possibility took hold, raised his own glass and said,

"Yes! To Bellaria. Bellaria di Rivergaro."

***

Bellaria di Rivergaro

Acknowledgments

ONE OF MY DEEPEST REGRETS is that most of the people to whom my gratitude is extended for their help with this book have requested to remain anonymous. My cousins in Italy, who are all the descendants of Emilio and Evangelina, provided me with a wealth of valuable information about the history of Bellaria, our family and the Val Trebbia region. I appreciate all of their help, but in particular that of one cousin and close friend who insists on anonymity. With sadness, I will honor his request.

My lovely wife, Judy, not only helped me properly structure the story with her many constructive and insightful suggestions, but also patiently supported me during the many hours that I sat at my computer station struggling with the substance of the book. I also appreciate very much her help researching the period of the story.

I thank my sister-in-law Janan Talafer, an accomplished freelance writer, for her review and critique of the first chapters of this book. Her suggestions helped me develop a more readable style for the story that was then unfolding. Lastly, I extend my gratitude to still another cousin, a direct descendant of a principal character in the story, who also has requested anonymity, for his extensive proofreading and editing on the original draft of this book. His incredible skills and gracious help were both invaluable and very much appreciated.

Bellaria di Rivergaro

Author's Notes

IN A WORK OF HISTORICAL FICTION, fact and fiction often can blend together in a way that makes it difficult to discern one from the other. So it was with the people, places and incidents portrayed in Bellaria di Rivergaro. Therefore, it may be appropriate to briefly separate what did happen from what might have happened in the story.

As I mentioned in the Preface, Emilio and Evangelina were real people. Emilio did meet Evangelina in Montechiaro and was, in fact, immediately smitten by her beauty. The first time he met her she was wearing a red dress. To the best of the family's knowledge, Emilio promptly decided that Evangelina was the woman he wanted to marry. It is uncertain where they became engaged to marry. However, the Pigazzano church was a popular place for locals to travel because of the incredible vista from its terrace. This is true today, just as it was over one hundred years ago. So, it is quite feasible that Emilio and Evangelina became engaged on that site, which they visited many other times later in their marriage. An alternate version of their engagement that has been handed down through the family is that at the time, engagements were solemnized in the sacristy of the church in Montechiaro.

Before his marriage to Evangelina, and for some time afterward, Emilio lived in Statto, a small hamlet across the Trebbia River from where he later built Bellaria. His parent's original house below the Statto Castle, the place where they operated the small store and Emilio and Evangelina's house, La Casella, all still stand. The latter is in particularly good repair. Modes of transportation using *calesse, barra* (a Piacentino word describing a certain type of work cart), and *barcone* are described accurately in the book. Further, Emilio and his brothers Giuseppe and Silvio were indeed *falegname,* carpenters, and built many *stalle* and *mulini,* as well as most anything made of wood or brick and stone, for their customers in the Rivergaro area.

Emilio acquired the Bellaria property from a local landowner, although the circumstances are unclear. His motivation for building Bellaria was much as described: a growing family, customers on the Rivergaro side of the river, the foresight to know that as he aged he would need a less taxing way to support his family, and an ideal location at the junction of two well-traveled roads. Young Luigi unquestionably helped his father, Emilio, and his uncles build Bellaria. That has long been a part of our family lore. Also, the incident when Silvio nearly severed his leg with an axe is true, although it is uncertain whether it was Silvio or Giuseppe who suffered the accident.

After Bellaria was built, it served as an inn and restaurant that was operated by the family until 1980, when it was sold to another party. However, in the early days of Bellaria, Emilio did obtain the postal substation franchise as described and one section of Bellaria, the lower level to the left of the main building, actually served as a stable, store (somewhat like a modern delicatessen) and later a bicycle and motorcycle shop. The family's quarters were on the upper floor of the building.

Luigi left Italy and immigrated to America for all of the reasons that were ultimately disclosed in the story. He was very close to all of his family, but perhaps especially to his little brother Giuseppe, who was devastated when Luigi left Bellaria. In his adulthood, Giuseppe named one of his sons Luigi in remembrance of his older brother.

Luigi seems to have been sponsored to America by Alberto Zanmatti, a cousin who owned and operated a grocery distribution business. In fact, a thriving business of the same type now stands exactly on the spot where Zanmatti's business was located. When Luigi first set foot on Manhattan, he spotted an ice cream vendor and made a bee-line to get his first taste of the American version of gelato. It is uncertain whether Luigi's first construction job was at the Singer Tower. However, as time passed he became a successful construction executive and provided general contractor supervision on many landmark construction projects including the Memorial Bridge connecting Washington, DC with Arlington, Virginia, many Republic Steel plants in Cleveland's industrial area known as the Flats, the Forest City Publishing Building in Cleveland, the Mackinaw Bridge in the upper peninsula of Michigan and the Chrysler Stamping Plant in Twinsburg, Ohio, at the time the largest manufacturing plant under one roof in the United States.

Throughout the story Emilio enjoys an occasional glass of "Gutturnio" wine. As explained in Chapter 16, Gutturnio is produced by blending and fermenting the juice from Barbera and Bonarda grapes. In fact, it was not until 1939 that the name Gutturnio first appeared on the label of commercially

Bellaria di Rivergaro

bottled wine (from the Manara di Vicomarino winery - Ziano) and only in 1967 was Gutturnio listed as a wine of controlled designation of origin by the Italian Ministry of Agriculture. However, that particular blend was commonly referred to as "Gutturnio" by locals such as Emilio well before 1939; thus, that is the name chosen for his beverage of choice in this story.

The short section that featured Enzo Ferrari, the famous Italian race car driver and founder of the Ferrari S.p.A. automobile company, was included in the story simply for fun. However, his father was the first person in Modena to own an automobile and traveled to places like Milan, Turin, and Genoa on business. It is at least feasible that a man of his fine tastes could have driven past Bellaria and stopped for an exquisite meal and comfortable lodging for the night! In addition, during World War I Enzo Ferrari served in the Third Alpine Artillery of the Italian Army. So, it is not beyond imagination that Enzo Ferrari might at one time have known or have served with Giovanni Tagliaferri, the Alpine Artillerist who was the nephew of Emilio.

The preponderance of family tradition holds that Elisa and Giovanni Guasconi met in Italy (possibly at Bellaria) before Elisa followed Luigi to America. Their first meeting at Bellaria is fictional. In one way or another, Elisa was reunited with Giovanni in America and became his wife; the marriage taking place at St. Ann's Church in Manhattan. Andrea was their only child. At age four he was taken by his aunt Giuseppina for what turned out to be a prolonged visit with his grandparents and other relatives in Castello San Giovanni and at Bellaria in Rivergaro. The U-Boat encounter of the

Bellaria di Rivergaro

Dante Alighieri is completely fictional. However, because of World War I, Andrea remained in Italy until December, 1919 when he returned to New York with Giuseppina. The description of the Christmas at Ellis Island is accurate, as is the compassion that the overburdened Ellis Island staff had for the plight of the immigrants from all countries. The sad, tearful circumstances of the death of Elisa are accurate and are based on Andrea's own written recollection of that event.

Arturo Bocchini was a notorious personage in Mussolini's Fascist government. Mussolini did appoint Bocchini as Prefect of Genoa and, of course, it would have been necessary for him to travel from Bologna to Genoa – likely by automobile. In that case, Bocchini could easily have been driven through Piacenza and Rivergaro past Bellaria. Who is to say that he did not stop there for a delightful pranzo? This entire scenario, of course, is completely fictional, as is the following event when the fascist thugs burst into Bellaria months later.

Although it cannot be found on the usual list of World War II prisoner of war (POW) camps in northern Italy, this writer found compelling evidence that there was a small POW camp located in an ancient abbey in Montechiaro. In fact, there are written reports showing that local partisans helped POWs from that camp escape into Switzerland. Interestingly, for a period of perhaps ten years or so, there was an oil field between Montechiaro and Bellaria as described in the novel. Equally compelling family lore indicates that Bellaria was for a period a "safe house" for Italian anti-fascist partisans and that at one point one or more members of the family were almost executed by German soldiers who believed that the family was helping local partisans sabotage the road between Rivergaro and Travo. However, the narrative about Sergeant Pilot Keith Henderson and his escape to Switzerland is fictitious.

World War II was a terrible time for most Europeans and not the least for Italians. Gratefully, the family of Bellaria escaped the worst of the deprivation and destruction that many other northern Italian cities and towns had to endure. Still there were shortages and hardships. For example, meat was very difficult to obtain. Antonio actually began raising pigeons that flew throughout the countryside feeding on whatever was in the fields. Many of them later wound up in the family's food pot as soup or stew!

Andrea served in the American Army as a translator during World War II. There is no evidence, however, that he passed through Rivergaro or stopped at Bellaria toward the end of the war as fictionalized. He remained close to the family at Bellaria (now in Rivergaro and Piacenza) for the remainder of his life, however, as currently does one of his sons – a cousin of mine.

During the post-World War II years, things in Rivergaro and at Bellaria were relatively quiet. The family, and Bellaria as a business, struggled to keep up with changing times. Several strategies to make Bellaria a viable business entity were developed and tried – most to no particular avail. The incident, in which the load of logs tipped over, almost crushing the three brothers, happened as described.

In America, Luigi and his son Emil became estranged. Prompted by his wife, Catherine, Emil changed his family name to Talafer from Tagliaferri, an act that further estranged him from his father. In 1965 Luigi died, followed by the death of his daughter Angelina in 1968. That left only Luigi's grandson *"Piccolo Luigi,"* the author, to continue the original family name among the descendants of Emilio and Evangelina in America.

Almost three decades passed before active contact between the family in Italy and the family in America was reestablished. By then, the ownership of Bellaria had passed from family hands to a third party. The Epilogue of the novel accurately describes how the story of Bellaria and its family was finally brought to a conclusion – at least for now.

Although it is no longer owned by the family that built it, the Bellaria of today remains a popular restaurant that is known for the quality of its food and service. Sadly, it is unlikely that many of its patrons know the history and the story of that special place called Bellaria – Bellaria di Rivergaro.

Bellaria di Rivergaro

About the Author

LOUIS E. TAGLIAFERRI is a retired management consultant, publisher, and author. He has written many articles that have appeared in professional and trade journals on the subject of leadership, team building, and communication, as well as seven non-fiction books. *Bellaria di Rivergaro* is his first work of fiction. Lou lives in Ponte Vedra Beach, Florida with his wife of 56 years, Judy. In his earlier years, he enjoyed sailing, flying, and playing golf. His current hobby is historical research and writing.

Bellaria di Rivergaro

The Bellaria family at the fiftieth wedding anniversary of Emilio and Evangelina, who are shown seated in the front row center.